DISCARD

THE DARKER CHASE

Also by Cap Daniels

The Chase Fulton Novels Series
Book One: *The Opening Chase*
Book Two: *The Broken Chase*
Book Three: *The Stronger Chase*
Book Four: *The Unending Chase*
Book Five: *The Distant Chase*
Book Six: *The Entangled Chase*
Book Seven: *The Devil's Chase*
Book Eight: *The Angel's Chase*
Book Nine: *The Forgotten Chase*
Book Ten: *The Emerald Chase*
Book Eleven: *The Polar Chase*
Book Twelve: *The Burning Chase*
Book Thirteen: *The Poison Chase*
Book Fourteen: *The Bitter Chase*
Book Fifteen: *The Blind Chase*
Book Sixteen: *The Smuggler's Chase*
Book Seventeen: *The Hollow Chase*
Book Eighteen: *The Sunken Chase*
Book Nineteen: *The Darker Chase*
Book Twenty: *The Abandoned Chase*

The Avenging Angel – Seven Deadly Sins Series
Book One: *The Russian's Pride*
Book Two: *The Russian's Greed*
Book Three: *The Russian's Gluttony*
Book Four: *The Russian's Lust*

Stand Alone Novels
We Were Brave

Novellas
The Chase Is On
I Am Gypsy

THE
DARKER CHASE

CHASE FULTON NOVEL #19

CAP DANIELS

ANCHOR WATCH
PUBLISHING
** USA **

The Darker Chase
Chase Fulton Novel #19
Cap Daniels

This is a work of fiction. Names, characters, places, historical events, and incidents are the product of the author's imagination or have been used fictitiously. Although many locations such as marinas, airports, hotels, restaurants, etc. used in this work actually exist, they are used fictitiously and may have been relocated, exaggerated, or otherwise modified by creative license for the purpose of this work. Although many characters are based on personalities, physical attributes, skills, or intellect of actual individuals, all the characters in this work are products of the author's imagination.

Published by:

** USA **

13 Digit ISBN: 978-1-951021-38-2
Library of Congress Control Number: 2022948578

Cover Design: German Creative

Printed in the United States of America

The Darker Chase

CAP DANIELS

Chapter 1
The Doctor Is In

December 2007

I felt and looked like an idiot in my flowing gown and silly hat, sitting on a folding chair in the middle of Stegeman Coliseum in Athens, Georgia, beside a hundred other clowns dressed just like me. The coliseum was capable of seating a little more than ten thousand screaming fans when the University of Georgia Bulldogs basketball team took the court, but in attendance for that day's festivities were fewer than one thousand non-screaming fans, most of whom carried themselves with at least some degree of dignity. I feared the eleven people whose invitations had my name inked inside left most of their dignity at home.

When the dean of the psychology department finally called my name, I sighed beneath my ridiculous hat and stepped onto the stage, almost furious at my beautiful wife for insisting that I take what she called "the walk."

"You've worked so hard, and it means so much. How can you not walk after all the time and sacrifices you made to get here?"

I never remember winning an argument with Penny Fulton, and that record wasn't going to change, no matter how much effort I put into my protest over what I considered to be a perfect waste of a perfect day.

The dean announced, "Doctor of Philosophy in behavioral and brain sciences, Chase Daniel Fulton."

I extended my hands, shaking his with my right and accepting the rolled and ribboned sheepskin with my left. Somebody took our picture, and I exited the stage, relieved beyond words that my "family" hadn't set off any fireworks or screamed something entirely inappropriate while I was taking "the walk."

Back in my seat with the papyrus unrolled, I had to admit—at least to myself—that Penny was right . . . at least partially. The thousands of hours I'd spent studying the behavior and yearning to understand the workings of the minds of some of the world's most atypical personalities weren't spent in the worn classrooms of the university; instead, those research projects were conducted under enemy fire, in the driest deserts and wettest rainforests across the globe. I learned far more standing toe to toe with madmen than I ever learned from the pages of any intellectual publication.

Dr. Robert "Rocket" Richter had been right all those many years before when he sat across from me at an ancient oak table in my favorite library on the UGA campus. He'd said, "You aren't going to learn how the human mind works in this compost heap of intellectual bullshit. We learn the ways of the mind by observing the behavior of its keeper."

I made a life, a living, and maybe even some small difference in the world, by doing what my beloved professor recommended. There is no better classroom than the field of combat between warriors bent on ending each other's time on Earth. That's where I learned about the man I am, and also where I learned what bravery, allegiance, and sacrifice look like in their rawest and purest form. The heroes who stood beside me when the daggers and arrows flew, demonstrated valor of the highest order, with no expectation or desire for recognition or admiration. They wanted only to leave the world a better and freer place than it was the day before, and if that freedom came at the cost of their lives, that was the price they were willing to pay on behalf of the throngs of men and women who would never see their faces and never hear their names.

Freedom, purely for freedom's sake, is the noblest of all pursuits, and the heroes who taught me that eternal truth were sitting a dozen rows behind me, watching me parade around like a clown in a wasted, useless ceremony, bestowing a collection of letters after the name of a man who would likely one day fall to the blood-soaked earth beside one or more of them in defense and preservation of what we love and hold most dear. Ceremonies and titles have never, and will never, make the world safer, nor mankind freer, for it is the blood of noble patriots and the tears of those left behind that change the world one stone at a time, until the weightiest of all stones rests upon the grave of the noblest of men and women.

Chapter 2
Don't Call Me Doctor

The two-hundred-mile flight back to Saint Marys, Georgia, seemed hardly worth starting the Citation's turbines, but our flying carpet doubled as a time machine. Instead of driving five hours, we would fly for slightly less than half an hour.

Clark Johnson—Green Beret, my former partner, and my current handler—stood at attention at the base of the boarding stairs before bowing deeply as I approached.

I caught his chin with three fingers and not so gently encouraged him to stand up. "Don't you do it! I mean it. Don't!"

His patented crooked grin said he couldn't resist. He motioned toward the stairs in his best Vanna White open-handed presentation stance. "After you, Dr. College Boy."

"I'm going to shoot you in the face if you ever call me *doctor* again."

"You only shoot who I tell you to shoot, and you should look at this from my perspective. I've got a bona fide doctor as a subordinate. What does that say about me?"

I gave him a shove. "It says you should've stayed in school."

"I went to school," he said. "It's called Fort Benning School of How Not to Get Dead When People Are Shooting at You, and it was just like college. My undergraduate work consisted of boot camp and infantry advanced individual training. After that, I got a master's degree in Ranger school, and finally my PhD at Special Forces Q-Course."

I had to agree. "Touché."

He threw up his hands. "Don't get all froufrou fancy on me. The Army didn't make me take French."

"Get on the airplane, and pretend to have some sense."

A flight of such short duration in the jet was surprisingly a lot more work than a long one. By the time we got to cruising altitude, we'd start our descent and fly an approach into our home airport. Clark may have sounded like a nutbag at times, but there was nobody I'd rather have beside me when workloads got heavy in a cockpit.

Disco was a better pilot than either of us, but he spent so many years alone in the cockpit of an A-10 Warthog that he tended to manage most of the responsibilities himself without needing—or wanting—any help from the guy in the other front seat. I loved flying with both of them, but I cut my teeth in high-performance aircraft with Clark by my side, so he'd always be my wingman.

* * *

Back at Bonaventure Plantation, the whole team had never felt more like a family than that day. Maebelle created one of her masterpiece dinners, and we devoured it for almost two hours before she presented the table with her world-famous cinnamon roll bread pudding with Blue Bell ice cream.

With bellies full and appetites sated, we laughed, joked, and truly enjoyed being together, just like the good old days before our lives became defined by our careers. We'd been fortunate enough to amass enough wealth to walk away from the business of beating back the wolves at the gate, but a spark that can never be quenched still burned in each of us to stand up when evil reared its head and bared its venomous fangs. As long as our bodies and minds could stay in the fight, none of us had the will, nor the desire, to turn our back on the freedom-loving world that demanded so much of us.

As the laughter and joy of simply being together under one roof, with no one lobbing mortars into our camp, reached its zenith, Clark's cell phone and mine rang simultaneously. The Klaxon produced by our phones could mean only one thing, and everyone at the table instantly knew our make-believe world of peace and prosperity had just been shattered by the cruelty of our reality.

Without saying a word, Clark and I rose from the table and headed for the library.

I pressed the phone to my ear. "This is Chase."

"Dr. Fulton, are you with Mr. Johnson?"

Clark and I said, "Yes, he's right here."

My phone went dead, and Clark thumbed his speaker button. "Okay, you've got us both, and we're level-two secure."

"Good evening, gentlemen," came the tinny voice through the speaker. "We have an assignment." Neither of us spoke, so the voice continued. "When was the last time you were on Saint Barthélemy?"

Clark and I shared a look, and I said, "I don't think I've ever been to St. Barts, and we learned earlier today that Clark doesn't speak French."

The voice seemed to ignore my attempt to lighten the mood. "Here's a little history lesson. Saint Barthélemy, officially referred to as Collectivité territoriale de Saint Barthélemy, is politically an overseas collectivity of France. That means the U.S. military and U.S. law enforcement can't conduct operations on the island or upon its territorial waters. That's where you come in."

Clark leaned back in *my* chair and crossed his feet on the corner of *my* desk. "So, you're sending us into a sovereign nation to conduct covert operations without the cooperation of that nation's government or people. Does that pretty much cover it?"

"Not exactly," the voice said. "If we, meaning you, accomplish the mission properly, the government will never know you were there, and the people will think you were godsent."

"So much for letting them eat cake," I said.

The voice said, "Marie Antoinette isn't exactly a factor in this one, but a man named Marcus Astor is."

I ran the name through my skull and kept coming back to John Jacob Astor, but I couldn't place Marcus.

My newly minted diploma didn't prepare me for the voice to say, "You're probably thinking about John Jacob Astor, and you'd be right, but I bet you're thinking of the wrong one."

"The wrong one?" I asked. "How many are there?"

"At least six," he said. "Because Marcus claims that his father was one of the illegitimate children of John Jacob Astor the Sixth, better known as the Titanic Baby."

Clark tapped a pen on the desk. "Is this history lesson really important to the mission?"

"Probably, but Mr.—excuse me—Dr. Fulton will be better able to make that determination when it's over. For now, indulge me while I pontificate."

Clark cupped his hands around his mouth and whispered, "Does that mean what I think it means?"

I shook my head. "Probably not, but I don't want to know what you think it means."

Turning my attention back to the phone, I said, "Forgive me, but why was he called the Titanic Baby?"

"John Jacob Astor the Fourth's wife, Madeleine Talmage Astor, was four months pregnant when the Titanic sank on April fifteenth, nineteen twelve, killing John Jacob. Of course, Madeleine survived, was rescued, and gave birth to Astor the Sixth five months later."

He paused, apparently to have a drink, then continued. "John the Sixth was a bit of a ladies' man and likely fathered several children out of wedlock—one being Phillip Astor, who, as fate would have it, is the father of our target, Marcus Astor."

Clark said, "I still don't see how any of this is relevant to our mission."

"You will, Mr. Johnson. A little indulgence is all I ask. Phillip is apparently Marcus's father, but he was killed under mysterious circumstances in nineteen fifty, only weeks after Marcus Astor was born."

"Mysterious circumstances?" Clark asked.

"Yes, it was reported that Phillip Astor was killed during a hunting trip in Colorado, but there was no evidence that Phillip ever spent a day hunting. In fact, he didn't own any firearms."

Clark turned his pen's attention from the desk to his two front teeth. "That is mysterious."

"Indeed, but it's likely unimportant as far as we're concerned, so back to the case at hand. Marcus was raised by his mother, Carolyn Willoughby, a lady of questionable morality, who told little Marcus of his glorious heritage as a descendant of one of the wealthiest families in American history. Of course, none of that wealth was passed down to Marcus, whose last name, according to his birth certificate, is also Willoughby, but that little detail didn't deter him from proudly proclaiming the Astor family name beginning in his early twenties."

I reached across the desk and grabbed a legal pad. "Don't stop now. It sounds like we're finally getting to the good part."

The man said, "I wouldn't call it the good part, but this is the part that leads us to your mission."

Clark said, "Wait a minute. You keep calling it our mission as if we don't have a choice."

"You're partially correct. Now that Stinnett is out of the game, you're the only team left with a ship, and this assignment can't be completed by a team of ground pounders."

"So, that's the catch," I said. "By accepting the ship, by extension, we're accepting all assignments requiring the ship."

"We made that clear when we offered the platform to you and your team, Dr. Fulton."

"Stop calling me doctor! And you did *not* make that clear."

"Well, we *assumed* you understood the responsibility that came along with the vessel."

"Assuming is a long stretch from making it clear. Wouldn't you say?"

"Okay, back to the mission at hand. Marcus Willoughby, aka Marcus Astor, is the CEO of a company called Astor Atlantic Holdings. Are you familiar with them?"

Clark answered for both of us after I shook my head. "No, we've never heard of them."

"There's no reason you should have," the man said. "The company exists for only one reason, and that's to move money between people who have it and people who want it."

"So, it's a bank," Clark said.

"Not remotely. The people who provide the money have specific expectations of the people who take the money, and transactions with those circumstances aren't always purely legal in most civilized societies."

"Enough with the vague doublespeak," I said. "Tell us exactly what you're asking—or ordering—us to do."

He cleared his throat. "Everything has a price . . . everything. We're talking about elections, multi-million- or multi-billion-dollar contracts, sales of companies or majority holdings within major companies, wars, treaties, and everything else you can imagine. It can all be bought for some price." He paused, and this time, if it was for dramatic effect, it worked.

Clark scowled. "This doesn't sound like the kind of thing we do. We kill people and break things. If anybody survives, we hand them over to somebody else. That's pretty much our job description."

The man said, "That *was* your job description. When the ship became part of your arsenal, that job description morphed into something new."

Clark cut him off. "We're a bunch of trigger-pulling knuckle-draggers, Scott. We're not the white-collar crimes division."

"If you ever use my name during any conversation we have again, do so having kissed Maebelle good bye, because you'll never see another sunrise."

I froze in utter disbelief, but little did I know what would happen next would be even more unbelievable than the man's unveiled threat against Clark's life.

My handler ducked his head and took a long, deep breath. "Yes, sir."

I couldn't believe my neck didn't break when I snapped my head around to eyeball Clark. He wouldn't look up to meet my gaze, and my blood ran cold.

Is Clark afraid of these people? Is the threat sincere? And is Clark's submission voluntary or forced?

Chapter 3
The Big Dog

The conversation, or perhaps our orders, continued. "Here's what we want from you. You're going to convince Mr. Astor you have money to invest. A great deal of money. And in return, you have an extravagant demand."

I tried to look away from Clark, but I couldn't do it. Seeing him subservient was a pain I couldn't endure.

"You want me to do this?" I asked.

"That's right," Scott said.

"I'm a thirty-three-year-old psychologist with a history of starting and ending fights. I'm not what you'd call a typical rich guy."

He said, "There's no such thing as the typical rich guy, and you'll do just as well as anyone else, especially since you understand the psychology of deception and influence better than ninety-nine percent of the world. You'll get a good haircut, a new wardrobe, and arrive in luxurious decadence. Play the part. Be seen. Dance, drink, and leave no question about your financial standing. Perception is fact, Dr. Fulton. Isn't that what your beloved Dr. Richter taught you?"

I tried to keep the bite out of my voice, but I failed. "Look, whoever you are . . . I've never refused a mission. I've never balked or hesitated. In fact, I've never considered giving anything less than one hundred percent and answering every call, but you're making mortal threats against my handler."

Clark raised his head with a look of horror on his face and pressed the mute button on the phone almost hard enough to drive it through the desktop. "Whatever you're doing, Chase, stop. You don't want to make an enemy of this man."

I tried to look as if I'd swallowed my pride, and he turned the phone back on. I said, "You're asking me to do something I've never been trained to do in a world I don't understand, for a reason I can't comprehend. I'm a simple man, and I do what I do for simple reasons. But none of those reasons has anything to do with money. I believe you, or someone, spent a great deal of time and money training me to do things very few people have the stomach for. At the risk of sounding overconfident, I've become extremely good at those things. That collection of skills—"

The man on the phone cut me off. "And there will come a time during this operation at which that collection of skills will be the only thing that can keep you alive, Chase."

Oh, so we've moved from Dr. Fulton to Chase.

"Now you have my attention," I said.

"I thought so. The concept for this operation has been in consideration for over a decade, but until now, it has been impossible with only one team. Before today, the size of the force required to conduct such an operation has been too large and diverse. Blending teams creates too much room for a leak."

"Slow down. I told you I'm a simple guy, and you're losing me."

"It's simple, Chase. Now that you have the vessel, a competent crew, and a capable, amphibious Action Team, you can conduct the operation without the probability of intel leaks. You know what they say about loose lips."

I pulled a bottle of water from the cooler. "Outline the op for me. What's the ultimate objective, and what are the essential steps to achieve that objective?"

The voice said, "Mr. Johnson, are you still with us?"

"I am."

"Good. We need a commitment to action prior to a full briefing. Are you prepared to commit to this mission?"

Clark turned to me with inquisition in his eye, and I slowly shook my head and said, "Not until I brief the team."

Clark gave a nod. "We're not ready to commit to action without involving the remainder of the core team."

The voice said, "Half an hour in the SCIF."

The line went dead.

Clark stood and headed for the door, but I caught him by his belt as he passed. "Oh, no, you don't. Put your butt back in that chair, and tell me what just happened. I've never seen you let anybody run over you like that."

He stopped in his tracks, but he didn't return to his chair. "Think of it like this . . . Before you went to The Ranch, you never knew people like us existed. The same is true for me when I became a project manager."

"Project manager?"

"That's my official title. Handler is just a term we use in the field."

"Whatever. Tell me why you didn't growl back when the big dog barked at you."

"When I became a project manager—handler—everything in my world changed. I now know things only a handful of people know. I've seen and heard things that can never be told outside the extremely tight circle. With that level of information, there is zero tolerance for dissension, and that is a level of responsibility that can't be appreciated until you've experienced it. Trust me. You do not want to become what I am."

I didn't like the side of Clark I was forced to witness, and for the first time in my career, I felt a sliver of distrust for the Board.

Clark, being a psychologist himself, even without the degree, saw that flash of distrust and laid a hand on my shoulder. "Don't let yourself do it, Chase. Keep the faith. We're on the right team, even if we don't always understand the plays the coach calls."

I released his belt. "I'll let you get away with that for now, but this is a to-be-continued conversation."

He shrugged, and we headed for the kitchen, where the rest of our "family" waited on pins and needles.

Penny was the first to speak. "When?"

"We don't know yet. But we have to make a decision."

I turned to Clark and raised an eyebrow.

He said, "Go ahead. There's nothing classified yet, but keep it tight."

"We've been offered a mission."

Hunter coughed. "Offered?"

"Well, sort of offered," I admitted. "The Board won't give us a full briefing until we commit, so I'll tell you what I know, and we can decide."

Mongo, our three-hundred-pound gentle giant, turned and admired Irina, his stunning Russian fiancée, and her daughter, Tatiana. They both wore looks of concerned understanding, and the big man said, "I'm in."

"Me, too," Tony offered.

I held up a hand. "Wait. I haven't told you anything about the mission yet."

Singer, our Southern Baptist sniper, gave me a wink. "You don't have to tell us anything about the op. If you're in, we're in. It's that simple."

"I appreciate that. I really do. But this will be our first mission with the new hardware, and the implication is that it'll be a two-part op with a waterborne element, as well as a ground op."

Hunter said, "Two great tastes that taste great together. Let's do it."

Skipper had been noticeably quiet, so I gave her a look and motioned with my chin to follow me. She did, and we stepped into the library.

"What's up?"

She sighed. "It's different now."

"Yes, it is. More than you know. But you're talking about Tony, right?"

She nodded. "You know I love you and all the guys, but with Tony, it's a different feeling. The thought of doing something to get him hurt, or worse, terrifies me."

"I understand, but he's already a good operator. He's strong, smart, fast, and fearless."

"He's also a rookie, and that fearless part is what scares me."

I took her hands. "Listen to me, Skipper. You're the best analyst any team could want. That brain of yours is a supercomputer beyond anything any of us can fathom. You're great at what you do, and there's no reason for you to ever doubt that. You don't get us hurt. You get us out of situations where we try to get ourselves killed. Don't change a thing. Just keep doing what you do, and we'll take care of Tony in the field. I promise you that."

She stepped in and wrapped her arms around me, and I returned her hug. With her face pressed into my chest, she mumbled, "Sometimes, I can't believe how far we've come since it was just the four of us."

I leaned back and cocked my head. "Four?"

"Yeah. You, me, Clark, and Anya."

I chuckled. "It's hard to remember back that far. Who knew we'd grow into anything like this?"

"You're telling me. We've got a hangar full of airplanes and a shipyard full of boats."

"Don't forget about the ops center upstairs."

"Of course. How could I leave that out? That reminds me. I've been wanting to talk to you about moving back down here. I'm working almost exclusively for you, and I don't rely on Ginger anymore. It just makes sense to be here instead of Silver Spring."

I nodded toward the door. "And, of course, this has nothing to do with young Tony out there, right?"

She blushed. "Well, maybe a little."

"Of course I'm supportive of you moving back down here. Pick a spot, and build the house you want. In the meantime, you're always welcome here at Bonaventure. We've got a few extra bedrooms, you know."

She squeezed me again. "Come on. Let's get back out there. I suspect we've got a briefing to do."

Back in the kitchen, the gathering had broken up. Penny, Irina, Tatiana, and Maebelle were missing, and Mongo was loading the dishwasher. Skipper and I helped clear the table. When the kitchen was returned to its pre-assault condition, I dried my hands and said, "Let's get upstairs, guys. The Board is waiting to hear from us."

Chapter 4
The Perfect Russian

With the team secure inside the ops center on the third floor of Bonaventure, Clark said, "I need to make sure we have a consensus before we go any further. There can't be any hangers. Is everyone in? If not, it's fine. I just need to know before we move forward."

Everyone confirmed, and the team became the epitome of e pluribus unum.

Clark gave the thumbs-up. "Okay, Skipper, ring their phone."

The man Clark had called "Scott" answered on the first ring. "I assume your team is assembled, unified, and prepared for the mission brief."

I clicked my pen and pulled my legal pad close. "We're ready."

"Good. We've wasted enough time already. Here is phase one. Arrive in Gustavia aboard a yacht we will provide. Spend half a week making yourselves seen, heard, and familiar on the luxury party scene. Ten million dollars U.S., and five million euros will be locked aboard the yacht's safe and will be used exclusively to bolster the ruse of your affluence. Are there any questions so far?"

Heads shook, and I said, "It sounds easy so far. Please continue."

"After you're underway, we'll deploy the *Lori Danielle* to lay off St. Barts, awaiting phase two."

The *Lori Danielle* was our newest piece of hardware—a nearly five-hundred-foot-long warship hiding behind the façade of being a meager research vessel.

"Once you've been sufficiently noticed, you'll make contact with Marcus Astor. You won't have any trouble picking him out of the crowd. A full dossier will be delivered to you when this briefing is concluded."

He paused, apparently expecting questions, but none came, so he continued. "Once contact has been made and some confidence established, you are to inform Mr. Astor that you are in the market for a rather rare piece of art—a Fabergé egg, to be precise." Again, a pause, but this one didn't go unused.

I said, "I thought all of the authentic Fabergé eggs were in museums or private collections."

Scott cleared his throat. "You would be mostly correct, but as is always the case, *mostly correct* equates to *wrong*. Seven of the fifty-two Imperial eggs are currently believed to be lost. You are to express interest in any of the sixty-nine original eggs, but primary interest in the fifty-two Imperial eggs."

I asked, "Do we think Marcus has possession of any of the eggs?"

"No, but we believe he has contacts who may be able to acquire at least a few of them. The one we want more than any other is the Third Imperial egg. If you don't already know, the egg was produced by workmaster August Holmstrom, we believe in eighteen eighty-six and eighty-seven, under the close scrutiny of Peter Carl Fabergé. It was produced under the commission of Czar Alexander III as an Easter gift to his wife, Maria Feodorovna. It is in the Louis the Sixteenth style and boasts eighteen-karat gold with sapphires and diamonds, but the real value is what's inside. When opened, the egg displayed a fourteen-karat gold Vacheron Constantin lady's luxury watch, with exquisite diamonds set in gold hands."

I said, "Forgive me, but the more you tell us about this mission, the less it sounds like something we're qualified to do. I can't imagine why you'd need an A-team to buy a Fabergé egg. This sounds more like an operation for—"

"This will be the last time you interrupt me, Chase. Is that understood?"

Clark looked up with lifted brows and terror in his eyes, but I didn't share his fear of Scott.

I said, "I'm in command of a team of highly qualified warriors. That makes me responsible for their lives. With all due respect, you don't have to look into the eyes of their widows when I fail to bring them home alive. I'm the one saddled with that responsibility, so I'll interrupt when I feel it is prudent and in the best interest of my team for me to do so. Now, you may continue your briefing."

Clark collapsed back into his chair, and Scott continued as if there had been no interruption. "As I was saying, phase one is all about establishing credibility. Once that is done, and we have the egg in our possession, we will have established ourselves as—"

I couldn't resist. "I hate to interrupt again, but you keep using the pronouns *we* and *ourselves*. Does that mean you'll be joining us for this operation?"

"Fine, Mr. Fulton. *You* and *your* team will have established credibility."

I raised a finger with the definite intention of interrupting again to correct his calling me *mister* instead of *doctor*, but Clark drew his knife, deployed the blade at the press of a button, and stuck the tip into the conference table with impressive force. Seeing his willingness to destroy the table, and by extension, perhaps also me, I refrained, and Scott carried on.

"After we—excuse me—after you have the egg in your possession, you are to express interest in a much more valuable piece. We want you to finance the overtaking and commandeering of a Moroccan warship, specifically, one *Descubierta*. It was a corvette originally built for the Spanish Navy in the late seventies, but then it was sold or traded to Morocco sometime later. Egypt ended up with two or three of them as well, but the *Descubierta* was the first of its class. At any rate, it was reconfigured and commissioned as a nearshore patrol vessel by the Moroccans. I'm sure you've put it together by now, but in case you haven't, I'll be glad to continue."

I tossed my pen onto the legal pad. "I'm simple, but I'm not stupid. You want to catch—actually, you want *us* to catch—Marcus Astor in the act of piracy against a warship on the high seas, thereby eliminating the protection he enjoys on the island of St. Barts. It's an excellent plan, but why not lead with that instead of the foolishness with the Fabergé eggs?"

"For the reason I laid out . . . To build credibility. If you're wealthy enough to chase a trinket, albeit a valuable one, you're wealthy enough to buy a naval corvette."

"Okay, I'll buy that. Where do we pick up our yacht, and when do we leave?"

"The departure time is up to you, but your yacht will be waiting in Miami. I think you'll recognize her when you see her again."

I ran through my catalog of yachts I'd likely recognize but came up empty. "Give us four days to research and train up, and we'll be ready to go."

"Very well. Other than the parameters I've laid out, the operation is yours, Mr. Johnson. Oh, and there's one more thing. We need an authentic native Russian speaker, preferably a woman, to scrutinize the egg and serve as a passable Fabergé expert in the short term."

I couldn't keep the smile from my face. "I know just the perfect Russian, and something tells me she'd love to get involved."

Scott said, "I thought you might. Feel free to bring her in at your discretion, Chase. And Mr. Johnson, do you have any questions or concerns?"

Clark scribbled a note on his pad and looked up. "Not right now, but I may have some before we go wheels-up."

"Not *we*, Mr. Johnson. You're not going anywhere near the heart of this mission. You're too valuable for the Board to risk losing you. I'm sure you understand."

"Of course," Clark muttered.

"Are there any other questions or concerns for me?" Scott asked.

I scanned the room, but no one's eyes showed any inquisition, so I said, "That's all we have for now. We'll direct any questions to Clark if they come up. For now, we'll await your call to action while we train up."

"Very well," he said.

After the line fell silent, I wasn't surprised to hear Hunter's voice before anyone else's. "Really? A golden egg? That's what we're doing now? Hunting the goose that laid it?"

I chuckled. "Not exactly. We don't care about the goose. She's long dead. But the egg apparently hasn't hatched yet. Skipper, can you dig up everything you can on the Fabergé eggs, with particular attention to the Third Imperial?"

"I'm already on it," she said. "How much do you want to know?"

"I want to know what it's worth and where it is."

"Oh, I've got that information right now. The experts' best estimate is something north of twenty million dollars, and it's been missing since nineteen sixty-four, when it was bought by an unidentified bidder for twenty-four hundred fifty dollars."

I scratched my temple. "What makes it worth twenty million if it brought less than twenty-five hundred at auction?"

Skipper shrugged. "This is two thousand seven, so nineteen sixty-four was a long time ago, and maybe the fact that it's missing makes it more valuable by mystique. I don't know."

I leaned back and stared at the ceiling. "I guess the Board thinks I can buy it for ten million or less since that's the cash they're sending with us."

Clark leaned in. "Are you talking to yourself or the ceiling?"

"I was really just thinking out loud. I'm still baffled by the whole idea of buying some obscure bejeweled egg as a setup to buy a warship."

He threw up his hands. "Ours is not to wonder why. Ours is but to put the cart before the mule."

I squeezed my eyelids closed and shook my head. "None of that is right . . . Nothing about it. I've decided you do that on purpose because nobody could possibly be that dumb and have stayed alive as long as you have."

He gave his patented crooked grin that melted women from Bangor to Bangladesh. "I'll take that as a compliment, College Boy. Thank you."

"You obviously don't know the definition of the word *compliment*, either."

Skipper knocked on the console. "That's enough foolishness. We need to focus. I'm obviously the only one qualified to be the voice of reason in this room, so we need to talk about Anya."

Anya Burinkova was the single greatest mistake I made in my early days as an operator. If there's a rule that comes before rule number one, it's this: do not fall in love with foreign operatives. I broke that rule and about a billion more because of the beautiful Russian assassin who'd been dispatched by the Kremlin to find, interrogate, seduce, and recruit me into spying for the Rodina. It didn't work out the way the boys in Red Square planned, but the captivating and deadly sparrow would be a part of my life I'd never forget.

"What about her?" I asked.

Skipper raised her eyebrows and huffed. "You're thinking about bringing her in to play the part of the Fabergé egg aficionado, and that's a terrible idea. If you don't agree, let's go downstairs and talk to your wife, Penny, about it."

"Where did you get that idea?"

"Because you said you know just the perfect Russian for the job. Who else could you possibly have been thinking about?"

I gave her a wink and turned to Mongo, our six-foot-eight-inch mountain of a man. "I was talking about his fiancée, Irina."

Chapter 5
Old Dogs

The next morning, the team, minus Skipper, started our day in one of my favorite places on Earth—the massive gazebo housing the eighteenth-century cannon overlooking the brackish water of the North River on the back lawn of my home, Bonaventure Plantation.

Hunter started our training meeting. "All right, fearless leader. How do we train up for a mission to buy a golden egg?"

"That part is easy," I said. "Skipper and Irina are managing the heavy lifting for phase one of the operation. She'll get Irina up to speed, and with any luck, Mongo's fiancée will turn out to be an actress worthy of the silver screen."

"Good," Hunter said. "I wasn't looking forward to learning to drink out of a tiny little teacup with my pinky in the air."

I stared at my partner, who'd fight a chainsaw just to say he did. "You've been spending way too much time with Clark."

"What?" Hunter said. "Isn't that what people who buy jewelry eggs do?"

"How should I know what they do? I probably know less about Fabergé than you."

He planted his hands squarely on his hips. "Do you even know how to spell Fabergé?"

"Sure."

"Then you're wrong. Just knowing how to spell it means you know more about these people than me."

"Fabergé wasn't people. *He* was a person, Peter Carl Fabergé."

He shook his head. "Are you proving my point on purpose, or just trying to show off?"

"Neither. But that's not what today is about. Do you know how to dance?"

His dissolution with Romanov-era, Russian bejeweled eggs melted into definitive confidence. "Have you seen *Dirty Dancing*?"

"Of course. Everybody's seen *Dirty Dancing*. Why?"

He shot a thumb toward the center of his chest. I choreographed it."

"You did not!"

He shrugged. "Yeah, well, I could have, but they didn't ask me."

I laughed. "Okay, I'll take your word for it. I don't think any of us wants to see a sample."

Hunter wasn't having it. He stretched his neck and waved his arms. "Step back and give me some room. And somebody give me a beat."

To my surprise and secret delight, Singer tapped one booted foot and mouthed a beatbox that would've been right at home on any hip-hop album. Disco, Tony, and Mongo joined in, clapping and cheering Hunter on. Disco occasionally clapped on one and three, but Singer encouraged him to get back on the two and four.

Hunter's performance lasted a minute and a half, and that was ninety seconds of my life I'll never get back. "Just stop. I've seen enough, and you guys should be ashamed of yourselves for encouraging him. Please, don't ever do that again, any of you. Especially you, Singer. How did you learn to do that anyway?"

"It's just rhythm, baby. I can't help it if Hunter and I are the only two who have it."

"No!" I demanded. "Just, no. Let's get to work."

With the raucous performance finally over, I asked, "Does anybody speak French?"

Singer straightened his shirt. "Yeah, a lot of people speak French. Like, a whole country of them. I think it's called France."

"I'm going to beat you to death with a coffee cup if you don't straighten up. Do any of *you* speak French?"

Disco raised a pensive finger. "I have a little French, but I'm not conversational, and it's been a few years. I worked with the French Foreign Legion for a few months and picked up enough of the language to get by."

"That's good news," I said. "We'll be operating on a French-speaking island. I suspect we'll be able to get by with English for the most part, but there may come a time when we need the local language. That's thing number one. Now, let's talk about thing number two, the ship."

I paused long enough to reset the mood and attention of my audience. "The Board said we're supposed to purchase the warship through Marcus Astor, but I don't like that idea. I prefer buying information and intel from Astor and taking the ship ourselves."

Tony stuck a finger in the air. "Maybe I'm wrong, and I know I'm the new guy, but isn't the whole purpose of the warship thing to catch Astor in the act of piracy so he becomes an international criminal and thereby no longer untouchable on St. Barts?"

"It is, but if we get involved, we can get word to the Moroccan Navy that we're taking the ship as part of an international sting operation. We might be able to convince them to surrender the ship without a fight, knowing they'll get it back after the operation. That would save lives, and if we can bring some of Astor's men on board for the raid, that's the tie-in we need to arrest our boy, Marcus, on an international warrant."

Singer asked, "When did we become international law enforcement with arresting authority?"

"Good point," I said. "But it's likely we can recruit some guys with badges to clean up behind us."

Heads nodded, and Tony asked, "Do we know anything about the Moroccan Navy? I mean, are they fighters, or are they likely to give up a warship when confronted?"

"We don't know yet. But we will soon. I've got Skipper on the research now."

He said, "She's a busy girl. Between bringing Irina up to speed on the eggs and researching the Moroccan Navy, she's covered up."

I chuckled. "Oh ye of little faith. That girlfriend of yours can juggle flaming swords, memorize the complete works of Shakespeare, and write computer code to balance the federal budget at the same time. Don't worry about her. She's more capable than all of us combined."

Muttered agreement filled the air, and I continued. "That brings up another point we need to cover. Mongo, we all remember Irina's surprisingly impressive performance on the firing range. She dismissed her prowess as having learned to shoot with her brother under their father's teaching, but I don't buy it. She's had some formal training from somewhere, and we need to know where, how, and when. Can you get her to come clean about that?"

Mongo sighed. "I'll do my best, but honestly, Skipper may have better luck than me. She's pretty tight-lipped about her life in Russia."

I pulled my phone from my pocket and had Skipper on the line in seconds. "Hey, I need you to pull a tooth for me."

"Sure, which one?"

"I need you to get Irina to tell you when, where, and how she learned to shoot, and don't let her blow you off with the story of shooting with her brother and father. That's bogus. No one in the former Soviet Union had privately owned firearms. I need to know what she knows and how she learned it if we're going to put her on the ground for this op."

"You got it, boss. No problem."

"Thanks, Skipper. You're the best."

"Yeah, I know. Bye."

"Okay, Skipper is on it. Does anyone else have anything we need to talk about before we go hot for the day?"

Everyone shook their heads.

"In that case, we'll start the day with a little run. Try to keep up with the guy with only one foot. Tony, you don't count. You're young and fresh out of The Ranch, but if anybody else beats me back here, you're exempt from tomorrow's run."

"What's the course?" Singer asked.

"I'll yell out the next point every time we reach an objective. The first objective is the southwest corner of the old paper plant. And . . . go!"

As expected, Tony leapt out to an early lead, but my plan to call out the points along the way forced him to stay within earshot of the rest of us. I set the pace, and we somehow fell into locked step as Singer started calling cadence like a boot camp drill sergeant. We sang and ran as if we were one well-oiled machine.

At the paper plant, I yelled out, "Oak Grove Cemetery, southeast corner."

We stayed in perfect step as we made the turn back toward the Saint Marys waterfront. Even though Tony could leave all of us in his tracks, he fell into close formation with the rest of the team, and Singer kept singing.

When we finally made our way back to the gazebo, we'd put just over five miles behind us in boots and cargo pants. Everyone was winded except for Tony, and I had questions for our new kid.

I grabbed his T-shirt and yanked him close to me. "Why did you do that?"

"Why did I do what?"

"Let me beat you!"

"I didn't let you beat me. I stayed with my team and accomplished the mission. Besides, I don't want to be excluded from tomorrow's run. We're a team, and I don't want to be left out."

I gave him a shove and turned to Hunter. "Take care of your boy."

Hunter pulled the former rescue swimmer aside, and I listened closely as my partner explained the world to the Coastie. "Well done, kid. You made the boss proud, and you proved you're a team player. You did the right thing, but if we get in a scuffle, don't you dare let yourself be average. You're a red, white, and blue bulletproof hero, and don't you ever forget it. You got me, swimmer?"

"I got you, Sergeant Hunter."

Hunter shoved him and stepped close as Tony scrambled to regain his balance. Hunter threw a right cross, and Tony ducked it, but his off-balance maneuver sent him to the ground, where he rolled onto his back and drew his pistol.

Hunter froze and stuck his hands in the air. "You're learning, kid. Now, holster that thing, get up, and dust yourself off. We've got work to do."

When Hunter and his charge returned to the gazebo, I said, "That's a nice little warm-up, don't you think? Now, let's turn some gunpowder into noise. What do you say?"

Our visit to the armory lasted only long enough for everyone to leave the bunker with two cans of ammo, a pistol, and a rifle. The shooting house Cajun Kenny built for us inside the former paper plant was a thing of tactical training beauty. The double-stacked railroad crossties stopped every bullet we poured into them as we cleared rooms, analyzed each other's technique, and spent five thousand rounds honing our close-quarter battle skills to a razor's edge.

"Nice job, guys. I don't know if we'll have to clear any rooms in St. Barts, but if we do, nobody short of a team of SEALs will be able to stop us."

Tony scoffed. "SEALs? Ha! We'd run through those guys like Chinese food through Hunter's guts."

Hunter eyed him. "First, don't ever disrespect the SEALs. They're some of the finest warriors on the planet. And second, Chinese food does that to everybody—not just me."

Tony threw up his hands. "Sorry, I hear you, and it won't happen again. But you're wrong about Chinese food. You've got a special relationship with kung pao chicken."

"It's called digestive efficiency," Hunter barked.

"Speaking of room clearing," Mongo said. "Hunter's guts—"

"No! Again, just no," I said. "None of us wants to hear the rest of whatever you were about to say. It's time for us old dogs to learn some new tricks."

Chapter 6
New Tricks

I gave a little nod to the North River flowing black and smelling the way only marshland can. "Gentlemen, today we're going to get wet."

Hunter and Tony grinned, but Disco the pilot, Singer the sniper, and Mongo the giant clearly weren't excited about the prospect.

Disco groaned. "You realize it's December, right?"

Mongo pretended to shiver, and Singer closed his eyes, presumably talking to God.

"I know what month it is, and I know exactly what the temperature of Cumberland Sound is, but we don't get to choose when and where we go to work. We just have to embrace the suck and soldier on, as Clark would say."

Tony scanned the area. "Speaking of Clark . . . Where is he, and why isn't he included in the fifty-five-degree dunking?"

"As far as I know, he's still sleeping, and he's not getting dunked because he won't be on the mission. You heard the guy from the Board. Clark's too valuable to lose. I do have a special guest of honor who'll you'll all remember, though. He's waiting for us on the boat."

Mongo said, "I'll bet I can guess who you called in, and if I'm right, the team will have an even number of feet again."

I gave him the pistol fingers. "You'd be right about that, and he's not a man who tolerates tardiness, so head for the boathouse, and let's fire up the Mark V."

Our Mark V patrol boat wasn't pretty, but it was, by far, the sexiest piece of hardware we owned. It had been an asset of SEAL Team four at Little Creek, Virginia, but they sucked every ounce of life out of the old girl and used her as a target for assault train- ing until she finally ended up aground and forgotten at Kings Bay Naval Submarine Base, which just happened to be our next door neighbor. With a pair of custom-built diesels, a new layer of radar- absorbing coating, and a brilliant cooling system designed and built by none other than Earl herself, the craft was back on the wa- ter and deadlier than it had been when it originally left the Halter Marine shipyard in Gulfport, Mississippi, in 1995.

With the beast's twin diesels purring like a pair of four-ton li- ons, we climbed aboard, and Tony took the helm. He gently mo- tored away from the Bonaventure dock and brought the fifty-five- ton water dragon up on plane. Tony and the Mark V made navi- gating the winding North River look like child's play while the rest of us enjoyed the ride provided by the pneumatic system de- signed to absorb the shock of even the worst of sea states and keep its passengers dry and comfortable. I fully intended to rob the team of both of those luxuries as the day progressed.

The southern end of the river emptied into Cumberland Sound, offering wide open, glassy water, which Tony took full ad- vantage of. We were soon racing across the surface at sixty knots, and it felt like a lazy Sunday afternoon drive. The day may come when I am no longer fascinated and surprised by the *Lori Danielle*, but it wasn't going to happen that day.

Our warship masquerading as a humble research vessel looked like a mighty wall of haze gray cutting across the sound in front of us. The same look I wore shone in every eye aboard the Mark V.

Hunter said, "I still can't believe she's ours."

"Neither can I, my brother. Neither can I."

"She's coming with us to St. Barts, right?"

"She is," I said. "But at least part of the team will be aboard a ship with softer beds and fewer deck guns."

He shrugged. "I don't mind the harder bed, especially if we need the deck guns."

"You make an excellent point."

He gave me a jab. "I usually do."

I called to our helmsman. "Lay us alongside the port stern quarter."

Tony called over his shoulder. "Aye, sir. Port stern quarter."

An enormous part of my civilian heart envied the time my teammates spent in uniform. I was a competent warrior, but there would always be that invisible line separating the veterans from those of us who played baseball instead of shipping out to boot camp on our eighteenth birthday.

Tony expertly matched the *Lori Danielle*'s speed, and Mongo and Hunter tossed the fenders over our starboard rail. Our expert helmsman snuggled us alongside the ship, and our crew secured the offered lines from above.

Tony listened to the commands of Captain Barry Sprayberry on the bridge of the *LD* and spoke into his mic. "Roger . . . Dead slow . . . Lines secure and taut . . . All stop, aye."

The splash of the *LD*'s anchor as it left its cradle and plummeted toward the muddy bottom of Cumberland Sound was louder than the engines of the ship. Two minutes later, with the anchor set and our bows in the wind, a pair of deckhands lowered a cage from the stern deck of the *Lori Danielle*, and my team climbed aboard. We were deposited on the deck seconds later, and Naval Special Warfare Operator Master Chief Deandre Lewis, Retired, stood at rigid attention on his one remaining leg he was born with, and the prosthetic attached at his hip. He offered a sharp salute, and I was once again reminded that I'd never been taught how to do that. That didn't stop me from returning the gesture of mutual respect to the best of my ability. Hunter took the opportunity to fine-tune my hand position, and we finally progressed to hugs and handshakes all around.

"Dre, the only one you've not met is the new kid on the block. This is Tony Johnson, former rescue swimmer and current protégé of Hunter."

Tony stuck his hand in Dre's. "Good to meet you, Chief."

"Call me Dre. My chief days are well astern. I don't think I ever had the honor of being plucked out of the water by you, but a few of your shipmates have yanked me from the jaws of hypothermia on the open sea a time or two. Thanks for your service."

Tony eyed Dre's prosthetic leg. "I think I'll keep calling you chief, and from the looks of things, you're the one who deserves the thanks for his service."

Dre knocked on his leg just below the hem of his khaki shorts. "What? This old thing? Ah, it was just a misunderstanding. You should see the other guy. To the best of my recollection, he's feeding the sharks on the bottom of the ocean."

We assembled in the crew mess, where Dre had a whiteboard set up, and he delivered a master class in waterborne vessel assault. When his briefing concluded, Dre motioned to me. "Come up here, Chase. Help me make a point."

"This can't be good," I said. "You're going to hurt me, aren't you?"

"I'm just a one-legged, washed-up SEAL, and you're a hard-chargin', high-speed door kicker. I can't hurt you."

I shook my head. "This is gonna suck."

When I reached Dre's side, he threw an arm around me. "Look at us. Chase is eight inches taller and has at least thirty pounds on me."

Before he finished detailing my physical superiority, he planted his prosthetic foot right on top of mine and leaned a shoulder into my armpit. No matter how hard I begged my core muscles to keep me upright, there was nothing I could do. I was flat on my back and regretting having been volunteered for the demo.

Dre offered me a hand and pulled me to my feet. "If you forget everything else I said, don't ever let this point leave your head. No matter how big, strong, or well-equipped, every ship has a weakness. Chase is a monster next to me, but his prosthetic foot and lower leg are his soft spots. The key to assaulting any ship is to first identify its weakness and then exploit the hell out of it."

When Hunter finally stopped chuckling at my baby giraffe impression, he said, "I bet you can't do that to Mongo."

Dre eyed our giant. "Every ship, regardless of size, has a vulnerability. Come on up here, Mongo. You're a big ship. Let's find your Achilles' heel."

The big man slowly shook his head. "No, thanks. I'm good."

Dre laughed. "What's wrong, big man? Are you afraid of a one-legged SEAL?"

"No, Chief. I already happen to know where my weakness is, and I'm not interested in having you exploit it."

Dre held up a finger. "Aha! We've now stumbled onto the second thing you need to remember. Come on up here, Mongo. I won't hurt you. I promise."

He sighed and rose to his full height, ducking as he moved forward to avoid hitting his head on the beams.

Dre waved a thumb between Mongo and himself. "There's even a greater mismatch between this Neanderthal and me, but watch."

The SEAL flinched toward the giant, and Mongo instinctually covered his crotch with both hands.

Dre patted him on the shoulder. "Thanks, Mongo. You can have a seat."

Mongo reclaimed his chair, and Dre asked, "Did everyone see what happened when I hinted at an attack?"

Hunter said, "Yeah, he defended his weak spot."

Dre snapped his fingers. "And that's precisely what the skipper of any warship will do when threatened. He will do whatever is required to protect his weakness. Most of the time, that means maneuvering to bring guns to bear on the threat. Do you want to get into a shootout with a Spanish corvette in open water?"

No one volunteered for the gunfight, so Dre continued. "That's right. You do not, so that means you have to identify the vulnerability before the skipper of the target vessel can hide it from you. I'll step into the ring with Mike Tyson if I can identify his weakness, and that's the attitude you have to carry into a waterborne assault. Know more than your opponent—especially where the guns are."

He erased the sketches he'd made on the whiteboard and turned back to face us. "Any questions on the academics?" No one spoke, so he said, "Good. Let's get wet and learn just how hard it is to take a ship at sea."

We made our way from the mess to the aft deck, where Tony was first to make a disturbing observation. "The Mark V is gone!"

Dre held up a hand. "Relax, boys. I brought a few friends along to make your day on the water a little more enjoyable. They're going to demo how an assault is supposed to look, and your captain is going to try to make them look like fools. Who are you putting your money on?"

Grumbling came as most of the team bet on the SEALs, but I said, "I've got a thousand bucks on Captain Sprayberry and the *Lori Danielle*."

Dre put on a smile. "I'll take that bet *and* your money, Chase."

"We'll see."

Dre was the only man on deck not searching for the Mark V. "Since this is going to look a lot more realistic than most civilian eyes can handle, we're taking the circus offshore, where nobody will call the Coast Guard. The last thing we need is a bunch of Coasties boarding us, doing our hair, and polishing our boots."

Tony perked up. "Hey! That's not fair."

Dre held up both hands. "You're right. I should've been more sensitive. I left out the part about them checking to make sure we have enough life jackets for everyone aboard."

Unwilling to push it any further, Tony made a mental note and swallowed his pride.

Dre pulled a radio from his belt and keyed the mic. "Deck to bridge. Take us offshore to the rendezvous point."

Once clear of the St. Marys Pass and into open water, the helmsman transformed our displacement hull into a flying fish by deploying the foils. With the ship making at least sixty knots, Dre sighed. "That's magic."

I had to agree. "And the skipper isn't pushing her yet. She'll make at least twenty more knots with all four power plants online."

He let out a long, low whistle.

I asked. "Are you still feeling good about our bet?"

"Speed comes with its own basket of weaknesses. I've still got money on the frogmen."

Chapter 7
Pay Up

With the east coast of Georgia well astern, Captain Sprayberry gave the order to land the *Lori Danielle*, and the helmsman dutifully obeyed, reducing the flying ship, once again, to a displacement hull and cutting her speed in half.

"It's time to watch the fireworks," Dre said from our position on the helicopter pad.

I made a mental note of the position of the mid-afternoon sun in the southwestern winter sky. "You may want to hold on."

Dre scoffed. "I've had my sea legs for twenty years. The necessity of me holding on ended a long time ago."

I shrugged. "Don't you mean your sea leg?"

He tried not to smile but failed. A second later, he wrapped his left hand around the rail. "What are you thinking?"

"If I were playing the aggressor, I'd keep the sun at my back and hit the stern hard."

He nodded. "Radar doesn't care about the sun. And what's the advantage of hitting the stern of a ship you want to seize and not sink?"

"Radar may not care about the sun, but the crew on deck does. They won't be able to see the aggressor coming out of the sun, and that will be at least a slight advantage for the pirates. I can rake the stern well above the waterline with heavy fire, eliminating anyone who wishes to shoot back. As long as I keep my fire above the engine room, my rounds won't affect propulsion or steering."

"Not bad for a landlubber," he said.

I pointed over our heads. "One more thing. I'd cripple the chopper early in the campaign. I don't need that thing raining down fire from above."

"That's good thinking. You obviously paid attention in class. Maybe you'll get a gold star by your name, after all."

As I scanned the sun-kissed southwestern horizon, expecting to see the bow of our Mark V at any moment, I was thrown nearly off my feet by a violent turn to the northwest. Pods that looked identical to inflatable lifeboat canisters burst open, revealing five M134 General Electric Miniguns capable of firing six thousand rounds per minute from each gun, giving the starboard battery a thirty-thousand-round-per-minute capability.

Although they weren't dispensing the tons of lead they were capable of sending into the air, the muzzle of each gun gyrated through its potential arc of fire in an effort, by the electronic fire control system, to lock onto the hull of the aggressor.

With a spray of white water roiling from its bow, our patrol boat sliced through the waves at sixty knots, closing on the *Lori Danielle* at an impressive rate from the northeast—the opposite direction I expected.

I bumped Dre's arm. "Why aren't the miniguns locking up the Mark V?"

"Because it doesn't want to be locked up. The material of the hull, the angles of the exterior surfaces, and the radar-jamming capability of your Mark V render the miniguns almost useless."

"Almost," I said. "But not quite. If the fire control officer takes manual control of the guns and targets by sight, the radar isn't necessary."

"You're right, young Jedi, but the speed of the Mark V makes manual targeting a real challenge, plus, the fifty-cal on the bow can do a lot of damage to those miniguns while they're trying to get radar lock."

The Mark V screamed down the starboard side of the *LD* and executed a maneuver I would've never dreamed of trying. The helmsman used the ship's wake to slow the momentum of the patrol boat just enough to throw the wheel hard over and crush the throttles to their stops, sending the stern of the Mark V into the air in an impossibly tight arc. When the stern landed, the bow— and its Ma Deuce fifty-cal—were bearing directly on the stern of the *Lori Danielle*, and anything or anyone occupying the fantail would've been cut to ribbons. As impressive as the maneuver had been, the follow-up left me in awe.

A SEAL with a massive weapon that looked like an enormous rifle with a claw protruding from the muzzle stepped onto the cabin top of the Mark V and fired, sending what was actually a grappling hook over our stern rail. The second the hook landed on the deck, a second SEAL yanked the slack line from beneath the rifle and made it fast around a cleat mounted high on the patrol boat. An instant later, the Mark V's helmsman pulled the throttles into reverse and stretched the line like a rubber band between the *LD* and the patrol boat. What I hadn't noticed was a second line run through a pully on the head of the grappling hook. A two-man team of SEALs mounted the taut line, and the lead man on the line clipped the smaller line to his harness.

The gunner who'd launched the hook lifted the small line from the deck at his feet and ran for the stern as fast as his boots would carry him. His motion pulled the small line and accelerated the pair of SEALs on the line toward the stern rail faster than they could've ever propelled themselves hand over hand. Before I could piece together what was happening, the two SEALs were on deck with short-barreled rifles at the ready and standing guard, while six more men made the crossing. Once the last man was aboard, he tossed the grappling hook overboard, and the Mark V backed away.

The eight men who'd boarded undeterred split into a pair of four-man teams and moved to opposite sides of the vessel as they made their way forward.

Dre keyed his mic. "Okay, guys . . . Knock it off. Knock it off. Knock it off. Exercise is complete. Recover."

I scanned my team to find each of their faces frozen in fascination. "I've never seen anything like that," I said. "I'm amazed."

"Don't be amazed, Chase. Be motivated. By the end of the day, we'll have your team moving just like us SEALs. It's not hard. It just takes timing, communication, and coordinated movement."

"It's still astonishing."

Dre did a little dance. "Shock and awe, baby. Shock and awe. Now, pay up. I want my thousand bucks."

"Will you take a check?"

He groaned. "No, but I'll give you a chance to win your money back, double or nothing, if you're man enough."

"I like the stakes, but what's the bet?"

He motioned toward the Mark V. "If you've got a man on your team who can make that boat dance the same jig my man just did in less than ten tries, you'll get your money back."

Little did he know he'd walked right into my trap.

"I've got a better wager for you. I've got a helmsman who can do it within three tries if you'll demo it one more time. And I've got twenty-five hundred bucks to back it up."

Dre repeated his dance. "Oh, you're on, and you're going down."

He yanked the radio from his belt and held it to his mouth, but I put a hand on his arm, stopping him from making the call.

"Give me twenty minutes. I need to run ashore and pick up my helmsman."

He frowned and lowered his chin. "Are you going to get a coxswain from the Navy base?"

"Nope, that would be cheating, and I'm an honest man. Wait here."

I hooked Disco's arm as I turned from the rail. "Get the skipper on the horn and let him know we're launching the chopper."

As promised, twenty minutes later, Disco and I set the chopper down as gently as a baby's kiss, and Penny stepped from inside.

She said, "I hear you've got a maneuver I can't do. Let's see it."

Dre's jaw dropped. "All right, all right. I see. You're bringing out the big guns. Let's see you do this."

Captain Sprayberry got the *LD* back underway, and the SEAL at the helm of the Mark V blasted off ahead of the ship. Just minutes later, the party started again, and we broke hard to port with the patrol boat coming on strong.

I said, "Watch what he does when he crosses the ship's wake."

Penny locked her laser focus on the helmsman and memorized his every movement as he repeated the reversing maneuver. If possible, it was even more impressive the second time.

Penny eyed Dre, then turned to me. "What's the bet?"

I said, "I bet him twenty-five hundred bucks you could repeat that maneuver within three attempts."

Penny rolled up her sleeves. "Double it if you've got the guts, and I'll do it on the first try."

Dre took a step back, "Okay, I've got the bankroll, but do you?"

Penny hooked a finger toward the helm of the Mark V, and the sailor brought the eighty-foot vessel alongside as if it were a toy. The crane operator deposited Penny onto the deck of the Mark V, and she powered away.

Our captain put the bow back into the wind and waited for the patrol boat to turn inbound. The whole sequence repeated, and Penny's unruly hair looked like a crimson explosion as she roared down the starboard side. The wake rose, and she cut the wheel with one hand while expertly working the throttles with the other. The bow rose, and the stern danced across the wake, almost bringing the jet drives out of the water.

When the stern came to rest, the Mark V was perfectly aligned with the *LD*, and her deck gun waited ominously to belch its deadly fire. She'd done it on the first try, but my wife wasn't finished showing off. She hammered the throttles, bringing the bow of the boat within inches of the stern of the *Lori Danielle*.

Penny surrendered the boat back to the SEALs and sprang from the bow rail of the Mark V and back on board the *LD* with a graceful leap. "Top that, boys."

She climbed back to the observation deck, where we'd watched the performance. When her foot hit the deck where we stood, she brushed an imaginary flake of dust from her shoulder and stuck out her palm. "That'll be five grand, thank you very much. Now, *you* pay up."

Chapter 8

Lap Crawler

Dre took Tony by the collar of his shirt and pulled him within inches of his face. "Can you do what she just did?"

Tony, unfazed by the SEAL's aggression, leaned back, straightened his collar, and shrugged. "Not on the first attempt, but give me time, and I could master it."

Dre studied Penny for a long moment before turning to me. "Is she operational?"

"Maybe. But I want everyone to learn the maneuver. In the heat of an operation, it's impossible to predict who'll be at the helm."

"That's part of the reason we're here. I don't understand why you were given the Mark V without any real training on the thing. I'll leave a man behind for as long as you want him to work specifically on boat tactics and handling, but Ms. Penny has a gift. Hold on to that one."

"Don't worry, my friend. I'm not letting her get away."

"I hear you," he said. "I don't think we need to waste the afternoon on small boat operation and tactics, though. Let's get your guys some hands-on experience boarding, assaulting, and commandeering. Will you take the ship from the Mark V or from the *Lori Danielle*?"

"I don't know yet. It's all fluid for now, so I don't want to rule out anything at this point."

"Good plan," he said. "Let's start with assaulting the *LD* from the Mark V. That water's cold, and your boys are going to get wet. Are you planning to suit them up?"

"They won't be wearing neoprene for the actual assault, so I say we should practice like we play."

"Good answer. They would get a lot of grief from these SEALs if they put on rubber suits."

I asked, "How did you get a team of SEALs on this one? I thought you and the Navy parted ways."

"None of the guys are active duty. They're all retired or separated. Most of them are doing private security work, and a salty old chief tends to attract a pack of strays. If you need any of them, I'm sure they'd be open to an offer."

"We don't have a SEAL," I said, "but our team is bursting at the seams right now. I'd like to collect a few names and numbers for the future, though."

* * *

We practiced covert boarding techniques first, and everyone stayed dry other than a little spray from some high-speed maneuvers in the patrol boat, but the hostile boarding techniques were a different story.

Dre stood on the stern deck of the *LD* with a firehose in his arms. "Gentlemen, this is your worst enemy during a hostile boarding. Hearing rifles crack overhead is terrifying, but until you've been knocked off the side of a ship in twenty-foot seas by one of these, you have no idea what fear tastes like."

My team listened intently, but the looks on their faces said they weren't buying what Dre was selling, and the SEAL noticed. He smiled. "Oh, goody. You don't believe me. This is my favorite part. Who's the best hand-to-hand fighter on the team?"

Everyone looked around, but no one raised a hand, so I said, "Mongo for brute force, but Hunter for speed and inside work."

Dre took three steps back and positioned his feet for a fight. "Okay, Hunter and Mongo, it is. If either of you can take this hose away from me, I'll eat my peg leg."

Hunter looked up at Mongo. "Let's do this."

Both warriors balled their fists and moved in on the water-bearer. When Dre opened the nozzle, he hit Hunter first, lifting him off his feet and planting him on his back six feet away.

Mongo's size and strength proved to be more effective. He leaned into the blasting stream of water and stayed on his feet, but his progress toward Dre was slow. Hunter gathered his wits and climbed back to his feet. Instantly developing a plan, he planted his hands on Mongo's hips from behind and pressed the monster toward the assaulting nozzle. Their combined strength and weight increased their closure rate, and Dre yelled, "Close your eyes, Mongo."

The giant followed the order, but he didn't know why until the blast of high-pressure water struck him in the face, sending him tumbling backward over Hunter.

With the two men defeated and dripping wet, Dre closed the nozzle. "Anybody else want to give it a try?"

Mongo struggled to his feet and offered Hunter a hand. They stood, looking like drowned rats, and Hunter asked, "What about a sidearm? Couldn't we put a double-tap straight up the stream and neutralize the threat?"

Dre said, "I could tell you the answer, but you'd forget it. Make your pistol safe, and show clear."

Hunter drew his Glock 17, ejected the magazine, and racked the slide, sending the chambered round into the air. He caught it and showed the ejection port to Dre.

He nodded. "Okay, holster, and this time, forget about trying to get to me. Just try to shoot me. I bet you can't."

The gleam in Hunter's eye said, *Oh, really?*

Dre ignored the look and scanned my team. "Tony, you're the rescue swimmer, right?"

"Yes, Chief."

"Good. Get behind Hunter, and rescue his pistol before it makes it to the bottom of the ocean."

"Aye, aye, Chief."

Tony moved reluctantly behind Hunter, and Dre opened the nozzle. The stream of near-freezing water filled the air in front of the men, and Hunter drew his Glock.

As the weapon came to bear on the nozzle, Dre shut it down. "What are you doing, Hunter?"

My partner shook the water from his face and lowered his pistol. "I'm shooting you just like you ordered."

Dre grinned. "But you're using both hands. How are you going to climb aboard a ship at sea with both hands on your pistol?"

Hunter hung his head. "You're right. Let's go again."

The water came, and Hunter drew. Dre shifted between blasts of water to the muzzle of the pistol and Hunter's face. It took less than a second for my partner to lose control of his sidearm, and it went skittering across the deck, right into Tony's waiting hands.

As Tony and Hunter recovered and wiped their faces, our soft-spoken sniper said, "Check your nine o'clock, Chief."

Dre turned to his left to see Singer in a perfect sniper's prone position with an imaginary rifle trained on the SEAL's chest.

Singer said, "Bang."

Dre turned to me and shot a thumb toward the sniper. "He's good."

"He certainly is," I said.

By the time the exercise had sent each of my men into the frigid North Atlantic at least a dozen times, Dre shut down the hoses and began his debrief as my team stood shivering in the December wind blowing across the deck. "Any questions?"

Not a shivering head or teeth-chattering mouth said a word, so Dre nodded. "Good. Get inside, get dry, and let's shove some calories down our gullets. It'll be dark in an hour, and that's when this little game really gets fun."

We dried, changed clothes, and ate ten thousand calories each.

Boarding the ship under the veil of darkness turned out to be easier and a lot drier than the previous attempts.

Dre asked, "What have we learned, troopers?"

"We learned we like this a lot better in the dark," Hunter said.

"Bingo!" the SEAL said. "Darkness is our enemy's enemy, thereby making it our friend. That's enough for tonight. Let's head home."

Penny took us home, and everyone slept on the ride. Back at Bonaventure, with the Mark V tucked safely in her home, we showered and collapsed into bed.

* * *

Breakfast was biscuits, sausage, and gallons of coffee.

Tony stretched and groaned. "Am I the only who's sore this morning?"

Disco laughed. "Wait 'til your age starts with a four, kid. You'll learn what the word *sore* really means. I'm not sure I can take another day like yesterday."

I shoved a bite into my mouth and wiped my chin. "I'm not putting us back in that cauldron today. Dre promises we'll stay mostly dry today unless somebody screws up and takes a fall. Tony, you're going to be safety most of the day. We're going to work on assaulting the Mark V from the *Lori Danielle*. If anyone goes into the drink, it'll be a nasty fall, and I want the rescue swimmer in the water, double-quick."

Tony said, "You got it, boss. There's one more thing we need to consider. If you do take a fall and end up between the hull of the *LD* and the Mark V, it's important that you dive . . . and dive hard. You can't survive, and I can't get to you if you get pinched between the two boats."

"I was just about to cover that, but it probably carries a little more weight coming from you. Does anybody else have anything?"

Skipper spoke up. "I have a gift. It's the schematics of the *Descubierta* when she was retrofitted from a corvette into a coastal patrol boat. They're hand-drawn but good quality, so I suggest studying them closely. And there's one more thing . . . Clark wants a status briefing by close of business today."

"We can do that," I said. "And nice job scoring the schematics. Those will come in handy. How's it going with Irina, our Fabergé egg expert?"

Skipper pursed her lips. "Interesting, to say the least. I think maybe you and I should have this discussion privately."

Mongo's ears perked up, and I motioned toward him and raised an eyebrow.

Skipper nodded. "Yeah, him too."

Mongo and I crammed another biscuit down our throats and followed Skipper to the library.

"What's up?"

Skipper put on her nervous look that's impossible to hide.

"Spill it," I said.

She squirmed. "Before I get started, Mongo, do you know Irina's full history?"

"I don't know anybody's full history except my own. How far back are you talking about?"

"Twenty years."

Mongo frowned. "She was a teenager twenty years ago."

"Yeah, I know, and I don't want you to be upset with her for not telling you everything. I pushed her pretty hard, and I dug up some stuff I shouldn't have been able to find, but that's what I do. Did you know she was recruited as a GRU officer?"

Mongo stood in stunned silence for several seconds before asking, "That's the Russian military intelligence service, right?"

"Sort of. Officially, it's the Main Directorate of the General Staff of the Armed Forces of the Russian Federation, formerly known as the Main Intelligence Directorate, thus the alphabet soup, GRU. That agency is the largest intelligence force of the Russian Federation, and they employ over twenty-five thousand Spetsnaz special operators like you guys."

"Like us?" I asked.

"Well, not exactly like you guys, but you get the picture. Believe it or not, the GRU has over six times more intelligence operatives deployed in foreign countries than all other intelligence agencies in the federation."

"I didn't know that," I said. "Are you saying Irina was Spetsnaz?"

"Not exactly, but she was trained by them and a few other agencies. She served for almost two years in the GRU before marrying her husband and getting pregnant with Tatiana."

I fell into my chair and locked eyes with Mongo. "Is she a spy?"

Mongo inhaled all the remaining oxygen in the room and landed in a wingback. "I can't believe this is happening again."

I leaned forward in my chair. "Slow down, big guy. Let's not convict her yet. Skipper said she worked for the GRU for a couple of years before getting pregnant. What happened then?"

Skipper closed her eyes, I assume to situate the pieces of the story into order. "You probably don't know the history I gave Special Agent White about Tatiana's father, Maxim Dmitrievich Volkov. It's a really long story, but he was what you might call a *damskiy ugodnik.*"

She paused while Mongo and I ran that one through our heads. Mongo shrugged just before I did, and Skipper sighed.

"I thought both of you guys spoke Russian. I'm so disappointed. It means ladies' man, or horndog, if you prefer. Anyway, *his* father—Irina's father-in-law—was a former communist party official, but his boys, Viktor and Maxim, weren't the best eggs in the nest. Viktor was a thief, and our boy, Maxim, well, he got himself shot by a red commie colonel for messing with his wife. When that happened, of course Irina fell out of favor with the Kremlin, as well, and she got kicked to the curb. Or at least that's the story I could dig up. If the story is true, she's clean, but if it's a cover story, she could still be operational, and we let her crawl right onto our laps."

Chapter 9

You Could've Led with That

Two immediate missions arose simultaneously, and the possibility of Irina Volkovna, Mongo's fiancée, being a Russian spy on the payroll of the GRU was not the more important of the two. My primary concern in that moment was the psychological well-being of my friend.

I looked up at Skipper from my desk chair. "If you wouldn't mind, let Mongo and me have a couple of minutes."

She put up no argument and vanished through the door, closing it behind her.

I didn't want the five hundred pounds of my mahogany desk between Mongo and me, so I stood and rounded my desk so the coming conversation wouldn't feel clinical. I nestled into the second wingback beside my friend. "Pick your head up, big man. Tell me the first thing you think of when I say Tatiana Volkovna."

Sheer willpower kept the tear from escaping the corner of his eye. "The way she smiles every time I see her."

"I want you to think about that smile, and listen closely to what I'm about to tell you. Will you do that?"

He nodded.

"Good. That smile from that teenage girl is the most genuine thing you've likely ever experienced. That little girl loves every ounce of your three hundred pounds, and she turns you—the strongest man I've ever met—into putty in her hands. She's precious and honest and sincere in that affection for you. And you feel exactly the same toward her. She brings a joy to your life you've never known, and you give her a sense of family and even a loving father she's never known."

He looked up wearing confusion in his eyes. "This isn't about little Tatiana, Chase. It's about her mother."

I gave a hint of a smile. "That's the only thing you've been wrong about in a long time. It's absolutely about Tatiana. The two of you fell in love before you ever knew her mother's name."

"Maybe you're right about that, but this is still about Irina being a spy."

"Here's why I don't believe that to be true. Irina loves her daughter more than she'll ever love you or anything else on this Earth. She may have been an operative of the GRU at some point in her life, but would she let the daughter she loves more than life itself fall in love with an American just so she could break her heart when the whole charade comes crashing down in the future? Irina knows you love her daughter as if she were your own child. The love of a mother for her daughter is something you and I will never be able to fathom. It's stronger than any bond you and I will ever feel. Is the woman you love cruel enough to crush her own daughter's heart when she delivers you and the rest of us to the masters at the Kremlin? Would Irina Volkovna—soon to be Irina Malloy—do that to Tatiana?"

He swallowed hard and let out the breath he'd been holding. "You're a wise man, Chase, and I'm a better person for having you in my life. Every man should be so lucky to have a friend and brother like you. Thank you."

I cleared my throat. "I want you to know that I wholeheartedly believe everything I've just told you, and I do not believe Irina is a spy, but—and this is a huge but—you and I both know what has to be done."

He whispered, "Yeah, but I can't do it."

"I'd never ask you to. It's too much, and you're too close. I'll do it, but I have to ask you to tell the biggest lie of your life."

His eyes snapped open. "A lie? What are you talking about?"

"I need you to make Irina believe you have no doubt. I don't want her to see any trace of betrayal in your eyes when she looks at you."

He smiled. "None of that's a lie, Chase. I do love her, and I don't believe she's capable of betrayal with me or Tatiana."

"That's what I hoped you'd say. Now, get out of here and send Skipper back in."

When a man Mongo's size gives a hug, there's no question about its sincerity, and that day, at that moment, I was the recipient of one such hug.

Skipper reentered the library and once again closed the door. "You were putting that psych degree to work, weren't you?"

"No, I was just talking with a friend and brother I love."

She settled into a chair. "That's what I thought. But our conversation is going to be a little different, isn't it?"

"Yes, but that doesn't mean I don't love you, too."

"Yeah, yeah, whatever. Let's get to it."

I slid a pad from my desk and laid it across my thigh. "We have to do it."

"I know, but that doesn't mean we have to like it. Is it going to be you and me?"

"At least."

Skipper raised an eyebrow. "Who else?"

I tapped on my legal pad. "Do you still have Anya's number?"

Skipper threw her head back and glared at the ceiling. "No, Chase! That's a terrible idea and an even worse plan. What about Penny?"

I chewed on my bottom lip. "If Irina is a spy, it doesn't matter what Penny thinks about how we clean it up. If she's a spy, we're all going down . . . and going down hard."

Skipper sighed as if accepting a death sentence. "Okay, but you're telling her, not me."

"You go make the call, and get Anya here as quickly as possible. I'll talk to Penny."

Skipper headed up the stairs to the ops center, and I headed for Penny's office. To my surprise, she wasn't there, so I trotted toward the kitchen.

"Has anybody seen Penny?"

Hunter pointed to the back door. "She's outside on a phone call. Is everything all right?"

"I hope so. But if I don't come back inside within five minutes, send lawyers, guns, and money."

"That doesn't sound good," he said as I slipped through the door and onto the back gallery.

Penny was in a rocking chair with her phone pressed to an ear with one hand and twisting her hair with the other. I always loved it when she did that. It was innocently sexy, and that's a special kind of sexy.

She thumbed the end button and dropped the phone onto her lap. "What's up? You look worried."

"You didn't have to hang up," I said. "I could've waited."

"No, it's fine. I was on hold anyway. They'll call back. Tell me what's going on. I don't like that look."

I slid onto the chair next to hers and took her hand.

She squeezed and said, "Oh, boy. The look was bad enough, but now you're holding my hand. Let's hear it."

The letters after my name and the weight of my college transcript should've qualified me to say something better than what fell out of my mouth, but education betrayed me. "I need Anya."

Penny jerked her hand from mine, lowered her chin, and raised an eyebrow. "Pardon me?"

"I need—"

"Oh, I heard you. I just don't believe you. You need Anya for what? You certainly don't need her for this mission. I suggest you start talking."

"Skipper uncovered something potentially disastrous for the team."

She lowered her chin even further. "Potentially disastrous is exactly how I'd describe this conversation so far."

I drummed my fingers against the arm of the rocker. "Irina might be a spy."

"Our Irina? Mongo's Irina? What are you talking about?"

In through my nose, and out through my mouth. Just keep breathing.

"We discovered that she used to work for the GRU. That's the Russian military intelligence. We might never have known if Skipper wasn't vetting her for inclusion in the mission. I want to take her to St. Barts with us, masquerading as a Fabergé egg specialist, but I can't if she's a spy. There's only one way to know. I have to pin her down and drill her. If she's a spy, she'll lie, and I may never detect it, but if Anya is in the room, she'll know the exact lie Irina has been programmed to tell. She'll see the signs, and she'll be the ultimate polygraph test."

Penny let her shoulders fall, and she slid her hand back into mine. "You could've led with that. It would've been a lot better than saying, 'I need Anya.'"

I hadn't expected to chuckle during the conversation, but I did. "I guess you're right."

She wrinkled her nose. "Yeah, I tend to be right."

"You're coming with us, aren't you?"

"Coming where, with whom?"

"To St. Barts, with the team, to drive the boat."

"I wouldn't miss it for the world. When will Anya be here? Because I'm not missing that for the world, either."

Skipper came through the door with relief in her eyes. "That went better than I expected."

I looked up. "Were you eavesdropping?"

"Duh, of course. I'm not brave enough to pull up a chair and listen."

Penny said, "It's okay. I'm not going to kill him, but I am putting you in charge of chaperoning."

Skipper gave the thumbs-up. "I've got you, girl. Don't worry."

"Just promise me one thing," Penny said. "If she looks good when she gets here—and God knows she's going to—please mess up her hair and spill something on her before you let her in."

Skipper winked. "Oh, you know I will. But speaking of getting here, Disco is on his way to the airport to preflight the Citation. Are you going with him to pick her up?"

Penny rose from her rocker. "Yes, ma'am. *We* surely are."

Chapter 10
Family Lies

Back through the kitchen door, we went to find four pairs of eyes staring in anticipatory fear, so Penny went first. "Relax, everyone. Your fearless leader isn't in trouble, but he is under scrutiny."

The eyes relaxed, the tension fell, and I pointed to Mongo. "You're in charge. Don't get anybody dead, and we'll be back by lunch."

By the time Penny and I arrived at the airport, Disco already had the Citation on the ramp.

I parked inside the hangar and stepped from the Suburban. "How does she look?"

He shoved his phone into his pocket. "Great. No squawks, and the flight plan is filed. I was just updating the headcount. Three up, four back, right?"

I motioned toward the vehicle. "Yep. Penny didn't have anything else to do, so I talked her into coming with us."

Disco nodded. "Yeah, right. I'm sure that's exactly how it went. It's nice of her to make the sacrifice."

Penny closed the passenger-side door and slid the strap of her oversized purse across her shoulder. "Yep, that's me . . . Sacrificial."

Disco pointed toward her satchel. "What's with the rucksack? It's just an up-and-back."

"You boys just fly the plane and stop worrying about my accessories."

I leaned on tiptoes to get a peek into her bag. "You don't have a gun in there, do you?"

She squeezed the top of the bag closed and made a shooing motion. "What are you, TSA all of a sudden? Just fly the plane."

I threw up both hands in surrender and turned to Disco. "We've been relegated to the status of hired help."

He shrugged. "What can you do?"

In perfect unison, Penny and I said, "Fly the plane."

So, Disco and I flew the airplane.

We landed at Washington Dulles International and taxied to the FBO, where we were met by a lineman directing us to a temporary parking position and a gentleman wearing a suit that only an FBI agent would wear. I bounded down the stairs and leaned toward the lineman.

He pulled away one muff of his hearing protection, and I said, "We're a quick turn. No services required."

The lineman chocked the nosewheel and placed an orange traffic cone in front of the Citation.

I crossed the tarmac and stuck my hand out toward Dudley Do-Right in the suit. "Chase Fulton."

He shook my hand and stared up at me through mirrored shades that were straight out of *Smokey and the Bandit*. "Special Agent McIntyre. Come with me."

I could have some fun with this guy, I thought, but the good angel on my other shoulder won the battle. "Nice to meet you, Agent McIntyre."

Penny fell in beside me, and the oversized bag, that was now missing, made perfect sense. Her hair and makeup were flawless.

"You look nice."

She shrugged. "I just brushed my hair and put on a little powder. I thought it might be windy and cold up here, so I didn't want my face to get windburned."

"Good thinking," I said. "It's certainly colder up here than South Georgia."

She shivered. "I don't like it. I say we spend as little time as possible this far north."

I slid my hand into hers. "I like the way you think, sweetheart."

Agent McIntyre held the door for us, and we stepped out of the cold wind and into the inviting FBO. I didn't want to admit it, but a legion of butterflies fluttered in my gut. The lobby was bigger than most fixed base operators I'd visited, but there were only a dozen people milling about. I picked out the pilots by their oversized watches and swaggers, thankful I had neither.

"I don't see her," Penny whispered.

The agent stepped around us and continued toward a back corner of the room, and we followed. When we stopped outside a door leading from the small corridor, he spun on a heel. "I need to see some identification for both of you. We were only expecting one."

"*We?*" I asked. "Who's *we?*"

He pulled a cred-pack from a pocket inside his jacket and let it fall open in front of my face. "The U.S. Department of Justice."

The other angel won that time, so I mirrored his performance and let my credentials fall open even closer to his face. "*Supervisory* Special Agent Chase Fulton, U.S. Secret Service."

The man shrank inside his cheap suit and thumbed a six-digit code into the cipher lock on the door. He held the door for me, and I stepped in front of him and held the door for my Southern belle.

I heard her before I saw her.

"Is Penny! Come, come. You must meet Penny."

I don't remember the last time I heard Anya's Russian-accented voice, but it had not softened. I stepped through the door to see the Eastern Bloc beauty leading a striking woman across the room by the hand. Anya never took her eyes off Penny, but the brunette in trail locked eyes with me.

I glanced across my shoulder as Special Agent Boy Scout pulled the door closed, leaving him and me locked inside a room with three of the most beautiful women anyone has ever seen. I suddenly hoped Singer was somewhere praying for me at that moment.

Before I could get anything to fall out of my mouth, Anya said, "Friend Gwynn, is Penny. She is wife of Chase. Is nice to see you, Penny. This is friend Gwynn."

Penny recoiled at the full-frontal assault but managed to stick out her hand.

The brunette shook it and said, "I'm Gwynn Davis, Anya's partner. I've heard a lot about you, and it's nice to finally put a face with a name."

Penny, being the chameleon she is, adapted in an instant and put on the Southern charm school smile like the master she was. "It's nice to meet you, friend Gwynn."

Their hands slipped apart, and Gwynn said, "Anya was certainly right about one thing. You are as beautiful as she described. All of a sudden, I feel like the short, dumpy girl at the party."

Penny took half a step backward toward me and glanced down at herself as if she'd forgotten how she looked in my favorite pair of blue jeans. "Stop it. I just threw this on and fluffed up my hair a little as we were coming off our plane. You're far from dumpy, but Anya and I tend to make most women feel short."

Anya finally peered around Penny and let herself smile. "Is nice also to see you again, Chase."

The flashbacks came in rapid-fire bursts: Seeing her for the first time, a decade earlier, from a mile away with my binoculars pressed tightly to my face at Belmont Park. The flowing, white cotton shirt over the orange bikini on the beach in St. Thomas. The blood pouring from her shoulder after the gunshot wound that should have killed her. Lying facedown on the trampoline and watching dolphins play in *Aegis*'s bow wake. And her battered body in the demolished prison van on the outskirts of Sol-Iletsk in Orenburg Oblast, Russia, when the men who would become my team of brothers-in-arms worked alongside me to extricate her from the notorious Black Dolphin Prison.

"Hello, Anya."

The moment may have happened in an instant, or perhaps we stood there staring at each other for a lifetime, but the real time warp happened inside the Citation on the southbound leg back to St. Marys: overcoming the nearly irresistible yearning to crane my neck and peer into the cabin where Anastasia Robertovna Burinkova sat only three feet away from Penny Thomas Fulton. Imagining the conversation, or, even worse, the cold silence between the two, made keeping my attention focused on the cockpit all but impossible.

* * *

Back at Bonaventure, Penny kissed me on her way out the back door. "Have fun with your other women. I'm going to play with the boys."

I settled into my seat in the ops center with Skipper on one side and Anya on the other.

The Russian started the ball rolling. "Tell to me why I am here."

"We're mole hunting," I said. "No, that's not entirely correct. We have no evidence there's a mole in our organization, but we've

come across someone who has the pedigree for it, and that someone came from you."

Anya cocked her head. "You are blaming me for mole?"

"No, that came out wrong. I meant you're the reason Irina
Volkovna is in the States, and that was an incredibly kind thing for
you to do. You changed her and her daughter's lives forever by
bringing them here. I'm not suggesting you knew anything about
her past."

Anya relaxed. "Good. What is inside her past you do not like?"

"Skipper will bring you up to speed on the facts before I tell
you what I want to do."

Anya spun in her chair to face Skipper, and the briefing began.
She ran through Irina's brief history with the GRU and the details
of how she fell from the Kremlin's grace. The Russian listened intently and made no effort to interrupt.

When Skipper finished, Anya pursed her lips. "I now understand, and is good reason for you to have maybe doubts. I think
also you want me to be inside interrogation of Irina to listen for
semeynaya lozh'."

"*Semeynaya lozh'*?" I asked.

"Yes, is translated to *lies of family* in English. Is cover stories we
are taught inside former Soviet Union and now Russia to tell to
interrogators when questioned or confronted. These things are
taught to all intelligence operatives in Russia so many times they
become true inside head. This means if we tell *semeynaya lozh'*
during polygraph, we have no reaction because we believe inside
our mind these things are truth."

I puffed out my cheeks and let out a long breath. "I didn't
know the part about the polygraph. That's deep."

Anya stared directly between my eyes as if I were the only other
human on Earth. She'd been taught the technique in State School

Four on the Volga River, where her youthful innocence was replaced with the dark soul of the Russian Sparrow.

"Don't do that," I said.

"Do not do what?"

"That thing with your eyes."

She smiled, and I turned to my legal pad.

Skipper snapped her fingers several times in rapid succession. "Focus!" She drove a finger through the air toward me. "You're married!" Then she turned the accusatory finger on Anya. "And you're . . . whatever you are. Stop!"

I tapped my pad with the tip of my pen. "We're going to have a talk with her."

Anya said, "This means interrogation, yes?"

"Not initially. We'll start with a nice, friendly conversation, and turn it into an interrogation only if it becomes necessary."

She let her eyes drift to the ceiling. "Am I only to watch and listen, or to also give questions?"

"That's the part I've not decided yet. You know more about Russian intelligence operatives than all of us combined. How do you think we should handle it?"

She stared down at the table. "I think is two ways to do this. First way is Russian way. I will strip her of clothes inside cold place and tie her to chair . . ."

"Stop right there. We're not doing that. What's the other way?"

"Is friendly approach. I will talk with her and be subtle. If she is spy, I will know, but I must know one thing . . ."

"What is it?"

She licked her lips. "What will you do with her if she is spy, and what about daughter, Tatiana?"

"There's another wrinkle in this," I said. "I assume you know Irina and Mongo are a thing."

"A thing?"

"Yes. He asked her to marry him, and of course she said yes. Mongo and Tatiana are almost inseparable."

"Yes, I know these things, and for him, I am very happy. And also for Irina and little Anya."

I chuckled. "We don't really call her that anymore."

"Yes, I think probably you did not, but this is name she had when I met her inside New York. She is brilliant dancer."

I leaned back and let my pen fall to the pad. "She got a full scholarship to Juilliard."

"This is wonderful for her."

Skipper slapped a palm onto the conference table. "Hey! Stop it. This isn't get reacquainted and hold hands. It's work. Remember? Spies, espionage, that sort of thing."

Anya said, "I am sorry. It has been long time since I have seen Chase, and I—"

"No!" Skipper demanded. "That's not what this is. Now, get back on task."

I shook my head at how easily I was distracted from the task at hand. "It's my fault. I'm sorry. It won't happen again."

"Yeah, I know," Skipper said. "I won't let it. Now, listen up, Anya. Our mission is to buy a Fabergé egg, specifically the Third Imperial egg, and we want to send Irina in under the guise of being a Fabergé expert when we make the buy. If she's a plant, we obviously can't include her, but worse than that, if she's a spy, we've allowed her into the circle, and we've got a lot of damage control to do."

Anya frowned. "You are to buy Fabergé egg? This is very strange mission. This cannot be all of mission. There must be more."

Skipper said, "As far as you're concerned, it's just about finding out if Irina is a mole. I can't brief you in on the full mission."

"I understand this, but why not just ask me to play part of Fabergé egg expert? I can do this, and you know I am not spy."

Skipper rolled her eyes. "I think you know why that's not possible. Let's get back to Irina. Here's what I had in mind, and it didn't include ripping off her clothes and tying her to a chair. I want to bring her in here. That gives us the home-court advantage. I don't think she's ever been inside the ops center. When we get her in here, I say we tell her what we know and see how she reacts. Hopefully, we're worried for no reason, but if it turns ugly, we'll have her pinned up so she can't run."

"This is also good plan," Anya said.

I nodded my approval and asked, "What about Mongo?"

Skipper said, "I think we need to keep him as far away from this as possible. You left him in charge, right?"

"Yeah, he's running the training today."

"What kind of training?" Anya asked.

I grinned. "Oh, no, you don't."

Anya smirked. "Was worth try, no?"

Skipper slapped the table again. "Hello! I thought you two agreed that we're not doing that personal thing."

"Sorry," I said. "I think we should bring her in right away. There's no reason to wait. If she's clean, it won't matter, and we'll have worried for no reason, but if she's a plant, the sooner we find out, the better."

"Agreed," Skipper said. "There's no time like the present."

Chapter 11
The Right Thing

I stood from my seat at the conference table. "I need a minute."

Leaving Anya and Skipper alone in the ops center, I stepped into the third-floor foyer and dug my fingertips into my scalp.

How did we get here? I'm about to accuse the woman Mongo loves of being a Russian spy, and I'm going to do it with Anya Burinkova sitting beside me. Anya, the woman who was the real Russian spy and who almost cost me everything. A decade ago, I was one millimeter away from being a professional baseball player, and now I'm making decisions and conducting investigations of national security in my house.

Skipper poked her head through the door. "Are you okay?"

"No, I'm not. This is too much. I can handle people shooting at me. I can handle airplanes falling apart around me at twenty thousand feet, but what we're about to do in that room . . . I don't think I'm capable of putting that woman through it. It's cruel to everyone involved, and it's going to drive a wedge right down the middle of our team."

She stepped through the door and closed it behind her. "What are you talking about? Is this about Anya? Is having her here making you crazy?"

I landed on one of the chairs resting by the wall. "I don't know. Maybe. You were there. You remember what it did to me."

Skipper nestled onto the chair across from mine. "Yeah, I remember, and it sucked. But look around you. We came out the other side, and look what you've built since then."

"It's not about me. It's about Mongo. What will this do to him? If Irina's clean, there's always going to be that lingering question hanging over their heads. She'll always want to know how her fiancé—or maybe husband, eventually—could let me question her about being a spy. And even worse, if she's dirty—if she's really a mole—Mongo is going to crash. I just don't think I can do it."

Skipper leaned back in her chair. "What would Dr. Richter do?"

I snapped my head around to glare at her. "What did you say?"

"What would Dr. Richter do? He's your mentor. What would he tell you if you could sit down with him right now?"

I crossed my legs, remembering the wisdom of Dr. Robert Richter in the classroom when I was an undergrad psych student at UGA. But as much influence as he had in those halls of pedagogy, his real genius showed itself outside the hallowed ground of Old Georgia when he led me by the hand from the world I believed was to be mine and into a realm of intrigue founded on the bedrock of the preservation of freedom. It would not be an exaggeration to say Dr. Robert "Rocket" Richter was more influential in molding me into the man I'd become than anyone else in my life.

"I'm going to the gazebo. I'll be back in an hour."

To my surprise, Skipper offered no resistance and stepped back through the secure door and into the ops center.

I brought an old trusted friend with me to the gazebo—a friend whose roots ran deep in the fertile fields of our closest communist neighbor to the south. I punched one end and toasted the other with the cigar lighter I carried in my right front pocket every day of my life. The aromatic white plume of smoke rose above my head and filtered through the rafters, finally disappearing and leaving behind little more than a hint it had ever existed. I wondered if my fate would be the same. Would I drift off into oblivion, having changed nothing at all in the world I left behind? Would I destroy the lives of three people I cared about by planting seeds of doubt and demonstrating that my priorities lie in political considerations rather than in the beauty of three people dropped into each other's worlds?

I pulled the cigar from my lips and examined the dark leaf wrapper. As I studied the lines, folds, and stream of smoke trailing from the ash, I could almost feel the tortured muscles in the tobacco farmer's back as he labored over the ground into which his father had poured boundless waves of toil and sweat and tears under the relentless thumb of a dictator who would never know the horrors of abject poverty and a life sentence behind the bars of oppression. One of the finest cigars on Earth rested beneath my hooked finger, and the family who grew, dried, and rolled the tobacco into the masterpiece earned less money the prior week than I paid for the single cigar. Yet somehow, they beat onward from day to endless day, surviving but never truly living.

I spent the forty-five minutes it required to turn the Cohiba from beautiful brown leaves into empty gray ash, as Dr. Richter whispered in my ear.

I climbed the steps to the Bonaventure's back gallery and discovered Anya and Skipper in the rocking chairs Penny and I occupied only hours before. "Get her over here."

Skipper gave me a look I couldn't define and asked, "Now?"

"Yes. I'm going to shower. If she gets here before I come out, send her to the gazebo."

Anya whispered, "What is he doing?"

Before the door closed behind me, I heard Skipper say, "He's doing the right thing."

By the time I'd washed the smell of cigar smoke from my skin, climbed into fresh jeans and a sweatshirt, and headed through the back door, I saw Irina Volkovna standing by the muzzle of the once-mighty cannon beneath the octagonal lines of the gazebo. Her delicate hands slid across the surface of the weapon that had once belched fire, smoke, and hell, sending men to their deaths in a thundering roar they'd hear throughout all eternity.

Skipper and Anya weren't on the back gallery, so I stepped back inside and found them in the sitting room. "I've changed my mind."

Skipper looked up. "About what?"

"About Irina. I thought the right thing was to cordially give her the opportunity to explain her past and convince me she was no longer working for the GRU or any other arm of the Russian government."

Apparently, I had Anya's undivided attention. "And now what have you decided?"

"I want you to attack her."

"Attack her? What are you talking about? I would kill her even if she is trained by GRU and Spetsnaz. Is this what you want?"

"No, of course not. I only want her to believe you're going to attack her. She's in the gazebo. I want you to draw your knife— I'm sure you have at least one—and lunge for her as if you were going to do the thing you always threatened me with."

She grinned. "You mean gut you like pig, yes?"

"Exactly. But don't hurt her. If she shies away, which is exactly what I expect her to do, we'll know she's precisely what she appears to be—a gentle, kind mother and fiancée. But if she fights back, she'll have some explaining to do."

Skipper frowned. "*This* is the plan you came up with after smoking a cigar for an hour and channeling Dr. Richter?"

"No, this is exactly the opposite of the plan I came up with and something Dr. Richter would never do, but I'm not him, and there's too much on the line to be docile. We have hard questions that must have honest answers, and there's no greater honesty than reactions to a life-threatening event. And who's a better life-threatening event than Anya?"

"I don't like it," Skipper said.

Anya stood. "I do not like it, either, but is perfect plan. Is brilliant, actually. I have only one question for you. What would you have me do if she counterattacks with gun or knife?"

Her question froze me where I stood. "I hadn't considered a gun. I don't know if she owns one, but Mongo practically has an armory, so she has access."

"Is very dangerous if we do not know if she has gun. If I am close to her, I can stop gun before she can pull trigger, but I cannot do this without hurting her badly. If is only knife, this is not problem. I can move, keeping cannon between us while I calm her down. She will not hurt me with knife, but gun is serious problem."

"Here's the plan," I said. "I'll go talk with her and give her a hug. If she has a gun, I'll sit down on the left side of the gazebo, but if not, I'll move to the right. If I sit down, do not come through the door. Do you understand?"

"Yes, of course I understand. If sit, do not come because she has gun. If move to right, make her believe I am trying to kill her. This is what you want, yes?"

"It's not exactly what I want, but it's what we need."

"I don't like it," Skipper said, "but I don't have to. I can't say I've got a better plan, but a lot can go wrong with this one."

"Nothing can go as wrong as having a Russian mole waking up beside one of our teammates every morning and passing everything we do back to Moscow."

The analyst shrugged. "I get it. What do you want me to do?"

"Follow Anya through the door and across the yard. If this thing goes south, you may be the only voice who can talk Irina off the ledge."

She sighed. "Oh, great . . . Now I really hate this plan. Let's go."

I pushed through the back door and bounded down the steps to the lawn. I made enough noise to cause Irina to look up. Seeing me coming, she smiled and cocked her head the same way I'd seen Anya do a thousand times. That could mean nothing or everything."

On the deck of the gazebo, I closed the distance between us, then I opened my arms, and she stepped toward me. We hugged, and I allowed my hands to quickly explore her waistline as I pulled away. Nothing. Glancing down at her shoes, I noticed the jeans she wore were too tight to hide an ankle holster.

"Thanks for coming." I moved to the right, and dread filled my gut. The horrible experiment I was about to conduct was either unforgivable or absolutely necessary, and there was only one way to find out.

"Of course, Chase. When Skipper called, in her voice, something was wrong. Mongo is okay, yes? He is not hurt?"

I tried to figure out a way to stop the line of cascading dominoes I'd just kicked into motion. "No, he's fine. They're offshore and training up for the mission. That's what I wanted to talk with you about."

The sound of the back door of the house closing sent my heart thudding as if it were going to leap from my chest.

Could I stop it now? Is there anything I can do to keep this from happening?

Irina and I looked up simultaneously to see Anya sprinting across the yard, and my stomach churned.

Anya left the ground three feet from the gazebo and landed on the deck with her fighting knife drawn and extended before her. I shot a look toward Irina, who'd just landed one foot on the solid oak carriage of the cannon. As Anya powered directly toward me, Irina leapt from the carriage and landed a thundering kick to Anya's wrist. It was a blow that would've dislodged the knife from anyone else's grip, but not Anya Burinkova's.

Irina landed on the deck between Anya and me, and she repositioned her feet into the perfect fighter's stance. As Anya stalked, Irina mirrored her every move, keeping herself precisely between the former Russian assassin and me.

Irina reached behind herself and let her fingertips touch my arm. "Run, Chase. She is trying to kill you, but I will not let her."

I was mesmerized.

Her instinct is to protect me from Anya?

Awestruck, I threw both hands in the air. "Enough! Anya, stop!"

Anya sheathed her knife and stepped back with both hands raised to shoulder height. "Who taught this to you?"

Irina glanced between Anya and me in choppy motions. "What is happening?"

I laid a hand on her shoulder. "It's okay, Irina. No one is going to hurt anyone, but I need to know why a simple Russian widow knows how to protect herself and me from a trained assassin's knife."

Her knees seemed incapable of supporting her weight, and she slumped against the cannon. Her Russian-accented English left her without the words she wanted and needed. "I am sorry. Is for me . . . I did not . . ."

Anya spoke in her native Russian. "Do not be afraid, Irina. Is okay. I was not going to hurt Chase. I only needed you to believe I would. You must now tell us how you learned to fight like this."

Irina's Slavic features seemed to soften, perhaps in shame or embarrassment, but I couldn't know for sure. She lifted her chin and looked at me only long enough to say, "Is okay in Russian, yes?"

"As long as you tell the truth, it's fine in Russian."

She seemed to beg her lips to move as she grasped the cannon as if it were her only lifeline. "I was afraid to tell to you truth. When I was young girl, I was very good gymnast, and I was afraid of nothing. Inside Russia, these are important things, and they sometimes get attention of government. This is what happened to me." She paused, seemingly sucking enough moisture into her mouth to continue. "Inside Russia, government does not ask if girl wants to become nurse or teacher when she has no fear and is strong. Anya knows these things."

Anya nodded but didn't speak, so Irina continued. "I was chosen by GRU. This is intelligence division of military. You know this, yes?"

I said, "Yes, I know the GRU. Go on."

"I was strong in training, and I learned quickly, but I did not have aptitude for killing, so I could not become what Anya was. I had instinct to defend. This is what you saw when Anya pretended to attack you. I could not let her do this. I care for you like brother."

My stomach turned, and I felt as if I were suddenly worse than the officials in Russia who turned the two women in front of me into machines. "I'm sorry we had to do this to you, Irina, but we need to know the truth. Are you still working with the Russian government?"

Her deep eyes widened in disbelief and agony. "No, Chase! I could never do this. I detest Russian government. I spit on them.

They turned back on me when Tatiana's father was murdered because of something terrible he did, but I was innocent. I had little daughter, Tatiana, and they would let me starve. Is only because of brother-in-law, Victor Volkov. Is only because of him Tatiana and I do not starve. He is terrible man, but he had only enough honor to feed his brother's widow and daughter."

Tears welled up behind her eyes, but she fought them back. "When Anya put him inside American prison for his crimes, I was afraid I would have no home or food for my daughter, but she gave to us home and money. I was so confused when she came for you with knife. I don't know how to tell to you what happened inside me, but I cannot let her hurt you. This makes sense, maybe?"

I said, "Yes, it makes perfect sense. Now, I need you to look in my eyes and tell me you are not an agent of the Russian government."

She raised her hands and held my face in her palms. "Chase, I swear to you, I am now American girl and will soon be wife of American man. You saw where my loyalty is when I believed she was going to kill you. I swear it on life of my only child, I am not agent of horrible Russian government. I am loyal to man I love and to family he loves. I was afraid if you knew truth, you would send me away, and this would break heart of Tatiana."

Everything inside me wanted to believe her, but I had to know, so I let my eyes fall on Anya.

She said, "Irina, I am sorry for what we did and especially for what I did. We believe you, and I am truly sorry."

Irina pushed herself from the cannon as her legs regained the strength to stand, and she reached for Anya. The two embraced and whispered in their native tongue.

I couldn't hear what they were saying, but if Anya had ever been sincere about anything in her life, the look on her face said that was the moment. And I believed both of them.

Chapter 12
Why Me?

With the performance complete, Skipper, Anya, Irina, and I sat inside the gazebo pondering the lives we left for the ones we'd inherited.

Irina spoke first. "I am sorry."

I was suddenly intrigued. "Why would you be sorry?"

"I forced you to do this because of my dishonesty. If only I had told to you in early times truth of what I was so many years ago, this would not be . . . Uh, I do not know English word. Is in Russian, maybe *trebuyetsya* or *neobkhodimyy*."

"Necessary," Anya said.

Irina nodded. "Yes, this is word, *necessary*. I am ashamed. I should have told Mongo. This thing you do when you go away, this is important, and I give to you only reasons to think maybe I am *shpion*, but I am not spy. For this, I am sorry."

Skipper's eyes met mine. She said, "Are you going to jump in or just watch the poor girl drown?"

Drowning was not an option, so I got wet. "Listen, Irina. Everything you're saying makes sense. You were a little ashamed about your history with GRU, but it's important for you to understand that we don't see that part of your life as being any reason to be ashamed. If anything, the training you received and the skills you developed back then make you even more valuable, and it means you're more like the rest of us than we thought."

She cocked her head. "And this is good?"

"Yes, it's very good. In fact, it's better than good. It means you're more qualified than we thought for what I have to ask you to do."

She furrowed her brow. "You have for me something you need?"

"Yes, we do. I don't know how much Mongo tells you about what we do when we leave."

"He tells to me not much, but because someone is always, uh . . . *injured* when you come home, I know the things you do are dangerous and important. If not important, it would not make sense to have danger."

"Yes, the things we do are dangerous and always important, although they don't always sound important or dangerous when we get our mission brief. This is one of those missions that sounds innocuous but may be far more dangerous than we suspect."

"And for this mission, you need me?"

"Yes, we do, but we don't need you as a grunt. We need you as a ruse."

Confusion overtook her expression. "Please forgive me, but English is still difficult to me. You say *grunt* and *ruse*, and I do not know these words."

Anya took the helm and explained the situation in their common language. As Anya spoke, Irina's eyes brightened and darted between the three of us.

Anya paused, and Irina laughed. "This is funny. *Grunt* is *pekhotinets*. It can be also *necessisitri* . . . No, wait. I have it . . . *Necessary*."

I joined the laughter. "Yes, *grunt* is a term we apply to infantry-men, and in English, it may sound derogatory, but when boots hit the ground, it's the grunts who get it done without complaining or giving up."

"Then this is term of honor, not *unichizhitel'nyy*."

"Yes, that's fair," I said, "but we need your acting skills—not your boots on this one. If you're interested, we'll brief you on your role in the mission."

Her eyes continued to widen with excitement. "Yes, of course. I am much interested."

I checked Skipper with only my gaze, and she gave the subtle nod to proceed.

"We've been assigned a mission to purchase a Fabergé egg."

Before I could say more, Irina flashed pale as if suddenly terrified, so I paused.

"Are you okay?"

"Which one?" she asked.

I leaned in. "Which one what?"

"Which egg are you to buy?"

"Oh, we've been instructed to take any egg we can get, but specifically, we are to pursue the Third Imperial egg."

Irina grimaced. "Is not possible. Third Imperial egg is lost."

Skipper's expression sent me exploring. "How do you know?"

Irina didn't hesitate. "When I was small girl, maybe eleven or ten, father took Alexi and me to see Fabergé eggs inside Kremlin Armoury Museum in Moscow. For little Russian girl to see this is *volshebnyy* and can never forget."

Anya said, "*Volshebnyy* means—"

"Magical," I said. "Yes, I know."

Irina looked anxious. "We will maybe see and touch egg for mission?"

I shrugged. "Maybe."

Her eyes flashed like those of a child in a chocolate shop. "Is also maybe for me to hold?"

I said, "You seem to know a lot more about these eggs than any of us."

"Yes, of course. I know all of eggs but have seen only those inside Kremlin Armoury Museum and once in Petersburg inside Blue Room of Naryshkin-Shuvalov Palace."

My heart pounded as if I'd just discovered a sunken Spanish galleon full of gold doubloons. "Could you spot a fake?"

Irina instinctually turned to Anya, who translated. "*Smogli otlichit' poddelku?*"

Irina nodded. "*Da, mozhet byt', no ya dolzhen snachala izuchit'.*"

Anya chuckled and pointed toward me. "Tell Chase. Not me."

Irina blushed. "I am sorry. Is exciting for me. Yes, maybe I can identify real egg from not-real one, but I must first study."

I asked, "How?"

She dropped her chin. "How what?"

"How do you study to learn to identify a fake?"

"Ah, I must go to Virginia, inside Museum of Fine Arts in city of Richmond, I believe. This is correct, yes?"

Skipper nodded. "Yes, there's a collection of eggs in the museum in Richmond, but there are three eggs in New York City at the Met."

Irina nodded. "Yes, inside Metropolitan Museum of Art are three eggs—Imperial Caucasus, Imperial Danish Palaces, and Imperial Napoleonic."

Skipper said, "You're really into these eggs, aren't you?"

"I told to you was magic when I was little girl, and magic never goes away."

I asked, "Why haven't you already been to the museum in Virginia and New York if you love the eggs so much?"

She stared at the deck. "Is not fair to ask for things for me. When I say something I want, Mongo gives to me always, and he is very busy. Is not for me to ask him for this."

Skipper huffed. "You and I need to talk when this is over. You're an American woman now. I'll get you straightened out. And you're definitely going museum hopping, starting today."

I held up a hand. "Before we get too carried away teaching Irina how to abuse her soon-to-be husband, let's refocus on the task at hand. The mission requires that we make the offer to buy an egg—preferably the Third Imperial—inspect it, authenticate it, and complete the purchase. What we need from you, Irina, is to play the part of the expert for the inspection and authentication. Do you think you can pull it off?"

"I do not understand 'pull it off.'"

"Sorry, it's easy to forget. Do you think you can do it?"

"I will never be expert, but with time inside museum and talking with experts, I am sure I can learn to know differences between real and not. This answers your question, no?"

"Yes, it does. And we'll make sure you get all the access you need in any museum you want to visit. We just happen to have an airplane to take you anywhere you want to go, and we've got friends who can open a lot of doors that would otherwise be closed."

Irina beamed. "This makes me so happy. Thank you for all of this. I wish you could see difference in life for me and Tatiana inside Russia and inside America. Is dreams coming true."

I relaxed in my Adirondack chair. "I think you and Tatiana are a dream come true for Mongo, and if you know as much about these eggs as you say, you're definitely a godsend for this mission."

She frowned. "Godsend?"

"Yes, it means a gift sent from God."

She smiled in silent acceptance of the compliment.

I replayed the past half hour in my head, and I couldn't believe everything we'd accomplished. "I do have one more question, but it's not for Irina."

Skipper and Anya looked up in anticipation, and I asked, "Why me?"

Skipper looked confused, but Anya did not. She said, "Plan was not so good, so I made it better."

"You made it better? And just how does attacking me make the plan better?"

Anya eyed Irina and then turned back to me. "I understand mind of Russian women. You do not."

I let out a chortle. "You're right about that, but it's not limited to Russian women. I don't understand the woman's mind of any nationality."

"Do not interrupt," she said. "Is important and is not matter of laughing."

I held up both hands. "Sorry."

"You are again interrupting. Do not do this."

I sat in silence, waiting for her to continue.

"Good. When you told to me plan to attack Irina with knife to know if she could defend herself, I thought was good plan, but not best plan."

"We've covered that. I want to hear why you thought it was wise to change the plan."

"You are again interrupting. Do not do this. I thought of plan from you, and I knew Irina would try to defend herself if I pretend to attack her, but this is instinct and natural. Anybody would do this. We have inside desire to stay alive, so we try to do this always. But is very different for other person."

She had my attention, and I was on the verge of doubting that I had any understanding of psychology at all.

She continued. "I decided this is poor test. Better test is if Irina will protect you, Chase. This is not natural instinct of Russian woman, or of any woman."

I held up a finger. "Wait a minute! You were coming pretty hard. What if she hadn't intervened?"

Anya shrugged. "Maybe you would react in time to stop me, but I believe you would not. I think you trust me, even though you believe this is not true. Maybe inside heart, you know I will not hurt you."

Skipper leapt to her feet. "Nope! You're not turning this into whatever that's supposed to be. The plan worked, no matter who came up with it or who changed it, and I'm not risking having Penny kill me in my sleep for letting you two play happy-wordsy-games. Not happening!"

Anya was good at many things, but she may have been the world's best at ignoring what she didn't want to hear.

As if Skipper weren't there, Anya said, "This reminds me . . . Is very important that I talk with you alone for only few minutes. We can do this, yes?"

Skipper stomped her foot against the decking of the gazebo. "Hello! No. Not how this works. You were here to help us determine if Irina was still working with GRU. You've done that, and now it's time to get back on the airplane."

Anya never lifted her gaze from me. "You are coming also on airplane, yes? Good. We will talk on flight."

"Chase has work to do," Skipper said, "and we have a mission you're not part of."

Anya checked her watch and mouthed, "Five minutes?"

I shook my head. "I can't, but you can tell Skipper anything you want me to know, and she'll pass it along."

She sighed. "No, I cannot tell to Skipper. Is only for you."

"I'm sorry," I said. "But those days are over."

She whispered, "Perhaps not as much over as you think."

Chapter 13
Shot Over the Bow

Skipper herded Anya from the gazebo and turned to Irina. "There's no reason to waste jet fuel. The Virginia Museum of Fine Arts is on the way to DC, so I recommend we make the trip as efficient as possible."

Irina glowed with excitement. "Yes, I will be ready in one half hour. This is fast enough, yes?"

Skipper chuckled. "Yeah, that'll be fine. We'll pick you up on the way to the airport." She turned to me and waved a hand at the North River. "Go. Take the RHIB and find your wife. I think they're working on Mark V tactics in the sound."

The look of emptiness in Anya's face left me longing to know why it was so important for her to talk with me before she left for DC, but no matter what it was she had to say, nothing good could've come of the conversation.

As usual, Skipper was right, but the lingering question remained . . . What was so important that Anya couldn't—or wouldn't—tell Skipper?

* * *

I climbed aboard my old friend, *Aegis*, our fifty-foot sailing catamaran, and made my way to the stern. I loved everything about the boat, but the feature I loved perhaps above all others is what *Aegis* was *not*—a weapon of war. She was purely a pleasure boat with no hardpoints for weaponry, no steel plating to ward off incoming fire, and if all was right with the world, she could sometimes make fifteen knots, but never more. Aboard *Aegis*, I couldn't run toward anything, but I could, at times, run away from everything. I'll never truly know what I was running from on that particular afternoon.

The mid-December wind was out of the north, making my sail down the North River an absolute joy. Once I backed away from the Bonaventure dock, I shut down the diesels and listened as only the sounds of the wind, the water lapping at the hulls, and the soothing hums of the coastal Georgia marsh caressed me into a world where beautiful Russian assassins don't exist, and the necessity for warships like the Mark V and *Lori Danielle* fades away into blinded ignorance and peaceful bliss.

It took an hour to sail into the Cumberland Sound and beat against the wind in search of my team, but I finally found them at anchor lying off the Kings Bay Naval Submarine Base. Bringing the diesels back to life, I furled the sails and let *Aegis*'s anchor taste the muddied bottom of the sound just south of the gray beasts of battle. I tied the RHIB to the stern of the Mark V and climbed the rope ladder to the *Lori Danielle*'s stern deck.

The instant my boots hit the cold steel deck, Penny said, "Hey, sailor. Fancy meeting you here."

I gave her a peck on the cheek, and she made a sniffing sound. "You don't smell like you got any Russian on you, so how'd it go?"

"She's not a spy."

"Which one?"

I laughed. "Irina. She's solidly on the good guys' team. In fact, she's better than just on our team. She's already a bit of a Fabergé egg specialist, or at least closer to an expert than any of us."

"What does that mean?"

I told Penny about Irina's childhood fascination with the eggs and her excitement about the mission.

She asked, "Did you brief her in already?"

"Not fully. So far, all she knows is that we're buying an egg and that she gets to play the part of the expert. She's on her way to some museum in Virginia to see their collection, and then she's going to the Metropolitan Museum in New York. Skipper's unlocking some doors for her with the exhibition curators at both museums."

"That's awesome, and I'm a little envious. I've never seen one. Have you?"

"Not hardly. What would make you think I've seen one? I'm about as cultured as an armadillo. You're the big Hollywood type, and I'm just a gun-toting psychologist."

She stuck her hands on her hips. "Don't talk about my husband like that, Chase Fulton. Do you really think I'd marry an armadillo?"

I pointed toward *Aegis* bobbing at anchor. "If he had a boat like that, you might."

She shrugged. "Maybe." She laid a finger against my chin and then slid it down my chest until hooking my belt. "Thanks for not running off with your Russian."

I grabbed her hand and pulled her against me. "She's not my Russian, and you're my home. I'll always come back to you."

She raised herself on tiptoes and kissed me. As she pulled away, she whispered, "I trust you, but not her."

"Speaking of trusting a beautiful Russian, where's Mongo? I

suspect he'd like to know he's not on the verge of marrying a hammer and sickle."

She threw a thumb over her shoulder. "They're inside doing sand table, whatever that means."

"Why aren't you in there with them? You're still going with us to St. Barts, aren't you?"

She dug the toe of her boot against the deck. "We need to talk about that. I got a call from a producer this morning, and I'm sorry, but I really need to be in LA on Monday."

I smiled down at her. "Never be sorry for being the hottest new screenwriter in Hollywood. It's your job, and everyone understands that. Especially me. We've got six sets of capable hands who can run the boat almost as well as you, but not quite. You go to LA, do your thing, and if we're still in the islands, you can come join us. I'm pretty sure we can find you a ride."

She threw her arms around me. "I love you, Chase. I'm sorry I was such a brat about Anya being here, but—"

"Stop being sorry. You're fine. If you're done out here for the day, why don't you take *Aegis* home? We'll meet you back at the house when we wrap this up."

"Thank you. I really love how easy you make my life."

"I don't do that. *We* do that. That's sort of how teams work."

She kissed me again. "I'll see you at home."

I watched her descend the rope ladder like a pro and bound into the RHIB. By the time I pushed through the hatch to the interior of the *Lori Danielle*, she was already hoisting a sail.

Mongo looked up, inquisition on his face, and I gave him the thumbs-up. He smiled as if he already knew the answer and dived back into the mission plan. I stepped close to what Dre may have called a sand table, but there was no sand in sight. The horizontal, digital touch screen displayed a satellite view of the coast of Tangier in northern Morocco on the Strait of Gibraltar.

Dre pointed out terrain features with a laser and started an animation of tidal flow into and out of the strait. He said, "What you have to understand is that seawater stands still, and the earth around it moves. Okay, that's not exactly how it works, but when the sun and moon are on opposite sides of the planet, that's how it works for a few hours. The key is to remember that this boat and the *Descubierta* will behave very similarly until the sea state breaks ten meters. Her bow is designed to cut through the weather, but this boat is not. Even with her impressive speed, ten-meter seas are going to feel like the end of the world in this thing."

Tony looked up. "Why would we consider seizing a ship in ten-meter seas anyway?"

"Look at you," Dre said. "The kid has his head on straight while the rest of you let me talk about theoretical stuff that's never going to happen. Now we know who the real seaman is in the group. The rest of you should be ashamed."

Mongo said, "Isn't there some phenomenon about different salinity and density inside the strait?"

Dre lit up the big man's chest with the laser. "And now we know who the academic is on the team. Yes, and thank you for bringing that up. The salt water does a strange thing in that part of the world. Inside the strait, the water is more dense and saltier than in the open ocean outside the strait. This isn't terribly noticeable in a vessel of this size."

Tony asked, "Wouldn't the increased density reduce our top speed?"

Dre pointed to our rescue swimmer. "That's not bad logic, but you failed to account for Archimedes' principle. The increased salinity and density of the water inside the strait causes the boat to ride a little higher in the water than it does in the less dense, lower salinity open ocean. This phenomenon is most noticeable on the Plimsoll line. With less wetted hull surface, the speed differential is negligible, but I like how you're thinking. Don't let this bunch of landlubbers turn you into one of them. Stay salty, young man."

Tony gave him a nod but nothing more, and the briefing continued for another half hour.

Dre concluded his sand table exercise with an admonition and a warning. "Boarding a hostile vessel on the open ocean is a dangerous endeavor, no matter how many times you've practiced and how sharp the team is. This team is as close to being SEALs as any civilian team I've ever worked with, so you're going to make it look easy, right up to the point when things start falling apart. Keeping your head in the game and your eye on the prize is the only way you get this done."

Singer scratched his chin. "But isn't the plan to have the Moroccans in on the ruse? The crew of the *Descubierta* won't be hostile."

Dre said, "That's the kind of thinking that'll get you killed in the operation. Every boarding at sea is hostile. Ask your rescue swimmer. Stepping from one boat to another, even in calm, flat water on a sunny afternoon, has a high probability of putting somebody in the drink. If you go in the water with those tidal currents in the Strait of Gibraltar, God only knows where we'll pick you up, and it's an even greater chance that you'll freeze to death before we find you."

Singer chewed on his lip. "You said *we* twice in that answer. Are *you* coming with us?"

Dre's shoulders rose and fell. "That remains to be seen. I'll have that conversation with Chase when we wrap this up."

Singer nodded. "I'm sorry I interrupted."

"Never apologize for a good question," Dre said. "This is serious business, even if the Moroccans are waiting with open arms. Do not relax, and do not take anything for granted, especially if this is a night op. It's one thing to steal a ship when the sun is shining, but quite another when your side of the planet can't see that sun. Any more questions?"

The faces of my team showed the look of men who definitely had questions, but probably not for Dre.

He said, "If not, that's all I have for you today. It's up to Chase, but I recommend at least two dozen more runs—half in daylight, and half in dark. It's impossible to practice too much."

Mongo raised a finger. "Before we secure for the day, it's one thing to assault the *Lori Danielle* from the Mark V fifty times, but taking a corvette hull is going to be dramatically different. Baseball players don't take batting practice with bowling balls. Isn't there a friendly ship somewhere on the East Coast we could use to practice assaulting an actual warship with the shape and size of the *Descubierta*?"

Dre closed one eye and stared at the overhead. "I can't speak for the Navy since I'm a washed-up old SEAL, but there has to be something in Norfolk or maybe Mayport we could borrow. The *Descubierta* is about the size of a Destroyer Escort. I can make some calls, but even if they have something, it won't be quick. The government doesn't do anything quickly except spend the money they steal from us."

I studied the faces of my men and stopped on our rescue swimmer. "You look like you've got something to say, Tony. Don't keep secrets. What's going on in your head?"

"I don't know. It's a crazy idea anyway."

"Those are my favorite kinds of ideas. Spit it out."

"When I was in the Coast Guard, I did eight weeks on a cutter named *Thetis*. If I'm correct, she was about eighteen hundred tons and a little less than three hundred feet. If I did my homework correctly, the *Descubierta* is around fifteen hundred tons, two hundred ninety feet, and draws twelve feet of water. I know they're not identical, but they're close."

I turned to Dre, and he threw up his hands. "I don't know. I was too short to join the Coast Guard. They told me I had to be at least six feet tall so I could walk ashore if the boat ever sank. I had to settle for the Navy."

Tony groaned. "Now I'm taking shots over my bow from a peg-leg squid. Will it ever end?"

"This is fun to watch," I said, "but if we're going to commandeer a Coast Guard cutter, I think we need to make some calls. Do you know where she's based?"

Tony said, "When I was assigned to her, she was in Key West, but that was four years ago."

Chapter 14
Twist and Shout

Clark sounded hungover, or maybe just sleepy, when he finally picked up the phone after half a dozen rings. "What?"

"Well, aren't we in a good mood this morning?"

He growled. "It's early, and I was up most of the night with my body rejecting whatever I ate yesterday. What do you want?"

"It's not early," I said. "It's almost six, but I guess in the world of the project manager, anything before ten is early."

"Just tell me what you want so I can tell you that you can't have it."

"This one's simple. We just need to borrow a Coast Guard cutter named *Thetis*." I spelled it for him since it was a two-syllable word, and I didn't want to overload his brain so early in the morning. "Tony said she was at Key West a few years ago, but he doesn't know where she is now."

The sounds of him yawning and stretching filtered through the phone. "She's still based in Key West, but I think she's on maneuvers off Puerto Rico. I'll find out. Why do you need a cutter?"

"We want to practice assaulting her."

"Hang on," he said. "Let me get this straight. You want to borrow a Coast Guard cutter so you can assault it? Is that what you're saying?"

"No! I want to practice assaulting it because it's similar in design to the *Descubierta*, and I want our training to be as real as possible. You know, it's the whole practice-like-you-play theory."

"Yeah, okay. Whatever. I'll see what I can do. If you don't hear from me within an hour, that probably means I've fallen back asleep, so call me again."

"Don't go back to sleep until you get us a cutter. I'm going to call you every ten minutes until you have one."

"Okay, okay. I'm up. I'll take care of it."

* * *

Thirty-five minutes later, my phone chirped, and I thumbed the green button. "I got you the boat, College Boy, but there's a catch."

"I'm a catcher, so let's have it."

"No, you *were* a catcher. Now, you're a shooter."

"You made your point, so let's hear the catch."

"The ship is in the U.S. Virgin Islands, and they won't leave the exercise grounds. You have to go to them."

"That's terrible. That means we'll have to spend Christmas in the Caribbean. I can't imagine a worse fate."

"You're not on vacation. You're going to work. How much time do you need?"

I thought about the timetable for a moment. "I want two weeks to polish the process and work through as many hurdles as we can. I don't want any surprises when we go hot for real."

Without hesitation, he said, "Two weeks, it is. No problem. Why don't you take the mission yacht instead of living on the *Lori Danielle*?"

"You're just full of torture for us this morning, but if you insist, we'll pick up the yacht and suffer through the anguish of roughing it for two weeks."

He snickered. "I hate to ask for so much sacrifice from you, but that's the way it has to be. Let me know when you're headed south, and I'll have the yacht crew light the fires and kick the tires."

"Maybe I'm wrong. I've not seen the yacht, but I don't think there are any tires to kick."

"Oh, you've seen it, but you may not remember. It'll be ready when you get here. Skipper briefed me on the Irina situation. I'm glad it worked out. Nice job handling that one."

"I can't take much of the credit. Anya put in the work."

"She didn't crawl into your pillowcase, did she?"

"What's that supposed to mean?"

He couldn't stop laughing at his own joke. "It's kind of like a nervous, long-tailed fiddler on a hot rocking chair. You know what I'm saying. Now, leave me alone. I'm going back to bed."

"How? How is it possible for you to be that—"

Before I could finish my question, the line went dead.

* * *

As usual, the team gathered in the Bonaventure kitchen for breakfast, and Hunter delivered two enormous bags of biscuits and hashbrowns.

"I've got some good news," I began. "Thanks to Tony's brilliant idea, the Coast Guard has agreed to let us attack the Cutter *Thetis* as much as we want. It'll be a joint training exercise in which we'll conduct boarding raids, and they'll practice repelling us. The ship is on maneuvers in the Virgin Islands, so this means we'll have to spend Christmas in the Caribbean."

Hunter grunted through his biscuit-crumb-covered beard and mustache. "Cool. When do we leave?"

"As soon as we polish off those bags of biscuits."

He wiped his face but accomplished little with the effort. "Great. Let's roll. We can eat on the way."

"Slow down," I said. "We've got plenty of time. Clark said we could have two weeks, but if we don't feel comfortable in that amount of time, we'll stretch it out until we're one hundred percent ready. And there's another little nugget I forgot to mention."

Heads came up, and chewing ceased.

"We're picking up the yacht in Miami on the way, so we don't have to sleep in the racks on the *Lori Danielle*."

Hunter began an exaggerated nod. "It's about time. I finally get to travel in the style I deserve."

I downed my last sip of coffee. "You're exactly right. I'm pleased to hear you approve."

Hunter said, "I was starting to get the impression you people don't know who I think I am."

"How could we forget?" I said. "Since you adopted Tony, the two of you will deliver the Mark V to San Juan while the rest of us have cocktails and Cubans on this mystery yacht."

Hunter covered his heart with both hands. "That's hurtful and downright mean."

"Feel free to swap assignments with anyone who's willing. I don't mind at all."

When the biscuit bags were empty, we cleaned up our mess, and the team headed for the back gallery while I briefed Captain Sprayberry on the new training mission. When I finished, he said, "We'll make ready for sea and stand by for your order to set sail."

"Set sail when you're ready, Captain, but plan for a stop in the sound at the mouth of the North River. We need to load a few tools aboard, and we'll meet you in San Juan."

"If that's what you want, I'll do it, but I can bring the *LD* up the river, right to your dock, as long as the tide is in."

"In that case, park her right out back, and send down the crane."

"I'll have her anchored off your back door in half an hour."

"Perfect," I said. "Make sure you bring the full complement, especially the purser, Ronda No-H. We'll hop from the Virgin Islands, straight to St. Barts, and she'll come in handy when the money starts flowing."

"Consider it done. Crew and officers are already on board, and we bunkered fuel overnight. We flew the chopper this morning, and the mechanic gave it a clean bill of health, so we'll weigh anchor within the hour."

"Before you go, I spoke with Dre this morning and told him we'd fly his team down, but have the quartermaster square them away with bunks when you get to Puerto Rico. They'll likely live on board for a couple of weeks."

"Yes, sir," he said. "No problem. Anything else?"

"That covers it. We'll see you in thirty minutes."

I poured a second cup of coffee on my way through the kitchen and heard a sound outside I couldn't identify. Pushing my way through the door, I discovered every head turned toward the south.

"What's that noise?" I asked.

Singer said, "I don't know yet, but it's getting closer. It almost sounds like zydeco music."

I hopped down the stairs and rounded the corner of the house to see a monstrous white car the size of a tugboat coming up the tree-lined drive. It was easily the biggest car I've ever seen. The morning sun gleamed off the hood and windshield as if it had just been waxed to perfection. The closer the land yacht came, the louder and clearer the music grew, and Singer had been spot-on. There was no longer any question what the sound was. It was Cajun zydeco, and I couldn't understand a word they were saying, but it was impossible not to tap my foot—the one that was still made of flesh and blood.

I had little doubt who was behind the wheel, even though I couldn't clearly see either of the occupants of the car through the glistening windshield. The car left the driveway and hit the grass fast enough to send me scampering behind the cover of the house.

When the beast of a car slid to a stop, both front doors flew open, and Cajun Kenny LePine and Earl at the End came pouring out. With the doors open, the zydeco fiddle and washboard exploded across the backyard.

Before my brain could process the overload of sights and sounds, Kenny grabbed Earl by the hand and spun her like a top as they broke into some sort of dance routine that seemed to be a combination of the Carolina Swing and two people being attacked by a swarm of hornets. They continued the spasmatic convulsion punctuated by sporadic twists and twirls, topped off with jubilant yells of excitement, until the song came to an end and they collapsed into each other's arms.

I shot a look over my shoulder at the gathered crowd on the gallery, clapping and laughing uproariously.

Turning back to the dancing queen and her boy toy, I said, "What on Earth was that?"

Cajun Kenny caught his breath just long enough to say, "Dat righ' der be some mo' kinda fine woman. I garun-tole you dat be da God's all-fired troof. I dun tole you, and can't nobody be denyin' dat. Jus' cast dem der eyes o' your'n on her fine self, you, and you be knowin' jus' right zackly what ol' Kenny be sayin' be noffin' but all da troof day is in dis here ol' world. I guar-ohn-tee."

All five feet and two hundred pounds of Earl collapsed against the fender of the car, and I lifted the water hose from its reel on the back of the house.

"Do you need me to hose you down, ol' girl? You look like you're on the verge of bursting into flames."

She threw up both arms. "Hit momma with a splash, Baby Boy."

So, I spritzed my favorite diesel mechanic.

Kenny leapt between me and the open front door of the behemoth of a car. "Woah, der, Chase. Don' be gettin' none dat hosebib water on da hupolstry. It be all original, don' ya know."

I released the nozzle, and Earl shook like a puppy shedding water from her dirty T-shirt. "Thank you, Stud Muffin. That's just what momma needed."

"What is wrong with you two?" I asked. "It's barely seven thirty."

Kenny pulled his pocket watch from his pants and popped open the cover. "Oooh, wee, you is right. It be gettin' late on up in da day, but ol' Kenny just can't bring himselfs to climb out dat bed in dese here mornings wiff my lovin' rubbin' dubbin' fine woman, me."

"I really don't need that visual, Kenny. What are you two doing this morning? You make it sound like a Saturday night on the bayou."

He spun on a heel. "Dat reminds ol' Kenny of a sumpin'. Does you knows whats I love most 'bout da bayou?"

Knowing I'd regret it, I said, "No, Kenny. Tell me what you love most about the bayou."

He clapped his hands. "Not only it be by me house, but it be *by-you* house, too!"

I threw up my hands as if I hadn't heard him tell that joke before. "That's too much, Kenny."

He slapped his knee. "I knows it be too much, just like my lovin' Earline, ya knows."

Earl finally recovered her senses and pushed off the fender. "I heard you're taking my Mark V across the ocean, and you know you can't do that without me lookin' under the hood to make sure them motors are just right."

"What would I do without you, Momma?"

"You'd have a pile of broken boats layin' all around you, Baby Boy. What do you think of my man's new ride?"

I let my eyes roam across the two acres of steel and yards of baby-blue upholstery. "That's quite a car. I'll give you that."

Kenny puffed out his chest. "Yes, sir, she do be dat. Dis here be a nineteen seventy-nine Lincoln Town Car, and just like ol' Kenny, me, she be all original."

I chuckled and eyed Earl and the Lincoln. "Well, Kenny, it looks to me like you've got everything any man could want."

Chapter 15
It's Good to Be King

After changing fifty gallons of oil, lubricating everything that moves, and installing a dozen new belts, Earl wiped her hands and declared the Mark V patrol boat fit for duty. "Where's that skinny wife of yours, Stud Muffin?"

"She's inside doing whatever women do before heading off to LA."

Earl leaned close. "You make sure she knows which side of her bread is buttered before she goes. You don't want her making googly eyes at any of them California surfer boys. Every girl loves fancy boats and airplanes, but a little lovin' goes a long way, and don't you forget it, Baby Boy."

"I'm not completely sure what that means, but I appreciate the advice. Where's Kenny? You didn't leave him unconscious in the engine room, did you?"

"Stop that. He's up in the rafters of the boathouse. Said he needed to take a look at something, but if you ask me, I think he just likes being up there so he can look down at me and know I'm his girl."

"I'm sure that's what he's doing. Listen, I want you to know how happy it makes me to see you and Kenny together. I never have any clue what he's saying, but that glimmer in his eye every time he sees you is impossible to miss."

She waddled toward me and threw her arms around me. "I would've never found that man if it weren't for you, and I ain't never been happier than I am with him. You know I love you, Baby Boy, but puttin' that man in my life makes you specialer than you know."

"Specialer? I'll take that as the best compliment I've ever received. I love you too, Momma, and you can dance to zydeco in my yard anytime you want."

She shot a look across her shoulder. "I'm gonna hush before you make me cry. Here comes my man now."

Kenny ambled up and threw an arm around Earl. "How dat boathouse been treatin' you? Is dey anyting you don't been likin' 'bout it, you?"

I pieced together his question and said, "It's perfect, and I'll never have anything else built by anybody but you."

He gave me a wink. "Das' smart thinkin' from dat head o' yours, you."

I nodded, pretending I had some clue what he said. "While you're both here, I need to ask a favor. We're going to be gone for probably a month. Would you mind looking in on the place every few days? We have the security system, but I'd still like for you to put eyes on the house occasionally."

"You got it, Baby Boy. We'll flog anybody who messes with Bonaventure."

"Flogging sounds like fun," I said. "But maybe running over them with Kenny's super-sized Lincoln would be more appropriate."

"Anyting for you, Chase."

With the Kenny and Earl show complete, I climbed the steps back onto the gallery. "It's time to stock the *Lori Danielle*'s armory. Can you guys get started on that little task? I'll come down and join you as soon as I get a couple of things done."

Hunter looked up through squinted eyelids. "Oh, sure. Put us to hard labor while you go in there to butter some bread or whatever Earl said."

I rolled my eyes. "Get to work, you lazy bum."

The team stood in unison, but I caught Disco's arm. "Not you, Flyboy. I need you to take the SEALs to San Juan."

I slipped my phone from my pocket and called Dre.

"Morning, Chase."

"Hey, Chief. I've got Disco gearing up to fly you and your team to San Juan. How soon will you be ready to go?"

He said, "That's a waste of money and time, Chase. We're frogmen, and frogs belong on the water. We're going to stay with the ship."

"All right. If that's what you want. Captain Sprayberry is making ready to weigh anchor now."

"Yeah, we know. We're already on board."

I hung up. "Never mind. The SEALs are riding the ship to the islands, but I'll need you to take Penny to LA on Monday."

Disco said, "I'm starting to feel like nobody loves me around here. I talked with Penny earlier, and she said the studio is sending a jet to pick her up, and now the SEALs are afraid to fly with me. I took a shower, so I don't think I stink."

I gave him a sniff. "You may want to consider another shower, but in the meantime, you can give the rest of the guys a hand with the weapons."

I found Penny packing a bag in our room upstairs. "You're packing early."

She looked up. "Yeah, I figured if you're leaving today, there's no reason for me to stick around until Monday. They're sending a jet to get me this afternoon."

I slid a hand around her waist, and she grinned.

"What happened, Big Boy? Did Earl's dancing get you all worked up?"

"Something like that. If you get finished early in LA, it'd be nice to have you join us in the islands, even if you aren't driving the boat."

She laced her arms around my shoulders. "Why do you think I'm going early? I have every intention of spending some quality time with my man in St. Barts. Who knows? Maybe I can even convince him we need a vacation house down there."

"Oh, so it's a need, huh?"

"You once told me that my wants qualify as needs. Were you just trying to score points, or did you really mean it?"

"Did it work if I was just trying to score points?"

She kissed me just below my ear and whispered, "You tell me . . ."

Twenty minutes later, I said, "I think you should learn to speak French."

She smiled but clearly wasn't following. "Why French?"

"Because when we buy *your* vacation house on St. Barts, the language will come in handy."

She nuzzled against me. "You're really racking up the points now."

A massive horn sounded from outside, and I pulled back a curtain. "Look. Did you ever expect to see anything like that?"

Penny leaned toward the window. "Oh, wow! I didn't know it was deep enough to get the *Lori Danielle* all the way up here. That thing looks huge sitting out there. What's it doing here?"

"We're stocking the ship's armory."

She slapped at my arm. "Are you serious, Chase Fulton? You put those boys to work loading guns and bullets while you came up here to . . . "

I pressed a finger against her lips. "It's good to be king."

"Yeah, well, your knights of the round table are going to dethrone you if you don't get down there and help them."

I pulled open the door. "As you wish, my queen."

When I descended the gallery steps, the massive ship at the dock wasn't the most surprising machine in sight. "When did we get a forklift?"

Singer slung a pair of long black rifle cases over his shoulders. "It apparently came with the ship. They lowered it down with the crane, and it saved us a bunch of work. We're almost finished."

I watched the forklift operator gently place a pallet of ammunition onto the cradle of the crane, and seconds later, the pallet was resting on the stern deck of the ship. He spun the machine around and scampered off the dock, back toward the basement armory at the north end of the house. When he reappeared, Mongo and Hunter were riding atop a second pallet of ammo like rodeo cowboys, with one hand gripping the handle of an ammo can and the other waving over their heads.

Hunter yelled, "Next out of chute number two, it's Hop Along Hunter and Mongo the Kid on a pair of bulls nobody's ever ridden to the buzzer."

I turned to Singer. "Would you please shoot them in the kneecaps?"

"I'll get right on that," he said.

I recognized the forklift operator as one of the ship's engineers when he eyed me with a questioning look. I gave him the nod he wanted, and less than eight seconds later, Hop Along and the Kid were bouncing off the ground, and the bulls still hadn't been ridden to the buzzer.

"Still want me to shoot them, boss?"

"I suppose we'll let them live to ride another day."

The crane operator hoisted the final pallet aboard, followed by the forklift and the rest of our team. I followed them to the armory, where the quartermaster handed me a clipboard with an inventory of every item that left the Bonaventure vault and found its way into the ship's armory.

"Is that sufficient, sir?" the operator asked.

"Don't call me sir. I'm just Chase, and the list is great. Thank you."

"It's what I do," he said.

Singer carefully locked his pair of sniper rifles, still in their cases, to a rack against the portside bulkhead. "I didn't trust our rodeo clowns to carry these aboard."

"I don't blame you," I said. "Speaking of clowns . . . Where's Disco?"

Singer signaled with his chin toward the bow. "He's probably flirting with the purser."

Surprised by the revelation, I said, "Ronda No-H? Are you serious?"

He chuckled. "I can't believe you didn't know. He turns into a smitten teenager every time she comes around."

"And is she okay with that?"

"How should I know? I'm a sniper, not the love guru. You'd have to ask her."

On my way to the purser's office, I passed our chief pilot. "Is everything okay up there?"

He blushed. "Oh, yeah. Everything is just fine."

I narrowed my eyes at him and kept walking.

"Come in," Ronda said when I tapped on her door.

"Good morning. I've got three things to discuss with you if you've got a minute."

"Sure. What can I do for you?"

"First, how much cash do we have on board?"

She spun and grabbed her mouse. "It looks like just over two million dollars. Is that all right?"

"For now, but let's try to keep at least four million if we can."

She pulled a leatherbound book from her top drawer and made a note inside. "I'll take care of it. What else?"

"We need to set up a couple of accounts on St. Barts as soon as we get there. In fact, I may send you ahead to get that done before we arrive if you're okay with that."

"I work for you, so I'll do whatever you need."

"Perfect. I'll get Disco to fly over to St. Barts from San Juan once we get settled in."

She blushed and tried not to smile.

"I guess that answers my third question."

"What does that mean?" she asked.

"I wanted to make sure Disco wasn't bothering you."

She looked away and continued blushing. "No, he's not bothering me at all. Do you think he might let me sit in the cockpit on the way to St. Barts?"

"From the look I just saw on his face, I'm confident he'll let you do anything you want."

She grinned. "He's sweet."

I laughed. "Sweet? I don't think that's what the bad guys call him when he shows up. I'll tell you this much about him. He may be retired Air Force, but he fights and shoots at least as well as he flies, so you're in good hands with him."

She cocked her head and raised an eyebrow. "Nice to know."

"I'll leave you alone. I'm sure you have plenty of work to do, and I have to go harass Disco a little. I'll be sure to tell him you think he's sweet."

"You do that."

Chapter 16

I Remember Her

With all the cards dealt and antes paid, I stood by the gazebo and came to a realization I found to be hilarious.

"Hey, Tony. Remind me how long our ship is."

He glanced up at the *Lori Danielle* and joined me in laughter. "I don't remember her precise length, but she's longer than the river is wide, and this is going to be fun to watch."

"Would you have brought her up the river?"

"No, and that's another reason I shouldn't be the skipper. Captain Sprayberry can do things with that boat I'd never have the guts to try."

Almost before Tony stopped talking, the *Lori Danielle*'s horn sounded one prolonged blast, followed by three short ones.

"That means he's backing away from the dock, right?"

Tony reached inside the gazebo and pulled two chairs to the edge of the deck. "It sure does, and I recommend we have a seat and watch the show."

I checked my watch and slid onto the chair. "We can't leave until he's out of the way, so I'll join you for the circus."

The *LD* picked up speed, running astern, and approached the first switchback turn in the river with far more speed than I believed she could survive. Tony and I leapt to our feet and ran down the riverbank to get a better vantage point.

Tony yelled, "He's gonna put her aground."

I yanked my phone from my pocket and hit the redial button, praying Captain Sprayberry would answer before sticking the props in the mud of the marsh, disabling our ship.

It rang twice before clicking to life, and the captain's calm, confident two-word answer filled my ear.

Without another word, the line went dead, and turbulent, muddy water boiled from beneath the *LD*'s stern. Her bow swung left, slowly at first, and finally arcing like the curl of a bullwhip as the horn let out a single prolonged blast that warned any northbound boater to make way because the big dog was coming around the bend . . . sideways.

Tony and I watched in utter disbelief as the captain pinned the bow exactly on course, down the river, and powered ahead as if he'd conducted the hair-raising maneuver a thousand times.

Tony tipped his hat. "I guess he didn't answer the phone, huh?"

"No, he answered."

"What did he say?"

"Watch this."

He shook his head. "Yep, you made the right call by pinning captain's bars on that man's shoulders."

"I think you're right, but you would've made a fine skipper, too."

"Maybe I can spend some time as first officer on that bridge in the future, but I'll never have the skill to oust him from the captain's chair."

"Speaking of skippers . . . I guess we should check in with ours before we hit the water."

She answered almost before it rang. "Save me! Irina is killing me with these eggs. I never want to see another egg. I never want to hear the word *egg* ever again. And most of all, I never want to eat another egg. This is insane!"

"It sounds like you're having a good time."

"No, I'm not! She's obsessed, and I'm bored out of my mind. Please tell me you're calling to order me home for the mission."

I snapped my fingers. "Consider it ordered. How soon can you be in Miami."

"Two hours after Disco lands in Richmond. Please tell me he's on his way."

"He's on his way," I said.

"I love you, and I'll see you in Miami this afternoon."

I pulled the phone away from my ear and stared at the lump of black plastic. "She hung up on me."

Tony said, "She does that. I take it you're sending Disco to pick her up."

Our chief pilot blasted off for Richmond, Virginia, the same time the rest of us pointed the Mark V's bow down the North River and put the town of St. Marys in our wake.

We passed the *Lori Danielle* just outside of the St. Marys pass where the river becomes the ocean, and the chilly north wind we'd enjoyed for the previous few days turned westerly. The change gave us a flat, smooth ride down the east coast of sunny Florida. The Mark V performed like a rocket ship, while the autopilot left us riding in comfort at seventy knots.

Every half hour, one of us would check the instrumentation and note our position, direction, and speed for the log.

When my turn to make the log entries came, I said, "Let's put a hundred bucks in the pot and see who can guess the closest to our calculated arrival time."

Tony won, of course, and Mongo argued, "Is that time to the sea buoy or the marina?"

Tony said, "The sea buoy. Surely you didn't think we were guessing the time to the marina. Nobody programs the autopilot all the way to the marina."

Mongo shrugged. "If you consider reaching the sea buoy the same as arriving, that must mean you'd be okay with me throwing you overboard at the buoy."

"You could try," Tony said.

Mongo reached out with both hands and cupped the rescue swimmer beneath his armpits, lifting him off the deck with ease.

Tony squirmed and twisted in a wasted effort to free himself from Mongo's paws. "Okay, okay. We can split the pot."

Mongo plopped Tony back down onto his seat. "That's what I thought."

We made the trip in just over five hours, and Mongo's estimated time of arrival was only off by three minutes. Clark met us at the Miami Beach Coast Guard Base because an eighty-foot-long military patrol boat gets a little too much attention at a civilian marina.

We climbed from the boat and onto the dock.

Clark said, "Welcome to Miami, boys. You look hungry."

A pair of Coast Guard sailors caught the lines thrown by Tony and Hunter and made them fast to a collection of cleats.

"Famished," I said. "Please tell me Maebelle has a big pot of something on the stove."

"Nope, not tonight. I'm sorry, but you'll have to suffer through someone else's culinary punishment this evening."

He kept staring over my shoulder until I finally turned to see what had Clark's attention.

I said, "Stop doing that. You're making me nervous. What's behind me that's so interesting?"

He pointed across the waterway and at the Miami Beach Marina. "Recognize anyone?"

I couldn't believe I hadn't noticed the yacht when we motored alongside the Coast Guard dock. "I remember her."

The rest of the team turned and followed my line of sight.

Hunter said, "Is that our yacht?"

I let my mind wander back to the earliest days of my career as whatever men like me call themselves. "That's a blast from the past, my friend. Anya and Dr. Richter and I ended my first official mission on the stern deck of that boat. She's the *Moscow Mule*. Two hundred ten feet of pure opulence. She belonged to a Russian oligarch named Dmitri Barkov. He's the man who killed Anya's mother back when Russia was still the Soviet Union."

"How do I not know this story?" Mongo asked.

"I don't know, but I watched Anya drive a nine-inch blade ten inches deep into his chest before we fed him to the hammerheads who love the taste of former Russian oligarchs."

"Ah, the good old days," Clark said.

I huffed. "They weren't that good. I screwed up everything I touched back then, and I should've been dead a hundred different ways. I guess it's true what they say about God loving drunks and fools, because back then, I was both."

Clark slapped me on the back. "You didn't screw up everything. You chopped up a Russian hit man with a boat propeller in Havana without getting caught or killed, so you did a few things right."

Mongo threw up his hands. "Again, how did I not know *that* story, either?"

I said, "Come on, big man. I'll buy you a sweet tea and tell you just how dumb I was back then."

We piled into Clark's crew van and drove across the MacArthur Causeway to South Beach, and my mind wouldn't stop playing memory reels. "I once drove the other way on this stretch of road at a hundred fifty miles per hour, with Skipper and Anya in the back seat and covered in blood. That's the first time I believed she was dead."

Tony perked up. "Skipper?"

"No, Skipper was fine. It was Anya's blood."

Mongo slapped the armrest. "Finally, a story I know! That's when you rescued her from the . . ." He paused and shot a look at Tony.

Our newest teammate said, "It's okay. I know the story, too. It was the time Chase, Anya, and Clark rescued Skipper from the porn producer."

"Man, you've been through some crap in ten years," Hunter said. "What would you do differently if you could do it all over again?"

I thought about his question and ran through the mental catalog of the bone-headed decisions I made along the way. "You know what? I don't think I'd change a thing, because everything I did back then led me to where I am and who I'm with today, and I can't imagine life without all of you."

We unloaded at the Miami Beach Marina, and Clark waved his access card past the reader. The gate swung open, and we made our way to the *Moscow Mule*, where we found Disco and Skipper enjoying a pair of cocktails and the afternoon Miami sun.

"What took you so long?" Skipper asked.

"We took the slow boat," I said. "But thanks for waiting for us for happy hour."

She held up her hands, feigning innocence. "I wanted to wait, but Diva Disco wouldn't hear of it. You know how he gets when he doesn't get his way."

"You have a point," I said. "I guess that means we have some catching up to do."

A young lady wearing a white apron over a black chef's jacket appeared on deck. "Well, hello, new people. I'm Kate, your chef. Are there any food allergies or food hatred I need to know about?"

I thought I detected the slightest Eastern European accent behind her American English, but I couldn't be certain.

I raised a hand. "No mayonnaise!"

She frowned. "You won't be able to taste the mayo in anything I prepare."

She uses contractions and articles naturally, but the nearly invisible accent is in there.

I gave her a nod. "Good. That means there's no reason to include it if you can't taste it. Other than that, we'll eat anything."

She said, "Fine. No mayo. How about dinner at seven before we shove off for Puerto Rico?"

Heads nodded, and Chef Kate vanished.

Disco pointed toward the bar. "They have a bartender, but I gave him the night off. If we're too lazy to make our own drinks, we don't deserve them."

I poured an Old Rip Van Winkle Ten Year and raised my glass. "Here's to living through the screw-ups and coming out the other side with scars and stories and surrounded by people you love as if they were family."

"Hear, hear!" came the chorus.

Rims were touched, and our family put another memory in the bank. I silently prayed we'd all come out the other side unscathed and closer than ever before.

Chapter 17
Made to Order

Dinner was classic seafood with an appetizer of broiled sea scallops served with candied bacon and a light honey glaze. The entrée of perfectly sautéed lionfish filets over lobster risotto, framed by grilled asparagus, melted in our mouths.

Chef Kate appeared on deck just as a steward lifted the final plate from the table. "I trust you enjoyed your main course."

If she was fishing for a compliment, she was about to land a whopper.

I rubbed my stomach and sighed. "It was unbelievable, Kate. Thank you. If every meal is like this, we'll be too fat to do our jobs in a week."

She bowed ever so slightly. "I'm pleased you enjoyed, but I do hope you saved room for dessert. I've baked a miniature chocolate lava Bundt cake with homemade vanilla bean ice cream and a raspberry glaze."

Sensual groans of delight rose from the table.

Kate said, "I'll take that as a yes. Port or coffee or both?"

"Both all around, except for Singer."

Singer smiled. "Yes, just coffee for me, please. I'm watching my girlish figure."

She almost curtsied. "Only coffee? No dessert?"

Mongo said, "Oh, yes. I'm having dessert. In fact, if you have an extra, I'll take it instead of the port."

"I'll see what I can do," she said before disappearing back into the yacht's interior.

Mongo met my gaze and then glanced over his shoulder. "Did you get a hint of the accent?"

"I did, but just barely. What are you thinking?"

"Maybe Chechen or Romanian. I can't be sure."

Skipper leaned in. "I caught it, too. What do you think it means?"

I said, "It probably means she learned an Eastern European language, first, but began speaking English before she was old enough to start school. Now that I know I'm not the only one who caught it, I'll check into it."

Clark tapped the base of his wineglass with a fork. "Don't get excited, College Boy. She sounds a little bit Russian because she *is* a little bit Russian. Georgian, to be precise. And I'm surprised you don't remember her."

"Why would I remember her? I don't think I've met her before tonight."

He leaned back. "Oh, you met her, but only long enough to shove her and the rest of the crew into a lifeboat when you took over this yacht."

"She's part of the original crew?" I asked. "Isn't that a little too close to the fire?"

"Yes, she was part of Barkov's crew, and she's not alone. The captain is also Georgian, as well as the engineer and one of the stewards, but don't get your apron strings in the custard. They've all been thoroughly vetted, and they're as American as you and me."

"Apron strings in the custard?"

"Yeah, you know what I mean."

The steward arrived with port and coffee only seconds before the miniature Bundt cakes were served. Conversation morphed into muffled moans of chocolate ecstasy.

When I was finally able to piece together a sentence, I raised my port glass. "Here's to apron strings in the custard and a well-vetted crew."

We touched glasses, sipped perfectly matured port, and watched the nearly full moon rise and claim the subtropical sky above America's southernmost metropolis.

The steward cleared the table, and I turned to Mongo and Tony. "All right, navigators. How long will it take us to make San Juan?"

Mongo lowered his gaze. "To the marina or the sea buoy?"

"Marina."

He said, "Sixty-one hours, thirty-five minutes."

Tony rolled his eyes. "You're getting senile, old man. This tub will do at least twenty-five knots, so we'll be safe and sound in San Juan Harbor in no more than forty-five hours."

Mongo chuckled and threw a monstrous arm around Tony. "I love you, kid, but you obviously didn't check the weather. We're beating into a twelve-knot headwind out of the southeast the whole trip."

Tony's head fell, and Mongo gave him a squeeze. "Don't worry, little fellow. You'll get old and senile like me someday, and just think how smart you'll be when it happens."

I called the table to order. "All right, let's talk business. We've all had a couple of cocktails, so the patrol boat isn't going anywhere tonight. Let's turn in early, get a good night's sleep, and head for Puerto Rico before the sun comes up. Are there any volunteers to take the Mark V to San Juan? If not, Tony and I will do it."

Hunter said, "I'll take my understudy and meet you there." He elbowed Tony. "Here's your chance to redeem yourself, kid. How long will it take us, non-stop, from here to San Juan in the Mark V?"

Tony landed a flat palm on the table. "I don't know, sir. I'll have to check the tides, sea state, and wind to accurately calculate our time en route."

Mongo clapped. "Well done, grasshopper."

Hunter slapped Tony on the back. "We'll be underway no later than zero-five-hundred, and I want to see you bright-eyed and bushy-tailed."

* * *

The sun peeking through my porthole drew me awake, and I was surprised to feel the yacht moving beneath me. I wandered onto the stern deck, wearing only shorts and a T-shirt, while the world was still sleepy and taking her first sun-kissed breaths of the morning. The air carried an unexpected chill, and I guessed it was near fifty degrees.

A steward I hadn't met the night before materialized beside me and handed me a mug of piping hot coffee. "Black, no sugar, right?"

"Yes, thank you. Am I the first one up this morning?"

"No, sir. Mr. Hunter and Mr. Johnson left an hour ago in the other boat, and I packed enough food for them for a full day."

I turned my gaze across to the northwest, where the outlines of a few of Miami's skyscrapers were still visible. "Thank you. I'm sure they appreciate that. I suspect the rest of us will be up and about soon. Is Kate working on breakfast yet?"

"No, sir. She'll make everything to order when you're ready to eat."

The next sixty hours of our lives were spent in the epitome of luxury, and I saw a side of the *Moscow Mule* I'd never considered

THE DARKER CHASE · 123

the last time I was aboard her. She'd been built to Dmitri Barkov's demanding specifications, and I had to admit his taste was spectacular.

The stacks of the Bacardi rum distillery came into view as we motored past the Castillo San Felipe del Morro that had been guarding the entrance to Bahia de San Juan since the fifteen hundreds, but that wasn't all that caught my eye. Apparently, our Mark V was making some new friends. She was nestled between a pair of nearly identical Mark V's at the Coast Guard Base, less than a mile from the fortress.

The captain and his crew executed a textbook example of a Mediterranean mooring at the Club Nautico de San Juan marina. He spun the yacht around in the basin just outside the marina, dropped and seated an anchor from the bow, and slowly backed toward the dock. The crew secured a pair of crossed stern lines, and the deckhand on the bow drew the anchor chain taut. The maneuver is a complex, intricate dance with four deckhands, wind, tide, other vessels, and finally, the maestro at the helm. The captain and crew of the *Moscow Mule* made it look easy, and Tony watched the show from the dock beside his mentor and my tormentor, Stone W. Hunter.

Hunter looked up and cupped his hands around his mouth. "Ahoy! What took you so long?"

The two crewmen who'd managed the stern lines deployed the gangway, and our team was, once again, whole.

Hunter snatched a handful of nuts from a bowl on the table. "How was the trip?"

"Better than yours," I said. "Did the boat do well?"

"Ran like a top all the way down. We only touched the controls to take her off the dock in Miami and put her alongside, right over there."

"Good. Have you made contact with our playmates?"

He chewed a few nuts and said, "Yep. They're ready when we're ready. They're a little over halfway between here and St. Thomas at a place called Savana Island. It'll take us about an hour to get there."

Thirty minutes later, we were clear of San Juan and cutting across the Caribbean Sea at seventy knots, with Tony at the helm. Just as Hunter predicted, we intercepted the USCGC *Thetis* five miles north of Savana Island, and I pulled on a headset from inside the pilothouse.

"U.S. Coast Guard Cutter *Thetis*, this is the American patrol boat off your port stern quarter."

A disembodied voice answered, "Good morning, patrol boat. This is the Cutter *Thetis*. We've been expecting you."

"It's good to be here, Thetis. Have you seen a perfectly harmless research ship called the *Lori Danielle*?"

"Affirmative, patrol boat. Your research vessel is tucked away in a small natural bay at the southwestern end of Savana. Why don't you check in with her, and we'll be lurking when you're ready to play?"

"Consider it done, *Thetis*. You can run, but you can't hide."

"We'll see about that, patrol boat. Happy hunting."

Chapter 18
They're Just Coasties

We rendezvoused with the *Lori Danielle* inside the inlet near Virgin Point at the southwest extreme of Savana Island, and to my delighted surprise, Master Chief Dre Lewis, Retired, stood in front of three former SEALs who were dressed from head to toe in solid black and kitted out as if charging into battle.

My headset came to life with Dre's voice. "No need to come aboard, Chase. We're coming down to you."

The crane operator lifted a blacked-out RHIB of some twenty-five feet and lowered it to the water with the SEALs on board. Dre and his team rounded the stern of the *LD* as the RHIB came up on plane. He brought the boat to a halt, with its portside tube resting against the Mark V, and tossed over a line. Hunter caught it and threw a couple of wraps and a cleat hitch with practiced ease.

Dre said, "Here's how things are going down today. Skipper's in the CIC, we've got four drones in the air prowling for the *Thetis*, and"—he paused to check his watch—"the satellite will be coming online any minute. Finding her won't be a problem."

We listened closely to Dre's briefing, then I asked, "Are you going to be neutral observers in the RHIB?"

He grinned and stuck a thick cigar into the corner of his mouth. "Not hardly, son. Today, we're teaching small boat tactics by baptizing you boys with fire. Now, get out of my boat."

My team stood staring at each other, unsure what to do. Dre and his four SEALs bounded over the gunwale and into the Mark V.

He said, "I wasn't playing. You guys can take the RHIB, or you can swim."

The six of us surrendered the patrol boat to the SEALs and slid over the side into their RHIB. The looks on our faces screamed full-blown confusion, and Dre finally took pity on us.

"Relax, guys. We're going to teach you a little move we like to call hide-and-peek."

I positioned Tony at the helm, Singer on the forward deck gun, Hunter and Mongo abeam the helm as scouts, Disco directly behind Tony in case our rescue swimmer needed to be in the water, and I took the stern.

Dre watched and made small adjustments to our positions. "Just remember to keep Mongo aft of the console. It's a big boat, but with three thousand rounds of seven-six-two under that deck gun on the bow, that big man is enough to submarine you until you burn off some ammo."

We conducted a comms check with Skipper in the combat information center aboard the *Lori Danielle*.

Dre asked, "Have you found the *Thetis*?"

Skipper laughed on the radio. "What do you think?"

"Let's have it," he said.

Skipper read off the cutter's coordinates, and we entered them into the nav systems of the RHIB, as well as the Mark V.

Skipper said, "She's tracking north at twenty-two knots, but I don't know for how long. I'll report speed and direction changes."

Dre stood on the elevated stern of what had become *his* boat, and stomped his boot onto the transom. "See my foot?" We nodded, and he said, "Keep your bow as close to this point as possible. Watch for hand signals for turns and speed changes. Do not . . . I repeat . . . Do not get more than one meter away from this spot, no matter what happens. Got it?"

Tony said, "Got it!"

Dre looked down at our sniper. "Singer, listen to me, and listen good. Do not sweep my men with that muzzle. Capisce?"

"Aye, aye, Chief."

Dre continued. "We're going to maneuver across the horizon in front of the cutter and then drive straight at them. They've got some of the best surface-detection radar on the planet, but your patrol boat is really good at playing invisible. That RHIB is not. That's why you have to stay exactly in our shadow. The Coasties can't see through us, so you're just as invisible as we are until we break formation." He scanned my team. "Any questions so far?"

"When do we break formation?" Tony asked.

"Keep your shirt on, swimmer. I'm getting to that part. As we approach their bow, we'll push the boat as hard as she'll go, and you do the same. You can keep pace with us. If you need to hang back to learn the boat on the way out, do it, but when the fun begins, you have to stick your nose right up our butt."

Tony nodded. "Roger, Chief. Will do."

"Now, with our seventy-five or eighty knots and the cutter's twenty-five, our closure rate will be over a hundred knots. Things happen fast at that speed. We'll rake their bow with fifty-cal and force them to keep their heads down. When we break to starboard, you break to port and rub that tube against that pretty orange and white hull until you make the stern. That's when you get to pull off that spinning turn we taught you. The difference is the RHIB will leave the water in the turn and come crashing down like twenty tons of bricks. It'll rattle your teeth, but you have to stay on the throttle. Don't worry if you hit the cutter. You can't hurt it with that little boat."

I looked up. "What are you going to do while we're dancing with the cutter's backside?"

"We'll be shooting, hooping, and hollerin'—whatever it takes to keep their attention on us and away from you."

I pulled off my hat. "I like this plan already."

"I thought you would. Once you and your men are aboard, peel off the starboard stern quarter a thousand yards or more. The boarding party should be able to take the cutter before the crew can man the battle stations. Move quickly and quietly. The rules of engagement are simple. If you touch a man before he draws down on you, he's dead, and he'll go to the deck. If anybody puts you in his sights, you have to do the same. Lie down on the deck and play dead."

"We're not going live-fire, are we?"

"Absolutely not. Every weapon will be clear and safe with no fingers on triggers. The same holds true for your team. Clear and show safe, then lock up the live rounds if you're going to carry your sidearms onto the cutter. This is a no-fire exercise from your side, so there's no reason to carry the extra weight of the weapons unless you're married to them and can't leave them behind."

I stared up at him through the morning sun. "You said you were going to rake their decks with the fifty-cal. Is it all simulated?"

"We're firing blanks. If the thing with the Moroccans goes right, you'll do the same to keep up the ruse. From their perspective, that fifty-cal deck gun will be belching lead like a fire-breathing dragon."

"This sounds like fun."

"It's not fun when the bullets are real," Dre said. "We know that from experience. In all honesty, you should be able to take the cutter without any casualties. They're just Coasties."

Tony gave Dre the single-finger salute, and the SEAL laughed. "We're on headsets underway and waterproof whisper-comms for the boarding. Ready to have some fun?"

Tony glanced back at me. "I gotta tell you, this feels weird assaulting my old shipmates."

I said, "Today, your old shipmates are bogies. Let's do it!"

Dre ordered his helmsman to move out, and Tony stuck our snout right in their blowhole.

"Don't you want to get the feel of the RHIB first?" I asked.

Tony didn't look up. "I think I'll be just fine. After all, I'm just a Coastie."

Skipper's voice filled our headsets. "Delta, Delta, Delta! Course change. Target vessel is now heading one-three-zero at twenty-five knots."

Dre said, "Roger."

Tony looked over his shoulder at me and yelled, "Somebody plot that position and course!"

The headset comms made communication possible, but not perfect. The roar of the twin outboards on the RHIB, coupled with the thunder of the Mark V only inches in front of our bow, penetrated the passive noise-reduction capability of the headsets.

I moved behind the console and tapped Disco to take my place at the stern. The ride in the wake of the Mark V was like sliding on ice, giving me the ability to manipulate the chart plotter with ease.

A few seconds later, I elbowed Tony and motioned toward the screen. "Take the helm."

I moved to the wheel as Tony sidestepped to study the plotter. A few seconds later, he groaned. "That's what I was afraid of. They're bearing on Salt Cay. That means . . ."

I said, "I know what it means. They're going to force us to guess."

He said, "Yep, and I'd bet your net worth they're going south of the island."

"Why would they go south? That's the busy side full of cruise ships and tourists. Surely they don't want us to put on a show in front of thousands of screaming fans."

"That's exactly why the skipper will choose the south side, because he thinks we'll guess north."

I tugged Tony back to the helm and stepped from behind the console. I looked up to find Dre staring straight back at me. He pointed north, then south, and shrugged. I pointed south, and he gave me a nod.

We ran as hard as the Mark V could move, and the RHIB never protested.

"I don't know where Dre got this RHIB, but we're keeping it."

Tony gave the thumbs-up and followed the patrol boat in her gentle turn to the southeast.

Stepping behind the windshield to soften the seventy-mile-per-hour wind noise, I pressed my transmit button. "CIC, RHIB."

"Go for CIC," came Skipper's all-business reply.

"Do you have satellite coverage yet?"

"I have partial sat coverage, but I'm re-tasking the drones to cover what I can't see. What do you need?"

I said, "I need a nice, quiet spot to kick some Coast Guard butt. Find me a playground."

"I'm already on it. He's obviously going south, right?"

"That's our guess."

While she worked, I studied the chart plotter and came up with the craziest plan my brain was capable of piecing together. I grabbed Tony's shoulder and drove my finger at the screen. "Can the cutter make it through that hole?"

He glanced down, but the demands of staying dead astern of the Mark V made it impossible to multitask.

He said, "Take the wheel."

I slid around him in the tight confines of the RHIB's console. "This isn't as easy as you make it look."

He ignored me and focused his attention on the chart plotter. After studying the picture, he stood up and grinned. "She'll fit, and I like where your head's at. I have the helm. I believe you have some coordination to do."

I surrendered the wheel and briefed the team. "All right, listen up. We're going to drive the cutter around his elbow and into his earhole. Dre, put us dead astern, out of sight, and match his speed."

The SEAL said, "What?"

"You heard me. Just do it."

He said, "You do know the idea is to get ahead of him, right?"

"That's exactly what I'm doing, Frogman."

We maneuvered exactly as I ordered, and I gave Tony a pat on the back. "It looks like you were right. She's slipping south of Salt Cay."

"And right into our hands," he said.

I keyed my mic. "As soon as she's south of West Cay, break cover, bear south, and triple her speed."

"She'll see us for sure," Dre argued. "There's no place to hide."

"That's what I'm counting on."

We trailed at twenty-four knots until the cutter was just past the break between Salt Cay and West Cay.

I said, "She's committed south. Break thirty degrees to starboard and all ahead full."

Dre followed my instructions, and Tony stayed pinned to the Mark V's stern. I watched Dre bend over the console, apparently studying the chart. When he stood back upright, he turned and grinned back at me.

Pushing the Mark V and the RHIB to their limits, we broke cover and showed ourselves to the Coasties on the cutter. Through the binoculars, I watched four lookouts on the cutter's starboard side point straight at us. One of the sailors stuck a radio to his mouth but never took his eyes off us.

I told Tony what I saw, and he said, "All that's left now is to figure out if the captain is a fighter or a runner."

"If he's a fighter, we'll break south and run like smoke and oakum."

I watched the cutter for any signs of it turning toward us to instigate a fight, but the captain held his course, just like I'd hoped. When the cutter's bow was less than a thousand yards from the Big Current Hole between Salt Cay and Little St. Thomas, I gave the order. "Hold your course, and go to the whip, boys!"

Continuing the overtaking maneuver, we showed the cutter's captain our stern, and he took the bait. Obviously believing we were running to turn about for a head-to-head encounter, the captain turned his nimble ship hard to port and stuck the bow in the four-hundred-foot-wide bottleneck that would take him and his ship north of the island. I prayed my gambit would work.

Spying the cutter's stern through my binoculars, I ordered, "Hold . . . Hold . . ."

When there was a sufficient chunk of earth between us and the Coasties, I said, "Come about to starboard!"

Dre made the turn, and Tony stayed on his heels.

I called to Skipper. "Watch him, and put the drones to the northeast, close enough to see."

"Roger," she said.

We rolled out parallel to our previous course and continued pressing the limits of the two boats.

Skipper said, "He's turning northwest."

I keyed my mic. "Put us between Salt Cay and West Cay, and keep it fast."

Skipper's voice echoed through my headset. "It's going to be perfect, Chase. Head zero-eight-five as soon as you're clear of the rocks, and you'll be on the cutter's bow at two thousand yards."

I said, "It's showtime, men!"

Dre plowed through the shallow water between the Cays and broke hard right as soon as he had the depth to do it safely. We followed with our bow almost touching his stern, and the big, beautiful, orange and white hull appeared exactly where Skipper said it would. We closed the distance in thirty-five seconds, and Dre's bow gunner opened up with the fifty-caliber deck gun.

We were close enough to see the forward lookout on the cutter dive for the deck. Dre's full-frontal attack strategy was working, and he continued to push the patrol boat toward the slicing bow of the cutter. At the last instant before impact, Dre broke right and raked the port side of the cutter with the thundering fifty-cal as Tony juked left and slid the RHIB down the starboard side of the hull of his former shipmates.

Amidships, Tony pulled the throttles back and leaned right. "Hold on!"

Just as we passed the stern, our helmsman cut the wheel hard over and gunned the throttles. The RHIB leapt from the water as if she'd been fired from a cannon, but Tony never flinched. He kept the throttles pinned until we crashed down less than a hundred feet behind the cutter. He closed the gap in an instant, and Singer fired the grappling hook across the cutter's stern rail. Hunter was first up the line, but Singer, Mongo, Disco, and I followed only a breath behind.

Chapter 19
Death from the Depths

The roar of the M2 deck gun on the Mark V thundered through the air, capturing the attention of almost everyone aboard the Coast Guard Cutter *Thetis*. The only eyes not turned toward the gun were those of my team.

Once Tony saw the team safely aboard, he broke off the starboard stern quarter and ran like the wind. He took the RHIB far enough off to make engagement from the cutter unlikely but kept her close enough that he could run back in to recover the team.

Hunter took point in our modified wedge formation, and Singer brought up the rear. We moved as if we were one body, each of us fully aware of the movement of the others and anticipating the next step. The hours spent clearing the rooms in the abandoned paper plant at Bonaventure had forged my team into a razor-sharp edge.

The starboard side of the ship was all but abandoned as the Mark V continued her pillaging on the port side. We encountered four men and laid hands on them long before they saw us. We left them lying on deck, simulating four kills before reaching the navigation bridge.

The bridge was accessible from three points: a wing from each side of the ship, and a hatch on the ship's centerline leading to the captain's quarters. We didn't have the time to prowl inside the ship to find our way to the captain's cabin, and moving to the port side, where the simulated lead was flying like gnats in a barnyard, was simulated suicide. The only remaining option was to storm the bridge from the starboard wing, and that's what we did.

Mongo filled the hatch with three hundred pounds of aggression and noise, and the rest of us followed. Scanning the environment, I counted five souls on the bridge: the captain, a helmsman, a navigation officer, and two enlisted lookouts with binoculars pressed to their faces. It took only seconds to gain full control of the bridge, but the chaos of five commandos storming a room the size of a walk-in closet left the Coasties chasing their tails.

With the captain's cooperation, we set the cutter adrift and ordered the crew to surrender. Convincing an American military crew to surrender anything is almost impossible, but to surrender their home that just happened to be an American ship, was bordering on an attempt to roll an immovable stone. Had the Coasties been firing live rounds, there would've been some casualties. My team would've gotten the Mark V chewed up pretty badly, with possibly a little blood on the decks, but all in all, the assault was impressive from anyone's perspective.

I called Skipper. "Exercise complete. Have the team form up on the port stern quarter for the after-action review."

We rafted up with the Mark V laying alongside the cutter's hip and the RHIB trailing by a painter from the patrol boat.

With everyone aboard the *Thetis*, I shook the captain's hand. "Thank you for letting us chase you around the Caribbean and climb aboard."

His red-faced expression never wavered. "Don't think you'll do it again. You can try a thousand more times, but if my crew surrenders this ship again, I'll keelhaul every man on board."

It took ten minutes to cool him down enough to have a conversation, but even then, he was a no-nonsense, steadfast officer who was determined to defend his honor.

I said, "You let me talk you into taking the exit at Little St. Thomas. If you'd plowed on, we would've had to back off and regroup."

"You don't have to tell me. I regretted that decision within seconds of making it. Then I let your drones talk me into turning northwest. I'm responsible for our failure, but it won't happen again."

We had a formal debrief that left the Coast Guard commander in slightly better spirits and Dre talking him into taking her back onto blue water for a capabilities demonstration of the cutter.

After the show, I sat on the console. "Are you familiar with the Descubierta-class of corvettes?"

He grunted. "Academically, only. I've studied them, but never been aboard, and never faced one broadside."

"How do you believe the corvette would perform beside your cutter?"

"They're slightly underpowered compared to my boat, but they displace a little less water. She'll turn tighter, but she's not likely to carry advanced weapons systems. She'll be reinforced near the waterline, and their deck guns are sometimes automated for remote firing capabilities."

I made notes and listened for half an hour. When I believed I knew as much about the Spanish corvettes as the commander could teach me, I thanked him again, and he offered his hand.

I shook it, and he yanked me close to him. "It won't happen again, so if you come at me, you'll have a tiger by the tail and one hell of a time dealing with the other end of him."

I'll never be sure if we abandoned the Coast Guard cutter or if we were thrown off, but either way, it wouldn't be the last time.

THE DARKER CHASE · 137

Back in our boats, we peeled off and headed for Mother, the five-hundred-foot Research Vessel *Lori Danielle* waiting patiently back at Savana Island. Unlike the Coast Guard crew, the team aboard the *LD* welcomed us with open arms as we rode the RHIB like an elevator beneath the ship's crane.

"Well done!" came Dre's compliment as soon as his foot hit the deck. "I couldn't have done it better myself. That was textbook, right down the line."

Instead of basking in his praise, I simply gave the chief a nod and headed for the mess. "Let's cram some calories down our throats before we get wet again."

Mongo put up no resistance. "That's music to my ears."

Before pulling off my whisper-comms, I said, "Hey, Skipper. Meet us downstairs in the crew mess. We'll have AAR and chow simultaneously."

Surprisingly, no answer came, but our analyst beat the rest of us to the table. It was lasagna, a salad, Texas toast, and roasted potatoes.

Disco pushed his potatoes aside. "They're trying to drown us in carbs."

Mongo shoveled another forkful into his mouth. "You're going to need those carbs, Flyboy. Something tells me we're not done for the day."

Disco eyed me. "Are we doing that again?"

I gave him a wry smile, and he pulled his potatoes back to the center of his plate.

Dre debriefed the team and pointed out a few small improvements we could make.

When the lasagna was gone, Tony spoke up. "I left a little gift for our friends on the cutter."

After our rescue swimmer shared his good news, Hunter knuckle-knocked the table. "Me and the kid have dibs on the diving. Somebody else gets to drive this time."

"I'll do the driving," I said. "This is going to be fun to watch."

It took Skipper less than two minutes to pinpoint the *Thetis*, and we were screaming across the water in the Mark V like a rocket sled on rails. As we put the cutter astern, I gave Mongo the nod, and he popped the first smoke grenade on the stern of the Mark V and sent a plume of black smoke trailing behind the patrol boat.

I pumped the throttles to simulate a pulsing engine. The urge to grab a pair of binoculars and put eyes on the crew of the Coast Guard cutter was almost irresistible, but I stayed the course and let the plan work as designed. I maneuvered to put the column of smoke between the cutter and the cockpit of the Mark V. "It's time to get wet, boys."

Tony and Hunter emerged from the forward cabin and crawled over the portside gunwale, keeping themselves pressed as tightly against the vessel as possible. Their full face masks with internal comms served not only to provide life-sustaining air from their rebreathers, but also a means to communicate with each other, as well as Skipper back in the combat information center on the *Lori Danielle*. They slipped into the water, their black dry suits protecting them from the December-chilled Caribbean water.

Phase one was complete. The ruse had begun, and we'd splashed our divers. Phase two was going to be harder to sell, but with the clandestine assistance of the former SEALs, it shouldn't be impossible.

Mongo's ingenuity was key to the second deception, and I gave the order. "Light the fire!"

Mongo positioned the asbestos-lined container above the engine room hatches and positioned the white phosphorous smoothly across the bottom of his cauldron. He poured on a generous dusting of iron powder to morph the flames into orange tongues, giving every appearance the Mark V was going down in flames.

I watched him carefully and couldn't resist asking, "Hey, witch doctor, do you need some eye of newt for that concoction? I think I have some in my rucksack."

He didn't look up, but I could almost feel his eyes rolling.

"No, but I could use the right foot of a village idiot. Got one of those?"

"Words hurt, Mongo. You could really use some sensitivity training."

He stood and tossed me his miniature torch. "That's a good plan. I think I'll go now. You can finish the fireworks."

"You know what? On second thought, I think you're exactly the right amount of sensitivity. Please, carry on. And here's your torch."

"That's what I thought."

He completed his deception and popped a white smoke grenade to blend with the black cloud already filling the air.

I pulled on the neoprene sock designed to keep my prosthetic foot dry and lifted the VHF radio mic. I coughed as if I were inhaling the life-stealing smoke. "Mayday . . . May . . ."

An instant later, orange and black flames danced skyward from Mongo's handiwork, and I handed out life jackets. "I never thought I'd have to say this, but it's time to abandon ship. Let's just hope the Coasties live up to their reputation."

We slid over the gunwale and into the chilly water, then activated our flashing lights as we held on to each other, forming a circle. The burning boat drifted slowly downwind, and we kicked away from the hull, breaking the first rule of water survival: never leave the floating remains of an abandoned boat.

As we cleared the bow, the instant Mongo saw the Coast Guard cutter turn toward us and accelerate through the water, he let out that enormous belly laugh I love so much.

I followed Mongo's line of sight and joined him in a laughing celebration. To my horror, I felt something powerful clamp around my one remaining flesh-and-bone leg, and I was dragged beneath the turquoise surface with a violence I never remember experiencing in the water. Fright and disbelief kept me from filling my lungs before my head was submerged and descending with speed. The absence of air in my lungs and the panic filling my chest became the greatest threat to my survival.

Why isn't my life jacket keeping me afloat? What creature could possibly be dragging me to the depths with such speed and violence? Can anything be done to stay alive? Have I drawn my final breath, and will I perish in the clear blue water of the Caribbean while perpetrating a ruse on the U.S. Coast Guard?

My knife!

If I can sink the blade of my knife into the skull of whatever creature has me in its relentless vise, I might get back to the surface in time to take another breath.

I extended my right arm to draw my knife and immediately realized why my life jacket was doing nothing to keep me afloat. It was gone. Not torn, ripped, or sliced. It was gone.

Nothing could be done about the missing jacket, but I could still fight. My vision was terrible without a mask, but I didn't need to see my attacker to bury my blade into its head until it released me . . . or until I'd expended the meager supply of air in my body.

The knife came clear of its sheath, and I pulled with every ounce of remaining strength in my leg to draw my torso close enough to the leviathan to launch my counterattack. At that moment, the most bizarre thought entered my mind.

If this thing bites off my only remaining foot, I would be a double amputee, but I would be alive. Perhaps slicing off my own leg makes more sense than attempting to kill or wound my attacker.

Suddenly, for no discernable reason, the creature released me, and I found myself at perfect peace, slowly floating toward the sun. I kept my knife locked in my iron grip in case the would-be killer returned, but I would never have to use the blade that day. My head broke the surface, and my lungs filled with precious air. My teammates greeted me with laughter instead of relief, and I was furious.

"What are you laughing about? I was almost killed! Did anybody see what had me?"

Disco caught his breath between outbursts of laughter. "Oh, yeah, we saw it. It was a hideous creature of the murky depths. It had to either be a giant squid or Hunter."

I yanked my life jacket from his hand, gritted my teeth, and tried not to laugh along with him. "He'll pay for this one. Mark my words. He'll pay."

Chapter 20
So Others May Live

With my heart beating in somewhat regular rhythm again, and my dedication to making Hunter regret his prank, I spun in a circle to put eyes on the Coast Guard cutter again, and to my delight, she was slicing through the water with a bow wave blooming from her snout.

"Here comes the cavalry," I said, still shaking water from my hair.

"How's this going to go down?" Disco asked.

I said, "I think they have rescue swimmers on board cutters, so they'll likely deploy a couple of swimmers and a RHIB to pick us up. While they're concentrating on saving our lives, Tony and his devil partner below will take full advantage of their misdirected focus."

Mongo corrected me. "According to Tony, they're actually called cutter swimmers when they're assigned to a boat. I guess that means they're only rescue swimmers when they jump from a helicopter."

"I don't care what they call themselves as long as they get us out of this water before we freeze to death."

"Freeze to death?" Singer scoffed. "It's gotta be eighty degrees."

I said, "According to the chart plotter on the Mark V, it's seventy-eight, and that's twenty degrees colder than our bodies want to be."

The cutter slowed as it approached, and a pair of swimmers in masks, fins, and snorkels stepped from a protrusion in the ship, slightly aft of amidships, and sliced into the water like the seasoned professionals they were.

Disco said, "That was Tony's gig in the Coast Guard, right?"

"That's right. I guess heroes come in all shapes and sizes, huh?"

"Indeed, they do, my friend. Indeed, they do."

The pair of swimmers approached with their snorkels protruding from their heads and brought themselves to a treading position a few feet away from us.

The first of the two men spat out his snorkel. "How many in the water, sir?"

I held up four fingers. "Four, and no injuries."

"Roger that, sir. We'll have you on deck in a couple of minutes." He spun and gave a series of hand signals to a lookout on board the cutter. When he turned back to find his partner treading water beside Mongo and laughing, the defeated look on his face said it all. "It's a ploy, isn't it, sir?"

I pointed toward the navigation bridge of the cutter. "It is."

Hunter and Tony stood on the portside wing outside the bridge, holding the captain and the navigation officer hostage.

The captain yelled down from his elevated perch. "Let 'em drown, Mikey."

The first swimmer gave a saltwater-soaked salute. "Aye, aye, sir." He turned back to me and smacked his palms against the water, sending a small wall of water crashing over my head.

The sound of the Mark V's turbo diesels turning fuel into horsepower thundered across the placid water.

I shot a thumb toward the craft. "That would be the SEALs bringing our boat back to us."

Dre brought the patrol boat to a stop only inches away, and we climbed aboard while the cutter swimmers returned to their home away from home.

"Thanks for putting out the fire," I said.

"No problem," Dre said. "That was beautiful. They should've never left that line hanging over the stern rail for Hunter and Tony to exploit."

I toweled off and turned to see the remainder of my crew stepping from the cutter's deck and disappearing beneath the azure surface. Tony was first to reach the Mark V, and he tossed his fins aboard and climbed the boarding ladder.

As soon as he was solidly aboard, I gave the order. "All ahead full!"

Dre stared back at me as if I'd asked him to lasso the moon, so I repeated my order. "All ahead full . . . now!"

He shoved the throttles to a stop, leaving Hunter alone, adrift, and absolutely understanding his punishment had begun. I waved as he grew smaller and smaller in the distance.

I relented. "Okay, go back and get him, but put him back in the water as soon as his feet hit the deck."

Dre nodded and returned to pick up my partner, and when we arrived at his side, Hunter said, "I get it, and I deserve it."

"Yes, you do," I said. "Now, get up here. We've got work to do."

He tossed his fins, and I caught them before he began his climb from the water. The instant he released the rail, Dre crushed the throttles, and Hunter catapulted backward, right back into the water. Dre stopped only feet away, and I yelled, "Sorry about that. It was just a little miscommunication. Swim back over here, and I'll help you up."

"You have my fins, and you're upwind. Come get me," he said as he rolled onto his back.

Tony watched the exchange as he shucked off his dry suit. "You're not really going to leave him out there, are you?"

"For now. He needs to feel the sting of retribution and my wrath."

Tony chuckled. "I'll add insult to injury." He donned his fins, mask, and snorkel and dived back into the water. When he reached his mentor, he spun him around and laced an arm around him. "Relax, sir. I know you're older and probably exhausted. Don't worry. I'm a rescue swimmer, and I'm here to get you to safety."

Hunter growled. "I'll show you safety if you don't get away from me."

"But, sir, I do this so others may live. I just need you to relax. I'll swim your old, tired butt back to the boat."

Hunter said, "So, that's your choice, huh? You're solidly on Chase's side in this? Okay, I can live with that, but I can also make sure you live to regret it. Now, give me one of your fins and get out of here."

Tony followed Hunter's order, and they returned to the Mark V unscathed.

* * *

Nine more days passed, and we assaulted the Coast Guard Cutter *Thetis* two dozen more times. We won some, but the Coasties got a little better after every attack, and by the end of the exercise, they were kicking our butts more times than not. After the final conflict, my team, including Dre and his former SEALs, settled into the officer's mess aboard the cutter for a final meal and debriefing.

With the groceries consumed, the skipper of the cutter said, "Gentlemen and ladies, it's been quite an exercise for all of us. I'd like to first thank our guests for showing us our weaknesses and helping us overcome them. Second, I'd like to apologize for any injuries or scorched egos my crew may have inflicted on your team."

I said, "No apologies necessary, Commander. We're big boys, and we—"

He held up a hand. "I think you misunderstand. I said I'd *like* to apologize, but I'm not going to. I hope it hurt and stung to the core because those are the lessons that will keep you alive when you do whatever it is you bunch of spooks are about to go do."

"Fair enough," I said. "And we appreciate those lessons. Thank you for everything. The training has been invaluable, and I want you and your crew to know you've played an enormous role in making the world a freer and safer place. You'll never see our faces on the evening news, and you'll never read about the things we do in the morning paper, but we'll take the lessons we learned here and turn them into agony for the enemies of freedom."

The commander nodded. "We couldn't ask for anything more."

* * *

With our wounds licked, boats fueled, and training complete, we settled back into the lap of luxury aboard the *Moscow Mule*. Cocktails and canapes arrived as if by magic, and Skipper said, "I just got off the phone with the egg princess, and she's ready to join us."

Disco sighed and stared into his smoked old-fashioned. "I guess that means somebody else gets to enjoy this while I go fetch the czarina."

Mongo leaned forward and stretched out an island-sized paw. "I'll take it, and a seat on the plane, if it's available."

He surrendered it to the big man. "If Chase doesn't need you, I'll be happy to have the company."

Mongo put on the puppy-dog eyes, and I relented. "Just go, but get back as fast as you can. We need to be in St. Barts, ASAP. In fact, we'll pick you up at Simpson's Bay on St. Maarten."

Skipper jumped in. "Irina will need a stop at home to grab some clothes. She's been museum hopping and probably doesn't have a party dress for St. Barts."

"No problem," Disco said. "I'm just a high-speed chauffeur."

* * *

Cocktail hour turned into dinnertime, and Chef Kate did it again. After gorging ourselves, I pushed back from the table. "I have to find a way to control myself. Eating like this is going to force me to buy bigger pants."

Hunter grunted. "Tell me about it. Nothing against Maebelle, but Kate's killing it."

I folded my napkin and laid it on my barren plate. "How far is it to St. Barts?"

"About a hundred fifty miles," Tony said, "but I'm not playing the arrival-time game with anybody but Mongo."

As if he were clairvoyant, the captain materialized. "Good evening, all. I trust your dinner was satisfactory."

I shrugged. "It was just okay. Nothing special."

He grinned. "I'll fire the chef, immediately." His almost invisible Russian accent was even more faint than Kate's.

I protested. "There's no need to fire the poor thing. She's doing the best she can. We'll make the sacrifice and suffer through the torture while she learns."

The captain said, "That is very sacrificial of you."

"That's us. Just a flock of sacrificial little lambs."

He nodded. "Indeed. Well, anyway, I came down to ask when you would like to weigh anchor for St. Barts."

"Funny you should ask. We were just discussing that. If you can make it happen, let's wake up anchored off Gustavia."

"As you wish," he said before disappearing.

Skipper wiped her mouth and threw in the towel. "I'm done. I thought I wanted dessert, but I was wrong. Okay, I mean I still *want* dessert, but I don't have any place to put it."

Hunter said, "I'm pretty sure it's a communist plot to destroy our team by obesity."

Tony poked Skipper's side. "The rest of us have been getting plenty of exercise, but I think . . ."

Hunter's eyes turned to beachballs. "Oh, this is going to be good."

Skipper grabbed a pair of knives and poised them to strike. Tony froze in fear for his life, and Skipper said, "Don't forget. I spent two days with Anya, so you have no hope of surviving if you finish that sentence."

Chapter 21
Let the Games Begin

We woke up anchored in a harbor, but the island was not St. Barts. A tender arrived at the stern of the magnificent yacht with Disco, Mongo, and Irina, making our team once again whole. Captain Sprayberry made the short run from Simpson's Bay on St. Maarten to Gustavia, St. Barts, and I fell in love immediately.

"What a gorgeous place."

Skipper leaned against the rail beside me. "It's almost too beautiful to believe."

"I guess it's like most places on Earth. Its appearance on the surface barely resembles the ugly truth that lies beneath."

She leaned back, still gripping the rail. "Philosophical *and* pessimistic—the dynamic duo of gloom."

I shrugged. "Maybe I'm just a little jaded from experience."

"I get it. But we pull back the curtain and peer into places most people never see."

"You're right about that, but not just places. We do the same thing in people."

"Yeah, I guess you're right. Does it ever end? Do you think there's life after this thing we do?"

"Now, who's the philosopher?"

She watched a dinghy motor past. "No, I'm being serious, for like Tony and me. If we, you know, get married or whatever, and he was a car salesman and I was a schoolteacher, we'd build a nest egg and retire someday. Does that ever happen for people like us?"

"It worked for Clark and Tony's dad. He's living the high life."

She said, "Yeah, but it's a lonely high life for him."

"He's never been alone anytime I've talked with him since he retired."

She laid a hand on my arm. "Come on, Chase. You're supposed to know stuff like this. Real loneliness has nothing to do with being alone."

"Now *you're* waxing philosophical. I guess we'll burn that bridge when we come to it."

We stood in silence, absorbing the apparent tropical paradise spread out in front of us, until her supercomputer of a mind came up with a nice change of subjects. "So, do we really get to play spoiled rich kids for the next two weeks?"

"I'm not sure we have enough cash to pull it off for two weeks, but that's the plan."

"I put together a list of nightspots where Astor is likely to party, and from what I've been able to find out, I'm not sure we'll survive it. The nightlife is amazing down here, especially when compared to what happens in St. Marys when the lights go out."

"How many clubs are on your list?"

"About a dozen," she said. "But I've narrowed it down even more by putting out some local feelers. I should get some input later today, and hopefully, I'll be able to pinpoint our boy's favorite spot."

I rapped on the mahogany rail with my knuckles. "Let the games begin."

The table on the upper deck beneath the shadow of the helicopter was set elaborately for breakfast, but we weren't the only game in town. There were at least three yachts that outshined the *Moscow Mule*, but that didn't stop the *Mule* from soaking up the sun and beams of jealous fascination from shore-bound tourists and the occupants of lesser boats at anchor nearby.

I thought back to how ridiculous I looked at my graduation three weeks before and felt even sillier in the wardrobe someone had curated for me. Pretending to be a trust-fund baby wasn't coming easily for me.

"I look like a jackass," were the first words out of Hunter's mouth when he appeared on deck wearing shorts that could only be described as pink.

I tried to contain my amusement but couldn't. "Yes, you do, but a quite fashionable jackass."

He took an aggressive step toward the table. "I'm going to kill you with one of those baby spoons. What are those things for, anyway?"

I picked up one of the ridiculous utensils. I don't know. Ask the steward or Chef Kate. I'm a one knife, one spoon, one fork kind of guy. I'm barely cultured enough to lick my fork clean between courses, but that's the limit of my vast dining etiquette."

He took a seat and accepted a cup of coffee from the steward. "Please tell me Mongo got a new wardrobe too."

I shrugged as the steward refilled my cup. "I've not seen him since we picked him up this morning, but I'm excited about it."

Almost before we could imagine how silly our giant would look in Polo and Gucci, the big man made his appearance wearing a bright yellow polo over a color of shorts I can't describe.

Half a step behind him was Tony in cargo shorts, a tattered Coast Guard T-shirt, and flip-flops. He stepped around the largest commando on the planet and said, "Check out Big Bird here."

Mongo grabbed the Coastie around his waist and hoisted him over his head. "Now I just have to decide which of my baby birds I'm going to feed you to."

"Put me down, you maniac!"

Mongo grinned. "Port or starboard?"

"Right here, right now," Tony demanded. Mongo obliged, and our youngest teammate crashed to the deck amid cheers and claps from a dozen watchers onshore.

Big Bird took a little bow and tipped his imaginary hat.

"Why aren't you dressed?" I asked as Tony climbed back to his feet.

"I'm not wearing that fruity garbage in my cabin. It ain't happening."

Before I could scold him, Skipper rose from the table, grabbed one of Tony's flip-flops, and set about wailing him with the rubber sole. "Get back down there, and get dressed like you've got some sense. You can either dress like the rest of your team, or you can dress like a steward and bring us drinks for two weeks. You pick!"

I could've berated him, and Mongo could've pummeled him, but neither would've been more effective than Skipper's admonition. Tony vanished in an instant, and Skipper took a seat at the table. "I swear, he's a twelve-year-old boy most days. I don't know why you put up with him."

I said, "I put up with him because he makes you happy, and he keeps Hunter out of my hair."

"Fair enough."

An hour later, everyone was appropriately dressed—even Tony —and breakfast was behind us.

I wiped my mouth and deposited the napkin onto my empty plate beside the unused tiny spoon. "So, Irina, tell us what you learned on your little field trip."

She beamed, and I feared we were in for a two-hour lecture on Fabergé eggs.

"It was *vse*!"

My brain whirled as I tried to remember that Russian word, but it wouldn't come."

"I am sorry," Irina said. "When I am excited and happy, I sometimes can only speak Russian."

"Never be sorry," Skipper said. "When I get excited, I can only speak English, so I understand."

Irina cocked her head. "You speak language other than English?"

"No, but especially not when I'm excited."

Irina smiled at both Skipper's joke and her willingness to soften her embarrassment. "You are funny one, Skipper. Thank you. Learning about eggs was amazing. I held seven of them with *these* hands." She held out her palms, and I could almost imagine her picturing the orbs back in her grasp.

"They are much lighter than I, uh . . . expected. There! I found word. This is for me celebration." She had a sip of orange juice. "I will not bore all of you with stories, but was for me wonderful, and I am now Fabergé expert. Maybe not really expert, but I can sound like expert for you."

A twin otter buzzed overhead and slipped behind the mountain above Gustavia. Hunter seemed unable to look away from the airplane as it approached.

Disco tapped my leg with the toe of his Italian leather loafer. "You want to try it, don't you, Hunter?"

"You know it, but I hear you have to have some kind of special training to land over there."

Skipper furrowed her brow. "What are you guys talking about?"

Disco pointed at the mountain. "Believe it or not, there's an airport on the other side of that hill, and it's one of the shortest runways in the world."

"Seriously?" she said.

"Yep, and Hunter's right. You have to receive and log specialized training for short field operations specific to that airport before they'll let you land."

Hunter nodded. "That's what I thought, but I'd love to give it a shot."

Disco said, "Maybe when this is all over, Chase will approve a trip down here in the Twin Otter or the Caravan."

"Consider it done," I said. "Do you know anybody who can do the training for us? It'd be cool to put that airport in our logbooks."

Disco brushed off an invisible flake of some nonexistent dust from his shoulder. "You just happen to have an instructor pilot on staff who's certified to conduct the training."

"No way!" Hunter said. "How'd you pull that off?"

Disco said, "After I retired from the Air Force, I did almost a year down here flying a Pilatus for an operation out of San Juan, and I ended up being a check airman for them for a couple of months. The pay was garbage, but the scenery was fantastic."

Hunter threw up his hands. "Oh, we are definitely doing this."

* * *

We spent the day exploring the harbor and the shoreline of the island in the yacht's tender. The beauty of the island's rocky coast was breathtaking, but in some ways, ominous.

Tony scanned the jagged shore. "You're not going to land even a small boat anywhere besides a beach on this island."

I watched the waves crashing over the razor-sharp rocks. "You're right about that. I wouldn't want to swim ashore and try to climb out on those."

The first officer from the yacht piloted the tender and gave us tidbits of local history as we explored. I wasn't sure if he was making it up or if he had volumes of Caribbean lore tucked away inside his skull.

It took a couple of hours to make our circumnavigation of the island, including a fifteen-minute stop in Baie de St. Jean to watch a Caravan and two Twin Otters land at the most intimidating airport I'd ever seen. But I would soon learn that Gustaf III Airport was child's play compared to the short, steep slope we were about to experience behind the curtain we'd wish could've remained closed.

Chapter 22
Look Who I Found

We did lunch ashore at Fouquet's Saint-Barth on Rue des Normands Gustavia, and we couldn't have chosen a better spot. The waitstaff spoke passable English, but we soon learned that Disco had been a bit modest concerning his level of fluency in French.

Our chief pilot pointed toward an item on the menu and asked, "*Le Jambon-beurre est-il aussi bon que la Boulangerie le Pain Retrouvé de la rue des Martyrs?*"

Disco and the waitress laughed and talked, and he even stood and hugged her at one point in the conversation while the rest of us stared in awe.

When the waitress left, Hunter threw up his palms in the universal symbol of *What the heck was that?*

Disco took a sip of his water. "What? She's nice."

"No, not the hug. She's cute, so the hug makes sense. But dude, you really speak French."

"Yes, I told you that before we started this mission."

"No, you said you speak a little French. You didn't say you could woo a French waitress. You're not just a flyboy. You're more James Bond every day, and obviously, French chicks dig you."

He blushed. "What can I say? Some of us have it, and some don't."

Skipper glared across her shoulder at the departing waitress. "If Ronda No-H finds out you're flirting with the locals, you're gonna get it."

Disco blushed even harder. "She's sweet, too, but let's not tell her about the waitress. I'm a little afraid of her."

"A little?" I asked. "You should be a lot afraid of her. She writes your paycheck every month."

"It's not the money part that scares me. It's the part about not knowing if she'll shoot me down if I ask her out."

I leaned back in my chair. "I just happen to know she wouldn't shoot you down, even if she had an antiaircraft gun, so you can relax and ask. But maybe it'd be best to wait until we wrap up this mission. I need your head in the game."

As he returned to his natural color, Disco said, "You always need my head in the game."

"And you never let me down. What did you order us for lunch?"

He put on his innocent schoolboy look. "How should I know? My French is terrible."

Our plates arrived, and corks were pulled. We ate for an hour to a rising chorus of sighs and moans of delight. Although I couldn't pronounce anything I put in my mouth, everything was amazing, especially dessert, but my favorite surprise of the outing happened as we stepped back aboard the *Moscow Mule*.

The first officer brought the tender to a gentle stop at the stern of the yacht, and Tony hopped out to tie off the lines. We climbed from the tender with our bellies full and our heads anxious for our first night on the town.

I climbed the stairs to the upper deck and found a gorgeous woman wearing part of a bikini and stretched out as if she owned the world. She was clearly soaking up the brilliant December sun and loving every minute of her stress-free afternoon.

She looked up and gave me a wink and the sexiest smile I'd ever seen. "Hey, sailor. Nice boat. I thought you wouldn't mind if I came aboard and made myself at home."

I stared down at the familiar freckles on her shoulder. "Mrs. Fulton, I've got a feeling you'd be welcome on everybody's boat—dressed or undressed—like that."

She stood, unconcerned about her top still resting on the lounger, and I shot a look around the boat before quickly stepping close enough to provide some cover for my well-exposed wife. "What are you doing?"

She giggled and waved a hand through the air. "You know what they say. When in Rome . . ."

"Yeah, I know what they say, but we're not in Rome."

She stepped against me, rose onto her toes, and kissed me as if we'd been apart far too long. "Yeah, but we might as well be in France, so when in France . . ."

I helped her replace and retie her top. "When did you get here?"

She glanced down where her watch should've been, but just like her bikini top, it wasn't where it belonged. "I don't know. Maybe a couple of hours ago. The captain told me you guys were gone to lunch, so I thought I'd take advantage of the free time and get a little sun."

"How was LA? Did you get everything done?"

She lifted a daiquiri from the small table beside her lounger and took a sip. "I got all of my stuff done. The rest is somebody else's responsibility, and I got a nice little surprise."

"Oh?"

"Yep. I sold a script I've not even written yet. How cool is that?"

"I don't know . . . Seven."

She screwed up her face. "Seven what?"

"You asked how cool it was, and that's the number that came to mind. More importantly, *how* did you get here?"

I flew to San Juan on the studio's jet and chartered a Pilatus over here. That's one sweet airplane. We should get one."

"Maybe *you* should get one. You're the one making all the Hollywood money."

She picked up a cover-up from the chair beside hers and wrapped it around her shoulders. "Maybe I will. Would you teach me to fly it if I did?"

"Nope, but Disco would. I've learned a lot about him on this trip, including the fact that he used to fly a Pilatus for a charter company out of San Juan. Maybe it was the same company you used."

"Maybe so. He's just full of surprises."

"Speaking of surprises . . . Do you know about him and Ronda No-H?"

She took another sip of her cocktail. "Yeah, everybody knows he's got his eye on her."

"Apparently, not everyone. I didn't know."

"I'm not surprised. For a spy, you sure miss a lot of what's happening around you."

Before I could answer, Skipper said, "He's not a spy."

Penny jerked her head around to see our analyst peeking her head through the hatch to the upper deck. "Hey, Skipper."

"Hey. I was just making sure you were dressed before I let the rest of the gang come up."

I turned to Skipper. "You knew Penny was here?"

"Of course I knew. Who do you think chartered her flight? Jeez, you'd make a terrible spy."

The rest of the team joined us in the sun, and Skipper called the meeting to order. "Guess who I found."

"Marcus Willoughby Astor," I said.

Skipper rang an imaginary bell on the table. "Ding! We have a winner!"

"First, how did you find him? And second, *where* did you find him?"

"The *how* I found him is easy. It's what I do. And the *where* I found him is at a club called Mauvaise Conduite on Rue des Dinzey."

Disco came to life. "I know that place. The name means 'misbehaving,' and that's what happens inside. It's not the kind of club you'll find in New York or LA., but for the islands, it's perfect."

"How do you know so much about it?" Skipper asked.

He held up his hands. "I've not always been the bastion of morality you see before you. I had my wilder days, but thanks to you guys, now I get all the excitement I need in real life."

I laughed. "Just like Skipper said . . . it's what we do. So, tell us about this place, Misbehaving."

"It's been a few years since I've been, but it's not very big, and it's definitely not a five-star joint. It's a one-room club with way overpriced drinks and all the debauchery you can afford. Now that I think about it, Mauvaise Conduite is the spot I'd guess Astor would hang out."

"I've got an idea," I said. "How about telling us stuff like this whenever it comes to your mind? Don't wait for Skipper to do all the work. If you think it, say it. You've got a better grasp on this whole St. Barts scene than the rest of us combined."

"Okay, but I'm pretty sure most of the stuff that jumps in my head isn't stuff you want me blurting out."

"Okay, maybe you should filter some of it, but when it comes to operational details, we need to know. A great idea left unspoken is far more dangerous than a terrible idea left unsilenced."

Skipper rolled her eyes. "There you go with that philosophy stuff again."

"Oh, come on. That one was top-shelf wisdom right there."

"It wasn't bad," she said, "but I can't wait to hear Clark screw it up."

Tony cleared his throat. "I'll take this one if you don't mind. I can foresee my big brother breaking that one down into something like this. Unsilencing terrible thoughts is always a good idea."

I laughed. "It's almost like Clark never left us, but let's get back in the game. We need an opening move tonight to get Astor's attention. Anyone have any ideas?"

Everyone seemed to be looking to everyone else until Penny spoke up. "I've never been to Sparrow School like Anya, but with my party dress and high heels, I'll bet I could get his attention."

Before I took my own advice and applied the filter, I said, "You're not really trained for this kind of thing."

Skipper plucked a piece of ice from her drink and threw it at me from across the table.

Penny laid a hand on my arm. "Oh, my darling Chase. How little you know. Every girl starts training for this the instant she learns every boy wants exactly what he can't have."

I sighed and stuck Skipper's ice cube in my mouth. "Does anyone have any thoughts on Penny's idea?"

Hunter didn't waste a second. "I'll tell you one thing. Every one of us would put a bullet down Astor's throat before we'd let him lay a finger on you."

Penny smiled and cocked her head. "Thank you, Hunter, and that's precisely why I'd feel completely comfortable—and safe—getting his attention for you."

I turned to our gentle little tour de force. "What do you think, Mongo?"

He pondered the question for a moment. "I'm with Hunter, except I'd stomp him to death instead of shooting him if he put his hands on Penny, or Irina for that matter, but he's apparently a party guy with a big ego, so naturally, the guy's going to pay attention when she walks by. As long as you don't send her in there without at least some of us, I don't hate the idea."

I repositioned myself in my chair. "I'll have to think about it before we put anybody at risk and before we know more about who and what we're dealing with. This guy isn't exactly running the general store in Mayberry. He's a big-time broker, and apparently, he's not afraid to mix it up with some serious players."

Tony stared across the table at Skipper, and the beam of sympathetic understanding came across his face. "Yeah, I'm with the rest of the guys. If it were Skipper going in there, there's no chance I'd let her go in without me."

Skipper lowered her chin and raised an eyebrow. "*Let* me? Is that what you said? Because I'm not the asking-permission kind of woman."

Tony recoiled. "I didn't mean it like that. I meant that I'd insist on going in with you. I wasn't trying to imply that . . ."

Skipper couldn't hold the stern face any longer, and she giggled. "Relax, Tony Tuna. I'm just messing with you. I think it's sweet you'd have to go in with me."

Relief overtook him, and he let out a long sigh.

I was thankful for the interruption because it gave my brain time to come up with a reasonable plan. "Remember, this isn't a democracy. As always, no one is required to go, but I'm the final decision maker on our op order."

Before I could continue, Hunter said, "We do this every time we get a mission, and you're supposed to be smart enough to remember how things happen. We're all in because we trust you and your plans. Just like Mike Tyson said, everybody's got a plan until they get hit in the face. Just tell us what we're doing, and we'll do it."

I said, "Fair enough. We're going in tonight for observation only. It'll be Disco because he speaks French, Tony because he's young, strong, and fast, Penny because we need to lay some groundwork in Astor's head, and me because I said so. We'll watch, listen, and learn, and that's all unless everything goes perfectly—in which case, we'll throw a little money around and parade Penny in front of him until he can't look away. After that, we'll bail out and debrief. Any questions?"

Skipper said, "Yeah, I've got a few. Do you want video and audio? I can send you in with some cameras and microphones they'll never see. We may be able to pick up some subtleties you might miss in the heat of the moment."

"I like that idea," I said. "What else?"

"They've got four security cameras at the Mauvaise Conduite —one on the front door, one at the bar, one between the two bathrooms, and one on the main floor. The one on the floor is terrible. Between the smoke and the lack of good light, it doesn't collect any usable footage. The one at the bar is pretty good, but the bartenders have learned to position themselves between the camera and the cashbox when they're making change. The one between the bathrooms is useless except to know how long somebody stays in the head. The one at the front door is the goose that laid the golden egg, if Irina will forgive the pun. It gets facial-ID-quality video of everybody coming and going from the club, with a timestamp. But there's a twist."

Singer asked, "How's it possible for one camera to capture their faces, both coming and going?"

"It's simple. They use a multi-directional lens, sort of like a fisheye without the distortion. It's an expensive piece of glass, and the camera isn't cheap, either."

I held up a finger. "Two questions. How do you know all of this already? And what's the twist?"

Again, she rolled her eyes. "Because I'm your analyst, and you only have the best of everything. I've been crawling around inside their network for over a week. We've got great Wi-Fi on the *Lori Danielle*, and it's almost as good on the yacht."

She paused to have a sip and continued. "The twist is that the timestamp isn't real, and it's super easy to manipulate. This means they can provide video evidence of someone coming, and/or going, into or out of the club at any time they want. Does that sound valuable to you?"

I said, "It does if you're selling alibis or setting up a blackmail scheme."

She snapped her fingers. "Bingo!"

"You never cease to amaze me, Skipper. You deserve a raise."

"That's what you keep telling me, but so far, my check always shows up with the same number of zeros at the end."

"I'll get somebody on that. Now, does anyone else want to complain about the working conditions or meager pay?" Hunter raised his hand, and I said, "Good. No questions. In that case, it's a yes to the cameras and mics. Let's get ready for a little clubbing."

Chapter 23
Trust Fund

Disco, Penny, Tony, and I traded our tropical daytime attire for equally ridiculous outfits that more than tripled the cost of our wardrobes.

I said, "I look like a trust fund frat boy, but these shoes are amazing."

Penny stared at the shoes and made her way to my newly trimmed beard. "I think you look pretty hot, and you're right—the shoes are great."

"Speaking of hot. You make that dress look like it was made for you."

"It was. It came from a tailor on Rodeo Drive. The studio expects me to look the part. Nobody wants to see a frumpy librarian type at a premier. They want beautiful people in beautiful clothes making beautiful movies."

I let my eyes linger and enjoy. "Well, they clearly got their wish with you."

* * *

Disco, Tony, and I hit the front door first, leaving Penny to make her grand entrance after we'd done some advance work in the interior of the club. It felt strange having someone hold a door open for us. We were far more accustomed to breaching with a shaped charge of C4, but the VIP treatment wasn't bad.

The bone conduction audio set Skipper glued to our scalps, just behind our ears, was some sort of wizardry I'd never understand. According to her, it worked by transferring the vibrations that make up sounds through the temporal bone and into our ears. It was terrifying at first, but after a few minutes, we fell in love with the technology, and the ability to hide an earpiece beneath our hair was worth its weight in gold.

Through the magical comms, Skipper said, "Remember, don't look up at the cameras."

"We're good at this," I said. "You don't have to remind us of the rules."

"Just don't forget to give your body cams a few seconds to adjust for changes in lighting before you do anything that needs to make it into the archives."

The body cams were tiny lenses affixed to the buttons of our shirts, and the microphones were tucked away in plain sight inside my watch, Disco's ring, and Tony's earring. The technology was fascinating, but the opportunity to make fun of Tony for wearing an earring was priceless.

Skipper's lenses adjusted faster than our eyes as we stepped into the darkened interior of the club. The music was loud but not obnoxious. The crowd was young, beautiful, and oblivious to our presence. It was impossible to tell where the dance floor ended and the tables began. I decided the tables were an afterthought because the real action was the sweaty bodies grinding against each other to the beat of the four enormous speakers mounted high in each corner of the room.

I leaned toward Disco. "Something tells me we're not going to get any quality audio in here."

He either didn't hear me or was mesmerized by the scene in front of us, so instead, Skipper's disembodied voice filled my ear. "Don't worry about the audio. I can filter out most of the music. Any sign of Astor yet?"

"Still looking," I said. "It's a little crowded in here."

That's when it happened, and I was immediately terrified. A well-manicured hand appeared from within the throng of gyrating bodies and grabbed Tony's shirt, popping off the top button and his body cam. The hand pulled our rescue swimmer into a pool he wasn't prepared to be in. An instant later, he was dancing—or doing something that may have qualified as dancing—and the hand that had plucked him from his status as innocent bystander to willing participant found its way around his neck. It was blaringly obvious that Tony fell perfectly into the age group and sex appeal requirements for acceptance into the soul of the club.

Skipper said, "What's happening? I lost Tony's body cam."

I reached for a transmit button, forgetting we were on open-channel comms. "He's doing some undercover work, but he's fine. You can consider his body cam out of service."

I expected her to have a dozen questions about Tony's situation, but just like the consummate pro she was, she merely said, "Roger."

Scanning the crowd as we moved, Disco and I waded through the ocean of bodies, making our way to the bar. The wall of bottles spoke volumes about the social and financial status of the club's patrons.

I elbowed Disco. "Check it out. There aren't any well drinks in this place. Everything's top-shelf."

Four bartenders moved in practiced coordination behind the bar, and just as Skipper said, they each found a way to put their backs to the camera every time the cash drawer came open. When one of the bartenders finally made her way to our end of the bar,

168 · CAP DANIELS

she eyed us carefully, and I feared we'd been made as a pair who didn't fit in with the young, hip club crowd. But instead of calling us out, she leaned across the bar and cupped a hand behind her ear. "*Qu'est ce que je peux vous servir?*"

I turned to my pilot and translator, and he said, "What do you want?"

"Scotch, rocks," I said.

Disco turned back to the bartender and held up two fingers.

A pair of drinks appeared seconds later, and I slid a hundred-dollar bill into the woman's palm. "Keep it."

She smiled and winked, and I discovered she was at least bilingual when cash was involved.

Being a few inches taller than most people in the club, I scanned the crowd in search of our otherwise occupied teammate. I found him sandwiched between two women who clearly weren't there to spread the gospel. I met his gaze, and he shrugged as if to say, *Somebody's gotta do it.*

I took my first sip and held my glass up to what little light existed. "This is nice. What do you think?"

Disco took a sip. "Very nice. I think I like this place."

I motioned across the room with my glass. "It looks like we're not the only ones who like this place. Is that our boy?"

He squinted and followed my line of sight. "If that's not him, it's his twin."

We moved diagonally through the crowd until we found ourselves in a somewhat quieter nook facing Astor and the crowd surrounding him. I reached overhead with my left arm and grabbed a shelf that had likely once held a speaker. That day, it held nothing except dust, but it allowed the camera in my watch to capture Marcus Willoughby Astor for Skipper.

"Yep, that's him," she said. "Are you ready for Jessica Rabbit and her hot little red dress?"

"Send her in."

The average age of the women in the club—and especially those surrounding Astor—was a decade younger than Penny, but when she strolled through the door as if she owned the place, the twenty-somethings in the room and the eyes of their men drifted to the door. She was ravishing and impossible to ignore. To me, she was the most beautiful woman on Earth in jeans, a T-shirt, and a ponytail, but that night, nobody could ignore the auburn-haired, statuesque beauty in the ten-thousand-dollar dress, and Astor's decision to look around his adoring fans at my wife made it clear he was not immune to her charms.

The crowd didn't exactly part to let her walk through, but she didn't struggle to find her way to the bar. By the time she reached the mirror-backed alcoholic dispensary, Disco and I were back on that side of the room and leaning against the polished bar, nursing our scotch. Penny caught the eye of one of the bartenders and raised a finger.

The young man with his shirt unbuttoned to his navel leaned close, and Penny asked, "English?"

He said, "Sure. What'll you have?"

She turned and pointed toward my glass. "I'll have what he's having, and put it on his tab, will you?"

The bartender glanced over at me. "It's cool to put her drinks on your tab, man?"

I let my eyes climb Penny's body as if I'd never seen the goddess before. When I made it to her face, she gave me a wink and mouthed, "Please."

I leaned toward the man behind the bar. "How much will you take in tonight?"

He shrugged. "I'll make five hundred or so in tips. Why?"

I said, "No, not you, brother. I'm talking about the whole bar."

"Oh," he said. "Fifteen grand, U.S."

I reached inside my jacket and pulled out two banded stacks of hundreds, then I dropped the twenty thousand dollars onto the bar. "Everybody's drinks are on me tonight. Especially hers."

It didn't take long for news of my generosity to make its way through the crowd, but the stunning lady in red didn't seem impressed. She worked the room like a pro and danced by herself, but somehow made everybody on the floor feel like she was dancing only with them.

Occasionally, she'd brush past me and let her hand linger against my thigh, or sneak a quick kiss behind my ear as if thanking me for the cocktails. The show was strictly for Astor's benefit, but I liked the attention.

Penny spent two hours in the club drawing just enough attention to leave a gentle impression on the party scene in St. Barts. She was the first of us out the door, but not before brushing her fingertips down my arm, pressing her lips to my cheek, and whispering, "Nice work, big spender. How would you like to wake up in my bed tomorrow morning?"

Before she pulled away, I said, "I wouldn't miss it for the world, Mrs. Fulton."

As she made her way to the door, Penny let her gaze fall on Astor, and he returned the glance. She smiled, and he raised a glass and offered a barely visible nod.

Twenty minutes later, I leaned into Disco. "Go ahead and make your exit, and take Tony with you. I'm going to see if I can get our boy's attention."

"Whatever you say, boss. Do you want us to wait outside for you in case something goes awry?"

"Yeah, but do it outside the camera's watchful eye. There won't be any issues, but it never hurts to have a friend or two lurking in the bushes."

I ordered another drink and parked myself well in sight of our target, hoping he'd take the bait. He did.

He eyed me almost to the point of becoming uncomfortable and then headed across the crowded room. I'd watched dozens of men come at me from every angle, with every sinister intent imaginable, but I'd never seen anyone working so hard to appear docile. He looked like a golden retriever anxious for me to throw a ball. So, I tossed one.

When he was three strides away, I extended my hand and leaned toward him. He shook my hand, and just like the golden retriever, he was almost drooling over the prospect of bringing back the ball.

"Name's Astor. Marcus Astor. Nice to meet you. You speak English, right?"

I turned my head to hear him as the rhythmic beat of the music blared over our heads. "Yeah, I speak English. Daniel Chase. And it's nice to meet you, too, Mr. Astor."

With my hand still gripped in his, he landed his left on my bicep and turned me toward the back of the club. "Why don't we step out back so we can get to know each other without yelling?"

I followed him through a well-camouflaged back door and onto a stone patio. His demeanor gave me no reason to suspect he was dangerous, but I was alive because I never let my guard down until I owned the environment and everything in it.

He pulled a pair of Cubans from inside his jacket, and I produced a punch and lighter. He appraised my tools and accepted the punch. "I like a man who's not afraid to spend a little money for a nice night on the town."

"It's just money," I said. "The whole purpose of having it is to be able to smoke cigars like these and buy drinks for girls like those in there."

He toasted the end of his cigar and slid the Xikar lighter back into my palm. With our Cubans producing the smoke and mouth-watering smell only the best leaves in the world can create, he said, "That was a big-baller play you made in there buying out the bar. There's a lot of money on the island, but I've never seen anybody pull that one just to impress a lady."

I did my best imitation of Clark's crooked grin. "Yeah, but have you ever seen a lady like that one?"

He curled a finger around his cigar and raised it in a wordless salute. "What brings you to the island, Mr. Chase?"

"Just Dan, please. Mr. Chase was my old man, and he's the reason I can buy out any bar in the world."

"Trust fund, huh? Nice."

I took a long draw and let the white cloud of communist Cuban smoke rise above my head. "Not hardly, my friend. He didn't leave me a penny, but the old warhorse taught me how to make it on my own."

He pulled his cigar from his mouth and raised an eyebrow. "Even better."

We stood silently smoking two of the best cigars on the planet until he asked, "How long are you in St. Barts?"

"Until I get a better offer or my boat sinks."

"Your boat?"

"I have a little boat at anchor out there. I don't really think she'll sink, but you never know. The world is full of jealous husbands and sore losers."

He seemed to enjoy my answer, but his eyes said he had a lot more questions. "The *Moscow Mule*?"

"That's her," I said. "You might say I have a weakness for rare, beautiful, Russian things."

"Is that so? The lady in red didn't appear to be Russian."

I gave him Clark's grin again. "She most certainly is a rare beauty, but you're correct. She's far from Russian. I've learned that waking up next to a beautiful American woman is far less dangerous than falling asleep wondering if the Russian beside me is going to gut me like pig while I sleep."

"Well, Dan, it's been a pleasure. Next time we find ourselves in the same club, drinks will be on me."

Chapter 24
End of the Innocence

The main salon aboard the *Moscow Mule* wasn't the ideal operations center, but it was, by far, the most comfortable. Just like in the ops center at Bonaventure, Skipper left no doubt who was in charge of the room.

"Listen up," she said. "There are ears and eyes everywhere on this boat. It's an environment we're not accustomed to, so let's keep our voices down, and if there's anything critical we absolutely don't want to risk being heard, write it down."

Hunter said, "You don't think the crew is spying on us, do you?"

"I always think everyone is spying on us. That's how we prevent being spied on."

"Point made."

Skipper cocked her head. "Imagine that . . . me being right. So, anyway, I know we're all tired, but we need to get the debrief done before we forget any details. I have everything recorded, but the audio from inside the club is a little loud. I'm working on isolating voice and cutting out the music, but it's going to take some time. Chase, do you want to go first?"

I slid forward and sat on the edge of my seat. "Sure. I think it went far better than expected. I didn't expect to make face-to-face contact with Astor on our first outing. I was surprised when he pulled me aside."

"Me, too," Skipper said. "I can't say I'm disappointed, but I'm definitely surprised. I captured all that audio perfectly, by the way."

"Good," I said. "I panicked a little when it came time to make introductions. All I could come up with was rearranging my name when I told him I was Daniel Chase. We should've worked this out ahead of time, but we're going to need a legend for my new name."

Skipper said, "Give a girl at least a little credit. I created the back story as soon as I heard you use the name. We're good. We'll go over the details later, but rest assured, when Astor's people start searching for the real Daniel Chase, I'll take them by the hand and lead them right down the path I built just for them."

"I should've known. For those of you who may not have heard my conversation with Astor, I laid the groundwork that I've made a little money, and I have an affinity for rare and beautiful Russian things."

Penny rolled her eyes. "Who doesn't know that about you?"

"Listen to the audio," I said. "I think you'll approve."

"Oh, I heard it already, and it was good thinking on your feet."

Disco jumped in. "Buying out the bar was a nice touch. What made you think of that?"

"I just thought about what a rich kid would do to impress the lady in red, and the idea popped into my head."

"It definitely got Astor's attention," Tony said.

Skipper gave him a look. "Speaking of getting attention, you certainly did your share of turning heads, Dancing Queen."

He threw up his hands. "I was undercover. What was I supposed to do?"

"You weren't supposed to enjoy yourself quite so much."

"It was work," he said. "I was only pretending to enjoy myself. In reality, I was surveying the room for potential threats and positioning myself strategically to spring into action at any moment if Chase needed my help."

Skipper huffed. "Really? That's the story you're going with?"

"For now. At least until I come up with something better."

"I'll deal with you later, Romeo. In the meantime, let's talk about our next move. Are we going back out tomorrow night?"

I said, "Before we move on to tomorrow, I think Penny deserves a hand for her Oscar-worthy performance tonight."

She batted her eyelashes and covered her mouth with the tips of her finger. "Aww, shucks. Little ol' me?"

Disco spoke up. "I'm starting to think you belong in *front* of the camera instead of at the writers' table in Hollywood."

"Stop it. I did enjoy myself tonight, though. It was pretty cool to be part of the team."

"It's far from over," I said. "We have to play the hand we dealt ourselves. If we're going to convince Astor to steal a ship for us, we have to stay the course."

"So, I get to play Ginger, and when we introduce Irina to Astor, she can be Mary Ann."

Skipper snapped her fingers. "We're getting off track. Are we going back out tomorrow night or not?"

I said, "I think it might be a good idea to lay off at least one night. I don't want to spook Astor. If we keep showing up everywhere he is, he might smell a rat."

Skipper nodded. "That's what I was thinking. I know this isn't a democracy, but if I get a vote, I say we disappear for a couple of days."

"Disappear to where?" I asked.

"Anguilla isn't a bad option."

Hunter cocked his head, and it caught my attention.

"What's happening in that head of yours?" I asked.

He said, "What if he bolts?"

"Why would he do that?" I asked.

Hunter said, "I don't know. People do crazy stuff. I just thought it might be a good idea for a couple of us to stay behind and keep an eye on our boy just in case he gets the urge to move on."

"Who do you have in mind?"

He scanned the team. "Tony's no good. Astor saw him already. It'd be better if Singer and I did it. He's never seen either of us, and we're pretty good at blending in."

Mongo landed an enormous hand over his heart. "That stings. I can't believe you don't think I can blend in."

Hunter chuckled. "You blend in just fine in a sequoia forest, but you weren't made for surveillance, you big oaf."

I gave Skipper a glance, and she said, "I like it."

"Then it's a plan," I said. "Pack a change of clothes and grab some cash. I don't want to leave a credit card trail."

"Speaking of cash," Hunter said. "I know Mongo is our mental heavyweight, but I've been thinking."

Mongo said, "Oh, this ought to be good."

Out of character, Hunter ignored him. "Who's funding this thing?"

A sigh rose from the team, and Skipper said, "I wondered who was going to be the first to bring this up. Why is it in the U.S. National interest to catch this Astor character?"

I leaned back and groaned. "I was so fixated on the surface warfare element of the mission that my brain didn't have time to question the motives."

"I have a theory," Mongo said. "I think Astor probably pulled a fast one on somebody way up the food chain, and that person has enough juice to convince the Board he needs to be taken down."

Hunter said, "If that's the case, why not just have him killed?"

Penny gasped. "America doesn't do that."

I loved that woman for a billion reasons, but her belief that we were still the world's good guys was near the top of the list. That, and the little red dress.

I took a long, deep breath and pointed toward Singer. "Professional killer, trained, paid for, and supported by the United States Government." Then I shot a thumb toward the center of my chest. "The first mission I was given out of training was to kill a Russian assassin in Cuba. Dirty deeds are never dirt cheap, but they are done, and you're sitting in a room full of people who do those deeds in the name of keeping the world's only remaining bastion of freedom afloat."

Watching the innocence drain from her beautiful eyes felt like being kicked in the gut, but I had to do everything in my power to make her understand what the men and women around us truly were.

"For freedom to exist and remain, warriors—men and women capable of doing terrible things for the best of reasons—must be willing to step outside the walls of that freedom and security and do things most people can't stomach. We're those warriors, Penny. It's not what we do. It's what we are."

I watched a tear fall from her eye, and she made no effort to wipe it from her face. "Thank you . . . all of you."

Singer said, "That's the thing, Miss Penny. We never ask for thanks. We only ask that everyone who loves the life we defend never forgets that life comes at a price—a price people like us willingly pay on their behalf."

The solitary tear that had fallen from her eye suddenly was not alone, and my beautiful wife would be forever changed.

* * *

When I crawled into bed after sending Hunter and Singer ashore with ten grand in cash and one of the *Moscow Mule*'s tenders, Penny took me in her arms and held me closer than ever before. I treasured her embrace, and every part of me wanted it to never end. She laid her face against my shoulder and whispered, "It's not fair, Chase."

"What's not fair?"

"It's not fair that they don't know. The people—hundreds of millions of them—will never know you and the rest of the team exist. It's not fair to you."

"That's the way it has to be, sweetheart."

She kissed me gently. "I understand now. I understand why you don't quit. We have more money than we can ever spend, but that doesn't matter to you, does it?"

"No. We don't do this for the money."

"That makes you the best kind of man there is, and I love you a thousand times more than I did this morning."

We drifted off to sleep with the drone of the engines humming three decks beneath our bed and Anguilla just twenty miles off the bow."

Chapter 25

Why Run?

The knock on our cabin door was clearly only ceremonial. Skipper pushed into the room before the echo of her knuckles ceased. "Chase, he's running!"

I leaned up and situated an elbow beneath me. "Who's running?"

"Astor. He took off in a helicopter from Gustavia ten minutes ago, and Singer got a beacon on the chopper."

I wiped my eyes and slid from the bed as Penny groaned. "What's going on?"

"Astor's on the run," I said. "Go back to sleep. We'll take care of it."

She stretched and slid from beneath the covers. "No, I'm coming, too. All for one, and one for all, right?"

"We're not the three musketeers, my dear, but you're welcome to come if you want."

Skipper was through the door and into the corridor before I could step into my pants. "I'm set up in my cabin."

I pulled on yesterday's shirt and followed her to the cabin she'd turned into a combat information center with computers, maps, satellite phones, and notes on every horizontal surface.

"Where's he headed?" I asked as soon as she slid in front of her primary keyboard.

"Wherever it is, he's not going far. His chopper is an old Bell Jet Ranger. That thing has a top speed around a hundred knots and less than two hours of fuel. If he's truly running, he's running toward something faster with more gas."

"Do you have comms with Hunter?"

She spun in her swiveling chair and stroked the keys. A chime sounded, and she motioned toward a thin microphone on a stand beside the computer. "It's not great, but it's what we have."

"Hunter, it's Chase. Are you there?"

"Hang on a minute!" he yelled into the radio.

Skipper said, "They're in the RHIB and headed for the *Lori Danielle.*"

I grabbed a satellite phone from beside the mic and thumbed Hunter's number.

Seconds later, he yelled through the phone. "We're headed out to sea at sixty knots, so I probably won't be able to hear you. Do you want me to slow down?"

"No, keep at it," I said. "We'll get the *LD* moving toward you."

Skipper shook her head and pointed toward a map screen. "Do you really think I wouldn't have already done that?"

The symbol for the *Lori Danielle* was making over fifty knots toward the RHIB, and Skipper slapped a hand onto the desk. "Got him! He's descending into Simpson Bay on Sint Maarten."

I yelled into the phone. "He's headed for Princess Juliana Airport."

Hunter yelled back. "We can't do anything about it in the RHIB, but if you can get them to spool up the chopper on the *LD*, I can get eyes on him."

When other analysts would panic, Skipper dug in her heels. She pointed toward a computer behind me. "Get on that keyboard. I've got a receiver set up for the tower and ground control frequencies at Juliana. Bring it up, and hurry!"

I hit the keyboard with both hands, and the screen came to life. With three clicks of the mouse, the tinny speaker came to life, and the early morning sounds of arriving and departing aircraft played in French-accented English from the tower.

"How did you do this?" I asked.

She rolled her eyes yet again. "It's what I do. Now quit wasting time asking me questions, and figure out how to get me on board the *LD*. I'm too limited here on the *Mule*."

As my caffeinated brain tried to piece together the puzzle Astor was building, Penny stuck her head into the room. "Anything I can do?"

"Yes," I said as I tossed a sat-phone to her. "Get Captain Sprayberry on the line."

Her eyes darted back and forth between Skipper and me until the analyst threw her a bone. "Speed dial seven."

"Captain Sprayberry? Stand by for Chase."

She stuck the phone between my ear and shoulder as I made notes on the pad in my lap. "Barry, have someone get the chopper spooled up. Singer and Hunter are inbound, and they need to fly the instant they hit the deck."

"Aye, aye. We have the RHIB in sight, and we're coming off the foils now. They'll be airborne in less than ten minutes."

"I need you to cut that time in half, no matter what it takes."

"Who's the pilot?" he asked.

"Hunter will be at the controls. I need your armorer to have Singer's three-three-eight Lapua unsheathed and in the chopper."

"Stand by, Chase."

I listened as he gave the orders and returned to the phone.

"Do you need any muscle?"

THE DARKER CHASE · 183

"We've got that covered, but thanks. I need you to put into Simpson's Bay and track everything arriving and departing. Who do you have in CIC?"

The captain said, "Alpha watch."

"Double the watch, and get the best and brightest in there. I'll put Skipper aboard the second it's possible. She'll want a solid briefing, so don't send up the B-Team."

"You got it, Chase. Your men are aboard, and the rotors are spinning. Anything else?"

"There's one more thing. Don't watch Hunter fly the chopper off the deck. It's not going to be pretty."

"Is he checked out in the Little Bird?"

"Not exactly."

"We have a ten-thousand-hour pilot on board. Want her? She's the one who's spinning it up."

I sighed. "You've got to let me know these things, Captain. I absolutely want her." I covered the receiver and tossed the other phone back to Penny. "Tell Hunter he's not doing the driving, and patch me through to the pilot."

"I don't know how to do that," she said.

"That second part wasn't for you."

Skipper said, "The Little Bird is up on mic one."

"Go for Little Bird," came the pilot's crisp call.

"Put my two men over Simpson's Bay in sight of Juliana. We're chasing a Bell Jet Ranger, unknown registration, but my men have put eyes on her once already. Hunter is in charge, and the sniper is Singer. They'll put you on target. Don't worry about busting airspace. We'll get you out of any trouble you stumble into."

In her no-nonsense tone, she said, "Roger. I've got a Minigun and a pair of Hellfire rockets. I'm not worried about airspace, sir."

Hunter's voice replaced the pilot's. "Why is Singer locked and loaded? Who are we supposed to kill?"

"Nobody, I hope, but it never hurts to have Singer's eye in a scope and a finger beside the trigger."

"Roger," he said. "We're airborne, and we'll be on target in three minutes."

Everything turned suddenly silent, and Skipper looked up. "Chase, why would he run?"

I tried out a thousand reasons in the seconds following her question, but only one thing stuck. "Maybe we're blown."

"But how?"

"I don't know, but that's all I can come up with. Maybe he's got feelers out and somebody found out the *Mule* isn't registered to anything real."

"That can't be it. I've got the registry clean."

Penny had been watching the back-and-forth between Skipper and me, but she couldn't hold her peace any longer. "What does that mean?"

"What does what mean?" I asked.

"Being blown," Penny said.

I said, "It means Astor knows we're not who we claim to be, and he may even know we're here to spring a trap."

"But he's not done anything illegal yet," Penny argued.

"Sure he has. Just not directly with us. He may think we're feds."

"So, are you going to shoot him if he keeps running?"

"No, we're not going to shoot him, but we may disable a boat or an airplane if it becomes necessary."

"If we do that, we'll be blown for sure. Who's to say he's not going to Sint Maarten to pick up a date? I know I'd be impressed if some guy picked me up in a helicopter."

I gave her a smile. "I just happen to have a couple of helicopters, so I may have to test that theory of yours."

Hunter's voice cut through. "We've got him, Chase. He shut down the chopper, and he's standing on the ramp with a phone to his ear."

I closed my eyes and drew a mental picture of the scene as a plan fell into place. "Find some high ground, and set up a firing position. Make sure Singer can disable the chopper, if necessary, but don't get caught on Sint Maarten with guns."

He said, "Singer's already picked out a spot. Do you want me with him in the FP?"

"Negative. You're airborne command and control until I can get Skipper in the CIC on the *Lori Danielle*."

His one-word reply demonstrated why Stone W. Hunter was the most solid operator in the business. When confronted with a change in battlefield roles, he simply said, "Roger."

"Let's go, Skipper. Penny, you man the radios from here. We'll be up and running in the CIC in fifteen minutes or less."

Skipper abandoned her chair, and Penny claimed it. Two minutes later, we were lifting off the helipad atop the *Moscow Mule*. The *Mule*'s chopper wasn't as nimble as the Little Bird from the *Lori Danielle*, but she didn't suffer from a lack of horsepower. When I pulled pitch and backed away from the ship in the AgustaWestland AW109E, the machine felt like a thoroughbred beneath me who was chomping at her bit to run. Once clear of the ship, I made the left pedal turn and lowered the nose. Both our airspeed and altitude rose at an impressive rate.

Skipper closed her checklist on her lap. "Are you going to bring the gear up?"

I reached for the handle. "It's easy to forget this thing isn't exactly a tactical piece of equipment."

She said, "It's nice. Now, get me to the *Lori Danielle*. We've got a lot of work to do."

The GPS tracked the position of the *LD* and took us straight to her stern.

I set up for the approach and stiffened in my seat. "This is my first time putting this one on a ship."

Skipper reminded me, "Yeah, and it's not exactly your ship. Would you like for me to get us an invitation on board?"

"I've got a lot on my mind this morning. I'm sure Captain Sprayberry would appreciate us asking permission to come aboard."

She pulled the microphone to her lips and gave me the thumbs-up. As we approached the deck, she pulled off her headset and unbuckled her harness.

"You might want to keep that on," I said. "I'm not sure how gentle this is going to be."

She looked across her shoulder and pulled the door release. "I don't plan to be in this seat when you finally get all the pieces to stop moving. I'm getting out as soon as I can survive the fall. Oh, and don't forget to put the gear down, Top Gun."

She wasn't kidding. I lowered the landing gear, and she stepped out when we were still six feet from the deck. I watched her disappear through a hatch with a pair of laptop cases slung across her shoulder, but she didn't see my flawless landing. Okay, maybe it wasn't flawless, but none of the important pieces fell off. After shutting down, I made my way through the same hatch Skipper had used and took the stairs down to the combat information center.

Skipper was in full battle rattle when I pushed through the door. She had her headset on with screens coming to life in every direction. Her ability to write with either hand while typing with the other was one of her top one thousand most impressive skills. A pair of technicians who'd been manning the console briefed simultaneously, and Skipper never missed a word. "Good. Now, get out."

"That was a little harsh, wasn't it?" I asked as I nestled in beside her.

Without looking up, she said, "I wasn't talking to you. They were just in the way." She motioned toward a monitor above my head. "Singer will be there in ten seconds, and Hunter will be on monitor four."

Sooner than she'd predicted, the first monitor filled with a digital video broadcast through Singer's rifle scope. "When did you set that up?"

"Stop asking questions, and start commanding the operation. Open-channel comms are up, and we're live."

Monitor number four filled with the view from the camera mounted beneath the nose of the MH-6 Little Bird and showed a perfect view of the Princess Juliana Airport on Sint Maarten.

Hunter's voice boomed. "Are you up, Chase?"

"Affirmative. We're up and running in the CIC. Tell me what I'm seeing."

"The maroon-and-white chopper next to the Citation on the right is our boy's ride. He just stuck his phone back into his pocket, and he's moving toward the terminal."

"I got him," I said. "Any idea what's happening?"

Singer said, "Are my comms live?"

"Affirmative, Singer. You're loud and clear. Send the sitrep."

He spoke barely above a whisper. "It wasn't a cell phone. It was definitely a sat-phone. My scope is a little better than Hunter's binoculars. He's not agitated, and he doesn't seem to be in a hurry. I don't think he's running."

"Roger." I turned to Skipper. "Do you have anything on the registration yet?"

She tapped a small monitor to my left.

I read the screen. "It's a local charter company based here on Sint Maarten."

Skipper said, "Astor likes the world to think he's a big baller, but he's still renting helicopters. Isn't that cute?"

The monitor caught Astor turning from in front of the terminal and shading his eyes from the morning sun with his hand.

"What's he looking for?" I demanded. "Find it!"

The chopper camera turned and focused southwest, but the resolution wasn't good enough to pick up anything in the air.

"I think I know," Skipper said.

"Spit it out!"

"There's a Gulfstream IV thirty miles out, and it's registered in St. Petersburg . . . not the one in Florida."

Four minutes later, the Gulfstream touched down and taxied to the ramp in front of the terminal. The door opened, and the airstairs unfolded.

I said, "Singer, get me close enough to ID whoever comes off that plane."

"Roger," came his soft response, and the scope video zoomed until I could read the sign inside the door warning the crew to close the door before flight.

I studied the screen and waited impatiently for someone to appear, but it didn't happen.

Instead, Hunter said, "Astor's on the move."

Singer smoothly swung his rifle to capture Marcus Astor strolling across the tarmac toward the Gulfstream.

I said, "Skipper, find that plane's outbound flight plan."

"I'm already on it, but there's nothing coming up. They're not going anywhere, Chase."

"Oh, they're going somewhere," I said. "They just don't want us to know about it."

Chapter 26
Changing Parameters

As is her typical posture in the heat of a mission, Skipper had her head buried in a monitor, one earphone of a headset over an ear, a keyboard in one hand, and her attention divided between no fewer than half a dozen monitors. Just like Singer was most at home behind his rifle with one eye trained on a potential target, Skipper was solidly in her element. As if speaking to everyone and no one at the same time, she said, "They're not going anywhere without gas."

"What do you mean?" I asked.

"She took off from London eight hours ago, and that's almost forty-one hundred miles. In perfect conditions, with no headwind, her max range is forty-five hundred miles, so she's not moving until she takes on fuel."

"And you're sure about London?"

She huffed. "Yes, Chase. I'm sure. Before that, she was in St. Petersburg. Would you like to know how much vodka they had on board?"

"I'm sorry. I'm trying to piece this whole thing together, and none of it is making sense."

"What do you think I'm doing?" she asked. "My brain sucks at not knowing what's happening. I need to be in the know, and I'm just as stumped as you."

I drilled my knuckles into my temples and begged my mind to churn out an answer. Laying a hand on Skipper's shoulder, I said, "Get Singer out of his nest and on board with us. If you're right about the fuel, and I'm sure you are, we'll have plenty of notice before they take off again."

"You got it."

Minutes later, Singer and Hunter came through the door and into the CIC.

Hunter said, "The chopper's back up, and you'll have video of the Gulfstream in a couple of minutes. What do you think's happening down there?"

Skipper tapped on a monitor to her left. "Check it out, guys."

We watched as Astor climbed the airstairs onto the Gulfstream.

I said, "I'd give ten thousand bucks to have a microphone on that plane."

Singer said, "Put me back on the ground, and I'll make that happen."

Skipper tapped the top of the monitor again. "There's no time for that. Look."

"Can you zoom in?" I asked.

She stroked a few keys. "A little, but not much."

Astor bounced down the stairs like an excited child.

I leaned toward the screen. "Can anybody make out what he's carrying?"

Skipper slid her glasses up her nose. "It looks like a briefcase in his left hand and a tube of some kind in his right."

I squinted. "A rifle case, maybe?"

Singer leaned in. "I don't think so. Unless it's disassembled, you couldn't put much of a rifle in that thing. It looks more like a fly rod case than a rifle case to me."

Skipper leaned back in her chair and took a breath. "Why would a Russian-registered jet fly all the way from St. Petersburg to bring Marcus Astor a fly rod?"

I gave the case and tube one more long look. "I think he's going to open up both packages and show us what's inside tonight."

Hunter grunted. "I hate it when you do that. It's like you can see into the future. How about giving us a peek behind the curtain?"

"Thirty-six hours ago, I told Astor I had plenty of disposable income and a taste for rare Russian pieces. He's in the business of separating cash from its owner in return for things that aren't easy to buy. I think he found a couple of items I can't resist."

Skipper let her fingers fly across the keyboard again and then clicked her tongue against her teeth. "There's still no outbound flight plan, but there is a tug headed for the Gulfstream."

"Get the chopper in as tight as possible," I ordered. "I want to see the crew and the passenger."

Skipper pulled her mic to her lips. "Barbie, get in tight on the crew and PAX when they come off the Gulfstream."

Hunter said, "Barbie? Really? Please tell me that's just her call sign and not her real name."

Skipper glanced over a shoulder. "I don't know. That's what she said her name was, but I've never met her. You two flew with her. Didn't you make introductions?"

Singer gave Hunter a shove. "He was too busy looking at her butt, and I was too busy looking for a firing position."

Skipper shook her head. "I'm telling Tina."

Hunter said, "I was making sure her pants weren't too tight to safely fly the chopper. That's all. You know . . . safety first."

Barbie lowered the nose and flew a descending approach to the taxiway beside the Gulfstream, and Skipper manipulated the camera to keep it focused on the airstairs. The first two men who descended the stairs wore dark jackets over blue Oxfords, but instead of businessmen's wingtips, they wore black, tactical boots with their trousers cut to fall across the boots.

I motioned toward the screen. "Spetsnaz or GRU?"

Hunter stared into the monitor. "Does it really matter?"

"Maybe not, but it would be nice to know who we're dealing with."

Skipper worked furiously at her terminal with a hundred keystrokes per minute and her mouse moving like a squirrel in the street. "I may have gotten clear enough video to do some facial recognition, but it's going to be slow. I'm putting my money on private security."

"You may be right," I said. "Get that facial recognition program running. Maybe we'll get lucky. Here comes the crew."

Two pilots dressed identically descended the stairs with flight bags in hand.

I asked, "Charter pilots?"

Skipper said, "There's no way to know for sure, but they don't have that military look to me."

"I agree. They move like civilian pilots, but only time will tell. Does anyone else have any suggestions before we pull off?"

Singer asked, "Skipper, can you track the plane without us putting a beacon on it?"

She grimaced. "Yes, but not in real time. I'll be at least a few minutes behind, and possibly as much as an hour behind depending on a ton of factors that would take too long to explain. It's always better to have one of our beacons on the airframe."

Hunter jumped in. "Drop us in there, and we'll have the Gulfstream wired for sound in an hour. Do you want us to use the beacon from Astor's Jet Ranger, or should we pull another one off the shelf?"

Skipper looked up. "That's up to Chase, but for my purposes, I'd much rather have a fresh one on the Gulfstream and keep the old one on the chopper so we can track both of them."

"Let's do it," I said. "Get Barbie out of there and back on board. I'll clear the helipad and put Hunter and Singer on the ground with the One-Oh-Nine."

Skipper keyed up. "Okay, Barbie, get out of there. The mission parameters have changed. RTB."

"Roger. Returning to base."

I said, "Get the *Mule* headed back for Gustavia, as well. We want to be easy to find if Astor comes looking."

Skipper said, "I'm way ahead of you, boss. The *Mule* is already en route. I'm staying here in the CIC, though. I'm no good on the yacht."

"Do you need any backup?"

"No, the onboard geeks aren't bad. They're good enough to come wake me up if something happens that I need to know about. I'll be fine."

The AW109E turbines whistled to life, and the main rotor turned into a whirring disk above our heads. "Where do you want to be?" I asked as I brought the landing gear up without being reminded to do so.

"Let's see where they put the Gulfstream," Skipper said. "She'll be a lot easier to mark if she's resting in a hangar. Getting a beacon on her while she's being tugged is probably impossible in the daylight."

As we climbed away from the *Lori Danielle*, all eyes were on the Princess Juliana Airport and the Russian Gulfstream.

Singer said, "It looks like they're headed for the big hangar at the west end."

Hunter agreed. "If that's where they're going, it's not the best scenario for us. That place isn't Fort Knox, but it's busy. Somebody will see us."

I flew a pattern around the airport and watched the tug operator pull the business jet through the massive doors of the hangar. "Looks like Singer was right again, and I've got a plan. Can you get eyes on the crew or two passengers?"

Singer shook his head. "All four of them disappeared into the terminal."

"Good," I said. "Get ready to play some word games, and follow my lead."

I keyed the mic and spoke in my best Russian accent. "Princess Juliana tower is helicopter four-three-one Mike Mike, and we make landing on west end of taxiway Alpha."

In better English than I expected, the tower controller said, "Helicopter one Mike Mike, proceed as requested. Wind zero-seven-zero and eight. Clear to land taxiway Alpha."

Normally, my reply would've been a courteous readback, but in true Russian fashion, I said only, "Roger."

The gear came down, and I stuck the chopper to the taxiway like an old pro. We taxied to the ramp in front of the hangar and shut down.

As we climbed from the chopper, I said, "Pretend like I'm in charge for once, and try to look Russian."

Singer laid a hand on my shoulder. "Maybe I should stay in the chopper for this one. You and Hunter might pull it off, but how many people do you know would believe I'm Russian?"

"You may have a point," Hunter said, obviously trying not to chuckle.

Leaving our sniper behind, Hunter and I strolled into the hangar as if we owned the airport.

A young man with greasy hands and stained coveralls approached. "Good morning. Are you looking for someone?"

His mildly French-accented English made him sound more like a waiter than an aircraft mechanic, but his youth played into our hands.

I put on my Russian face and scowled at him. "We work for Mr. Petrovitch, and he insists we much inspect landing gear of airplane. He is not happy with landing."

"I am sorry, sir, but you cannot simply come into this hangar and . . ."

I put a palm on his chest. "You are making mistake, but if you must be big man and stop us from following Mr. Petrovitch's orders, this is up to you. Give to me name, and I will make sure he knows who stopped us. He is very busy man and has no patience for petty things. You will soon understand this."

The man stood in silent disbelief, so I took a fistful of his coveralls and shook him. "Give to me name, immediately. We do not have time for this."

He pulled away. "I am only mechanic, but I am not supposed to—"

"Give to me name."

"Okay, fine. But do it quickly."

I scowled and pushed by him. "We will do thorough inspection and will take necessary time."

Hunter didn't speak, but the look on his face was likely more effective than my accent and empty threats. When we reached the Gulfstream, he whispered, "Mr. Petrovitch? That's the best you could do?"

I shrugged. "I panicked a little, but it worked, didn't it?"

"Yeah, until that guy finds out the owner of this airplane is some guy named Bill Smith."

"Something tells me that kid isn't going to do anything to risk bringing Mr. Petrovitch down on him."

Hunter had the beacon installed and camouflaged in minutes, and we set about pretending to inspect the landing gear.

On our way out, we passed the young mechanic, and I said, "We will tell Mr. Petrovitch you were very helpful."

He waved a hand. "No, just forget you ever saw me, okay?"

"As you wish."

We climbed back aboard the chopper and lifted off as if we had a thousand legitimate reasons to be there. The 109 made me look good again as we made our approach and landed on the *Moscow Mule*'s helipad.

Inside the main salon, we briefed the rest of the team on the morning's excitement, and a steward stuck his head into the room. "Would anyone care for a cocktail before lunch?"

Hunter held up a finger. "I think maybe I could go for a Black Russian."

Chapter 27
Caveat Emptor

Lunch on the stern deck brought the team back together and delivered a surprise none of us expected so soon. The number of boats scampering about on the Bay of Gustavia, St. Barts, was a study in extremes. From luxurious yachts like the *Moscow Mule*, to wooden tenders powered by the muscular backs of singular rowers, and everything in between, dotted the perfect blue backdrop. I wasn't lost in the bevy of boats on the bay, though. One particular craft had my undivided attention.

The glistening deck of an antique mahogany boat polished to perfection glided across the water as if floating just above it. Barely leaving a wake astern, the classic epitome of elegance wafted ever closer to the *Moscow Mule*, and I was mesmerized and unable to look away.

Penny apparently noticed my condition before anyone else. "Is everything okay, Chase?"

Without a word, I raised a finger and pointed toward the approaching boat.

She said, "That's gorgeous. What is it?"

"Trouble masquerading as opportunity."

Soon, the entire team was focused on nothing except the

gleaming wooden hull, and just as I expected, she came to a hover only inches from our lowered swim platform at the stern.

"Monsieur Chasse," came the call from a gentleman standing in the beautiful craft.

I shot a look at Hunter, and he drew his pistol from the ankle holster hidden beneath the cuff of his pants. He gave me a nod, and I stood and approached the stern rail. Hunter stood three feet to my left with his hands crossed at his belt buckle and the pistol hidden behind his palms. If there was a man on Earth who was a better off-hand shot with a small pistol than Clark Johnson, it was Stone Hunter, and that knowledge gave me the confidence to face the calling man in the boat without a hint of fear. There was nothing he could do that Hunter couldn't do faster and more accurately, so I leaned on the rail and responded with one of the seven French words I knew. "*Oui?*"

"*Monsieur* Astor *aimerait vous voir. Il croit qu'il a quelque chose qui vous intéressera beaucoup.*"

I turned to Hunter. "Did you get any of that?"

"I think he said something about a croissant."

Disco came to our rescue. "He said Mr. Astor would like to see you. He has something you'll be interested in."

I waved for him to join us at the rail, and he did. I said, "Work it out, but don't sound too anxious."

Disco nodded, and I returned to my seat, leaving Hunter and our only French-speaking teammate negotiating a trap designed to make me the rat, and something perfectly irresistible, the cheese.

Mongo's eyes never left Hunter during the conversation. The big man's instinct to protect those he loved was even bigger than the body in which it resided. If Hunter flinched to raise his pistol, Mongo would undoubtedly shove as many of us behind him as possible and explode into the fight. That can't be taught. It's woven into the psyche of men who are, at their core, sheepdog. On the surface, they're perfectly peaceful, and sometimes even jovial, but beneath their fluffy exterior lies the spirit of a killer who will sacrifice everything he is and everything he owns to keep his sheep alive and unharmed. If ever a true sheepdog lived, he was Marvin "Mongo" Malloy.

The tension of the moment finally broke when Disco turned from the rail, leaving Hunter still watching Mongo's wolf drift away. With the classically beautiful boat showing us her stern and growing smaller by the second, Hunter turned from the rail and rejoined the team.

"Okay, let's have it," I said.

Disco took a sip of his tea. "It sounds harmless on the surface. Astor wants to meet with you to show you something. The guy wouldn't give me any details other than the fact that Astor believes you'll love what he found for you."

I scanned the combat-hardened eyes of the operators at the table, representing the decades of experience in situations that seemed perfectly harmless until they turned into trainwrecks, and those eyes said caveat emptor.

"One at a time," I said. "Mongo, you first."

He shook his head. "I think we're looking at this through the wrong lens. Every one of us has spent his adult life pursuing, catching, and ending bad guys on the orders of those above us. This mission bears one extreme difference than all of those other missions we've accomplished. In every case, when we were in uniform and sent out to capture or kill a target, that target was willing, capable, and sometimes anxious to turn around and shoot at us before we could shoot at him. That's not what this is."

He had not only my attention, but also that of everyone at the table.

The anticipation on our faces encouraged Mongo to continue. "This guy isn't a shooter. He's a businessman. First, he probably doesn't know we're chasing him and likely thinks he's pursuing us. He's in the business of separating wealthy buyers from their cash. In this case, it's Chase. If he had the slightest idea that we were here to nab him or lure him into a trap, he'd vanish like smoke in the wind."

He paused long enough to let that thought soak into our ironwood heads before motioning across the bay. "He just sent his messenger boy to deliver an invitation to dinner. Unless he's a cold-blooded killer, that wouldn't happen. There's nothing in his dossier that even hints at that. This guy's a greedy middleman, and we're treating him like a warlord. It's the wrong approach."

Hunter blew out the breath he'd been holding. "I don't know. It's a new situation for us. It's a new situation for us, but I believe it's a bad move for us to think this guy isn't a threat."

I turned to my moral compass and spiritual advisor with a face full of questions.

Singer said, "Maybe Mongo's right. But you're the psychologist, Chase. What do you think?"

"When the only tool you own is a hammer, you see every problem as a nail. I think maybe we need to open our toolbox a little wider and see what else we have in there. We've got Irina, our Russian art historian. We've got—"

Irina raised a finger. "I am not art historian. I know some small things about some art and some history, but I am here only to pretend to be expert on Fabergé eggs."

"Yes, but you know far more than you're willing to admit. Maybe it's modesty, or maybe it's something else, but playing dumb is not one of your strengths."

She shrugged and ducked her head.

I moved on. "Between the *Lori Danielle*, the Mark V, and the people on this boat, we've got all the muscle and firepower we could need, but all of that qualifies as a hammer. We're looking for screwdrivers and wrenches."

Disco rarely offered opinions on tactics, so I was surprised when he said, "Maybe we're not looking for tools at all. Maybe we're looking for *assets*. Forgive me for saying so, but a couple of nights ago at the club, Penny proved she's got assets in spades. In my opinion, it'd be foolish to move ahead without at least dangling those assets in front of Astor to keep him on his heels. Men don't think straight when beautiful women are around. We all know that."

"He's right," I admitted. "Penny, you're a killer at the helm of a boat and especially with a red-hot horseshoe. One particular farrier learned that lesson in our barn. But when a woman who looks like you winks and waves, a man's resolve turns to mush."

"Chauvinist much?" she asked before laughing. "I'm just kidding. Of course I'll do whatever you need, be it driving a boat or shaking my *assets*, as Disco so eloquently put it."

I leaned back and stared into the bright blue heavens above me. An occasional white cumulous cloud drifted by on the midday, tropical breeze, and my thoughts turned from hammers to sawbucks. "Let's have it, Disco. What did you commit me to with Frenchy McFrench?"

He said, "I committed you to sunset cocktails right here on the *Mule* tonight to have a look at whatever Monsieur Astor has to show you. Are you okay with that?"

"More than okay. That's what I would've set up if I could speak French."

Hunter jumped in. "By the way . . . McFrenchy, as you called him, may not speak English, but he can read it."

"How could you know that?" I asked.

"While I was assessing the threat, I noticed the English edition of today's *Wall Street Journal* tucked into his seat."

"Nice eye."

He tipped an imaginary hat. "Thank you."

"So, how do we play it?" I asked.

Before any of the hammers could open their mouths, Penny said, "I just happen to make a very good living setting scenes, so I think we play it like this. Have Mongo welcome Astor and his security contingent on board as a not-so-subtle show of force. Put Hunter and Singer in adjacent corners, looking like Secret Service. You and Disco play host, just in case Astor starts speaking a language you don't know, College Boy."

I pointed an open hand to my wife. "You need to stay away from Clark. He's rubbing off on you."

She gave me a wink and never slowed down. "Astor is obviously going to present you with an opportunity to purchase something he had flown in from St. Petersburg. When he does, I'll arrive with cocktails for the gentlemen. I think I'll wear my LBD this time. You know, the one you like so much."

I couldn't deny how much I loved seeing her in that one particular little black dress.

"That'll give you a moment while Astor will be distracted—forgive my confidence—and you can examine whatever trinket he puts in your hand. When my part of the show is over, you can finish with the perfect little Russian cherry on top."

"Russian cherry?"

She pointed to Irina. "Yes, sir. She may be the big brain when it comes to Russian art history, especially Fabergé eggs, but I'd bet she has an LBD of her own. Plus, she's got the added benefit of the Russian accent that we all know no man can resist." She ran a hand down my arm. "Isn't that right, Chasechka?"

I slid my chair away. "This is starting to feel a little close to home."

Penny giggled. "Relax. I was just telling you how I'd write it if it were in one of my screenplays."

Hunter stuck a toothpick into the corner of his mouth. "She's not wrong."

"I like it," I said. "We're well covered if things get out of hand. We look like we know what we're doing, and we've got enough razzle-dazzle to keep the party hopping. I say we do it just like Penny laid it out. Any more ideas?"

"I've got one," Disco said.

"Let's have it."

"I'm not the ground operator you guys are, so I may be way off the mark here, but I think I know a way to find out just how much of a threat Astor is, if any."

"We're all ears."

"How about we find out where Astor is and show up to deliver him to the yacht in the One-Oh-Nine? That accomplishes two things. It establishes you as a serious big-money player, plus, it traps him on our yacht with no means of egress other than jumping overboard. Would any of you take an offer like that?"

I gave our chief pilot a nod of respect. "Well done, Flyboy. You're starting to think like a ground-pounder. If Astor is a threat, there's no way he'll get on our chopper to be flown to our boat. If he's as dangerous as we hammers need to believe, he'll turn down the ride and find his own chariot to the party. I love it, but let's take it one step further with one more distraction. Does anybody know if Barbie is checked out in the AW-One-Oh-Nine?"

Chapter 28
Provenance

Disco spent the afternoon getting Barbie, the *Lori Danielle*'s pilot, up to speed in the AgustaWestland 109E, while Penny and Irina went ashore just in case one of the hundreds of little French boutiques had a better LBD than the ones they already owned. After a dozen approaches and landings on the yacht's helipad, Disco signed her logbook and declared Barbie more than competent in the luxurious helicopter.

Skipper made short work of finding Marcus Astor and even had a local courier service deliver an engraved invitation for cocktails aboard the *Moscow Mule*, with livery service provided.

Skipper said, "Not only did he accept the invitation, but according to the courier, he did so with *la vive émotion*. You'll have to ask Disco what that means, but I took it as a good sign."

The sun approached the western expanse of the blue sky, and I gave the pep talk. "It's almost showtime. If our theory is correct, Astor clearly isn't savvy enough to fear being stranded on our boat, but we're all alive because we think every door is a trapdoor. So, with that in mind, keep an eye out for avenues of egress—new boats lingering nearby with crew on board, eyes ashore that are paying us a little too much attention, and generally anything that makes your gut tighten up. Any questions?" None came, so I gave the order. "Go get him, Barbie."

"Yes, sir, but I do have one question first."

"Shoot."

"If he has, uh, associates, how many should I bring?"

"Great question. Give him two bodyguards and one assistant. Any more than that would make the chopper uncomfortable, and we want Mr. Astor to feel right at home."

Barbie launched and hovered the chopper sideways to the port-side of the yacht to avoid blowing the contents of the stern deck around.

I shot a thumb toward the helicopter. "She's good."

Disco nodded. "She certainly is."

"Are you sure it's Ronda No-H you're interested in, or does Barbie have your attention now?"

"Anybody can learn to fly a helicopter," he said. "But have you seen that thing No-H does with her eyes when she's supposed to be working, but she's really daydreaming?"

I had to laugh. "No, I'm afraid I've not seen her do that, but you've obviously been paying attention."

He grinned. "Besides, Barbie's a child. According to her ID, she just turned thirty."

"And she'd probably kill you if she knew you told anybody," I said.

"Consider it classified information."

* * *

Barbie returned with only two additional souls on board the 109, and she performed a similar maneuver as her departure to preserve Penny's pristine screenplay setting. Mongo escorted Astor and his plus-one from the helipad to the stern deck.

Every Southern courtesy inside me wanted to leap to my feet and shake hands at the base of the stairs, but the role I was playing demanded that I make them come to me. As they approached the table, Astor stuck out a hand.

I shook it and ignored his tagalong. "Nice to see you again, Mr. Astor. Won't you please have a seat."

He turned to the gentleman behind him, who suddenly looked far superior to a pair of bodyguards. His stance and the bulk of his shoulders revealed he spent at least as much time in the gym as he spent following Astor around.

"This is Mikhail. You can think of him as an *opekun.*"

Mikhail didn't offer a hand, and I wasn't surprised. Astor took a seat, but his man did not. Instead, he backed up several paces and stood like a statue holding the briefcase and the tube I'd seen on Skipper's monitors the day before.

The head steward materialized beside our table. "What may I bring you, gentlemen?"

I motioned toward my guest. "What's your pleasure, Mr. Astor?"

"Perhaps a good scotch, if you have it."

The steward bowed. "Oh, we have it, sir. Coming right up."

I eyed the case and tube across Astor's shoulder with Hollywood anxiety, and he noticed.

"Don't be too anxious, Daniel. May I still call you Daniel, or do you prefer Mr. Chase while we're doing business?"

I pulled my attention back to the table. "We're not doing business, Marcus. We're having a cocktail and watching the sunset."

The steward returned and placed two tumblers on the table and presented the bottle to me. I was suddenly impressed by my own liquor collection aboard the *Mule*. I nodded, trying not to appear in disbelief.

He poured two fingers into each tumbler and took a step back as a second steward slid a small table to his side. The man placed the scotch on the newly set table, and the two disappeared.

I lifted my glass and raised it to eye level. "To new friends, sunsets, and old things, be they scotch or"—I glanced across his shoulder again—"antiquities."

"Hear, hear," Astor said, and touched his glass to mine. He inhaled the whiskey and opened his eyes in surprise. He held the glass toward the setting sun and examined the honey-colored whiskey that had spent over half a century confined inside a cask in the Scottish aging house.

Astor allowed a sip of the scotch to linger on his tongue before swallowing. A smile of mischief crossed his lips, and he angled to see the bottle that was placed just out of his reach. He stared toward the bottle with the same interest I showed the items that Mikhail guarded. "Magnificent. I've never tasted its equal. I must know."

"It's the Glenfarclas Sixty-Year," I said as if I'd been drinking bottles of the fifteen-thousand-dollar whiskey for years.

With a tilt of his head and a drop of his chin, he said, "You're clearly a man of spectacular taste."

"As I told you before, I like rare and beautiful things."

"If I'm not mistaken, I believe you also mentioned that you like those rare and beautiful things to be Russian in origin."

I took another appreciative sip and found myself momentarily lost in the depth and complexity of the scotch. "Few cultures appreciate truly beautiful things the way the Russians did, especially at the turn of the century. The previous century, of course."

"Of course," he said as he motioned for Mikhail to approach.

The man stepped forward and hesitantly handed the long tube to Astor. "Thank you, Mikhail. Don't worry. I'm not going to damage it."

Mikhail stepped back but never took his eyes from the tube in Astor's hand.

I cast a look at Mikhail. "You used the Russian word for *guardian* when you introduced him. Do you speak Russian, my friend?"

Astor almost blushed. "I'm ashamed to say that I do not. That is just the word Mikhail insists on calling himself, so I thought it appropriate, even though until this moment, I didn't realize it meant *guardian*."

"Well," I said, "one doesn't need to speak French to love great wine."

He raised his glass. "Nor Gaelic to appreciate such scotch."

"Indeed. Don't keep me waiting. What's in the tube?"

He almost smiled as he held up the fiberglass case. "Oh, this, you mean? It's just a simple little trinket I picked up in Eastern Europe. Do you know Rasputin?"

"Not personally. But I know he was the Mad Monk who found his way into the court of Czar Nicholas II and his wife, Alexandra, where he found favor—especially from the czarina."

"It would appear you do know your Russian history. What would you say if I told you I held Grigori Rasputin's walking stick in this case?"

I eyed the tube as I swallowed the final sip of scotch from my tumbler. "I'd say you've been swindled, Marcus. Providing provenance for something as common as a Siberian peasant's walking stick would be an even greater miracle than turning this entire bay into sixty-year-old scotch."

His countenance remained stoic as he held an open hand across his shoulders and Mikhail laid a pair of white cotton gloves in his palm. He laid the tube across his lap and pulled on the gloves. With the rolling of six tumblers, he aligned the proper sequence, and the clasps sprang open. He pulled a second tube from within the first and laid the larger one at his feet. The smaller case un-screwed at a joint, revealing a cloth-wrapped object.

"This is turning into a *matryoshka*," I said, and for the first time, Mikhail's expression cracked. I could've sworn he almost smiled.

Astor looked up. "I'm afraid the two of you have me at a disad-vantage. *Matryoshka*?"

"Think of it as a puzzle," I said, and Mikhail reclaimed his stoicism.

Astor unwound the cloth from the twisted, worn handle of the walking stick. By the time he'd fully unwound its binding, the age of the piece was obvious, and I reached for the artifact.

Astor recoiled. "Not without gloves, until it is yours, Daniel."

"If my historian can establish provenance, Marcus, it's already mine."

He relaxed. "In that case, I suggest you get your historian on an airplane headed for St. Barts."

I lifted and examined my empty tumbler, the signal for Penny to make her appearance. "In the meantime, does Mikhail have an extra pair of gloves?"

The *opekun* stepped forward and produced a second pair of gloves.

I took them and pulled them onto my hands. "*Spasibo*, Mikhail."

Again, without a word, he nodded as Penny emerged through the doorway in a dress I'd never seen, and Astor forgot all about the artifact of the Romanov era in his hands.

If it were possible for Penny Thomas Fulton to look more beautiful than she did at that moment, my eyes couldn't survive such a moment. Every curve, and every long, toned muscle cried out to be admired, and her perfect smile punctuated the look with Southern charm and elegance. She lifted the bottle from the steward's table and poured until our tumblers were half full, then she let the back of her hand trace the side of my face. "Is there anything else I can do for you?"

In practiced apathy, I shook my head, and she turned to leave the deck. As Astor watched her go, I examined the walking stick with my layman's eye and determined it to genuinely be at least a hundred years old, if not more.

Penny's practiced, intentional snail's pace gave me the extra seconds I needed to brush the clasp of my watch against the bottom of the cane, marking it with a microscopic dose of luminol and nitrophenyl pentadiene, commonly referred to as NPPD or Cold War–era spy dust. Under ultraviolet light, the base of the cane would glow like a lighthouse, giving me the ability to tell if the cane I held that night would be the same piece of aged oak I'd eventually buy at Marcus Astor's outlandish price.

With Penny beyond the darkened glass, Astor swallowed hard and turned back to me. He watched me examine the item, but his mind had followed my wife's curves back into the main salon. After a long moment and an admiring sip of the scotch, he asked, "How long will it take your historian to arrive?"

I made a show of checking my watch. "Oh, if my calculations are correct, she'll be along very soon."

He raised an eyebrow. "She? Indeed. You seem to have no shortage of beautiful and capable women around you, Daniel. First, your pilot, then the lady in red turned lady in black. I can hardly wait to see this historian of yours."

"How many times must I tell you, Marcus? I have a voracious appetite for beautiful things."

"Surely you don't consider these women to be things . . . mere possessions," he said with an air of judgment in his tone.

I lifted my glass from its bamboo coaster. "I do not collect beautiful women, if that is your question. I merely enjoy surrounding myself with things that bring me pleasure, and the lady in black tonight . . . well, she, my friend, is the epitome of pleasure."

Before he could come up with a response, Irina Volkovna stepped through the door that had absorbed Penny only moments before. She wore a dark pencil skirt beneath a silk top that draped perfectly across her figure. Shorter, thinner, and with characteristically sharper Eastern Bloc features, Irina was an entirely different kind of beautiful, and I laughed silently at the thought of what Mongo would do to Astor if he touched her. Visions of the big man ripping Astor's arm from his shoulder and beating him to death with the separated limb wouldn't leave my mind.

"Marcus Astor, meet Irina, my historian."

He offered a gloved hand, and Irina ignored him.

In Russian, she asked, "What is that supposed to be?"

Mikhail frowned, and I suddenly realized Irina may believe she and I were the only two Russian speakers on deck.

I held up the cane and motioned toward its guardian. Although my Russian wasn't native like Irina's, it was certainly passable. "Rasputin's walking stick, and Mikhail over there, its Russian guardian, is quite particular about how it is handled."

She let her eyes dart ever so quickly to the Russian and back. "I see."

She pulled her own pair of gloves from a small bag. With the gloves in place, she slid a pair of magnifying eyeglasses onto her face and turned on an LED light built into the glasses. She handled the cane with practiced precision, examining every angle, scar, twist, and point of wear.

She pressed the cane beneath her nose and inhaled deeply, and I had no way of knowing if it was all for show or if Mongo's fiancée knew enough to authenticate the Mad Monk's alleged walking stick.

She held the cane at arm's length and said, "Please stand."

I wondered which one of us she was talking to until I remembered Astor didn't understand a word she was saying, so I placed my tumbler back on its coaster and stood.

Irina took my hand in hers and wrapped my fingers around the cane, then she pulled a napkin from the table and carefully laid it on the deck. "Place walking stick here, and stand naturally."

Astor grunted. "Can she speak English?"

Irina frowned down at him. "Yes, but is not necessary."

He turned to Mikhail. "If she's going to speak Russian, you will have to translate for me. I must know what's happening."

Irina rolled her eyes. "Fine. I will speak English when I know correct words. When not, I must speak Russian."

"Fair enough," Astor said.

Irina watched closely as I placed the foot of the cane on the cloth napkin and stood with the well-worn handle comfortably in my grasp. She stepped back and examined me and the cane from several angles until Astor said, "What is she doing?"

Irina placed her hands on her hips and faced him. "Do you know how tall Grigori Rasputin was?"

Astor turned to Mikhail, but the Russian offered nothing. "How should I know?"

Irina nodded. "Exactly. These are things for people like me to know. He was one hundred ninety-three centimeters."

She held out both hands toward me. "Mr. Chase is one hundred ninety-five centimeters, and walking stick is comfortable length, so is not evidence of . . . I am sorry, but I do not know word. In Russian, is *proiskhozhdeniye.*"

"Provenance," I said.

She continued. "Yes, is not evidence of provenance, but means is possible for person of same size as Rasputin and Mr. Chase to use walking stick."

"There you have it," Astor said.

I returned the cane to Irina's hands and reclaimed my seat. "There I have what? A long walking stick?"

Irina answered before Astor. "Is also wood from Quercus mongolica. This means tree that made walking stick is native tree inside Siberia, where Grigori Rasputin was born in eighteen sixty-nine in village of Pokrovskoye, on Tura River near Ural Mountains."

Astor shook his head. "How can you know all of this?"

"Is historical information, and I am historian. It is possible I am wrong, but I must take tiny sample of wood to see under microscope to be certain."

Mikhail stepped forward. "*Net! Vy ne mozhete povredit' artefakt.*"

"I will not damage artifact," she said. "Look. This has been done at least two times in past. Look here for tiny spot deep inside carving."

She handed her glasses to Mikhail, and he studied the groove in the wood. "Yes, I see small spot."

Irina rolled the cane over and motioned to another carving. "And also here."

"I see," Mikhail said. "If this is what you must do, you will do in same small mark."

"Of course this is what I will do," Irina said. "The reason two marks exist is because first sample mark could not be found by second person to take sample. I am very good at this, but I do not have tools to do this tonight. We must keep artifact, or we must meet again tomorrow. Is up to you."

Chapter 29
Up in Smoke

I was still uncertain precisely what role Mikhail played in the trans-action between Marcus Astor and me. He was silent during most of the discussion, but when Irina revealed the need to gather a non-destructive microscopic sample, he bolted into action and ap-peared to do so from a position of authority. Something made me believe there was more to the mysterious Mikhail than he wanted me to know.

Money doesn't create character. It reveals it. When a person suddenly finds himself in possession of a great deal of liquid assets, his true personality rises like butter from churned milk. It was time to give Mikhail a good churning and see what floated.

I said, "Marcus, before you make your decision, let's talk money. If your price is outrageous, or if my offer is offensively low, there's no need to study the walking stick any further. Irina has better things to do than analyze an object that is never going to be bought or sold."

Astor fidgeted in his chair and waved a dismissive hand. "Men like you and me don't squabble over money when an object is clearly one of a kind. A thing has value. It's that simple."

I smiled, crossed my legs, and lifted my tumbler. "You've clearly misjudged the kind of man I am, Marcus. A thing, indeed, has a value, but that value is never the same to every man. You are clearly not the owner of the staff. You're simply brokering a potential deal."

I paused and stared at Mikhail. "Whoever owns the thing continually sets its value by determining the lowest price he would accept from someone wishing to buy it. If this thing is genuine, I want to own it. All that remains is the difference between what the owner will accept and what I will pay."

I turned my attention back to Astor. "When I purchase things, I do so at a price no higher than the MAP—that's the minimum acceptable price from the seller's perspective and the maximum acceptable price from my point of view."

He bit his lower lip for a moment. "In that case, all that remains is for you to divulge your maximum acceptable price."

I took another sip. "I left out one critical element in the pricing puzzle. As you've gathered, I'm a man of considerable financial means, and I've deduced that you are a man of considerable connections. Men like us don't have time for petty bickering. When I make my best offer, it's just that, my best offer, and I will make no other offers. I expect the same from you. I would suspect it's a safe assumption that you don't get paid unless you close the sale. That detail puts you in an interesting little pickle because you get to make the decision about who shows his hand first."

He pressed his palm to his chest. "Me? I get to decide which of us makes the first move?"

"No, Mr. Astor. It's not the first move. It's the only move. You tell me your seller's take-it-or-leave-it price, or I tell you mine. There's plenty of whiskey left in that bottle if you need another drink and a little time to think it over."

He gave the bottle a look and then turned his attention to the sliding glass door into the main salon. "Do I have to pour my own?"

For a second time, I lifted and examined my empty glass, and for a second time, my beautiful wife made her appearance. This visit, however, was a little different than the first. This time, both she and Irina were side by side, and Astor was forced to make a gawking choice.

He made the correct decision. Penny's visit lasted only long enough to pour, wink, and disappear while Irina kept her spot on the deck. Astor had his cake and ate it, too.

While he was still imagining the little black dress, I said, "There's one more choice to be made. Leave the staff with Irina and me, or bring it back tomorrow."

"That one's easy," he said. "But, of course, it's not up to me. That's a decision you must make, Mr. Chase."

This guy is better than I expected.

He said, "If we reach an agreed price now, pending the outcome of your historian's vetting process, Rasputin's walking stick remains with you. Otherwise, it goes with me."

Ah, nice touch of neurolinguistic programming there, Marcus.

Calling it Rasputin's walking stick rather than a mere staff or cane was obviously designed to plant the seed of authenticity in my brain, but it didn't work.

I slipped a hand inside my jacket and withdrew a pen and notepad. Covering the pad with my left hand, I pulled off the top sheet and wrote a number on the slip before folding it in half. Sliding the small sheet across the table, I said, "Now, write down your number."

He covered the pad and quickly wrote a number, then folded the paper and slid it to me. I lifted the rectangle of white paper and tucked it beneath one corner of my coaster.

"Aren't you going to look?" he asked.

"Since I'm enjoying our little dance, I'd like to increase the stakes."

He enjoyed another sip. "How so?"

I pulled a cigar lighter from my pocket and slid it across the table. "If you'll burn my offer without looking at it, I'll pay the price you wrote down right now with no further vetting of the artifact."

He stared at the lighter and subconsciously increased his breathing rate. After another sixty seconds of silence, he took a drink, lifted the lighter, and sent my offer up in smoke.

I pulled the folded paper from beneath the coaster and handed it to Irina. "Bring Mr. Astor that amount of cash, and secure Rasputin's staff somewhere safe."

She did as I ordered and returned with a zippered, locking cash bag moments later. Astor handed the bag to Mikhail. The Russian took it and laid the worn case he'd been holding onto the table in front of Astor.

Marcus patted the case. "Well, that was fun. How do you feel about dessert?"

I rubbed a hand across my stomach. "I have a voracious appetite, my friend. What do you have in mind?"

By way of an answer, he rolled the combinations into the pair of locks on the case and opened the top, revealing a revolver and a dagger.

I leaned forward and peered into the case. "What are these?"

"Take a good look, then have your historian tell you the story of Rasputin's assassination."

Intrigued, I reached for the revolver, but Astor closed the case. "First, the story."

I slid a chair away from the table and motioned toward the seat. "Please, Irina, join us and regale us with the story of the Mad Monk's final hour."

I prayed a silent prayer that Irina knew enough of the history to sound convincing.

She slid onto the seat, removed her gloves, and crossed her legs in an elegant display of Eastern European etiquette. "I will try to tell story in English. After exhibiting considerable influence over Czar Nicholas II and his wife, Alexandra, Grigori Rasputin grew to be hated and mistrusted by many nobles and also right-wing politicians. In early morning of December thirty, nineteen sixteen —of course, this is seventeen of December in Russian calendar— Prince Felix Yusupov, Grand Duke Dmitri Pavlovich, and Vladimir Purishkevich insisted Rasputin come with them to Yusupov's home, Moika Palace.

"Once there, he was given sweet cakes and Madeira laced with cyanide. This is part where story has many versions. Some believe cyanide had no effect on Rasputin, making Prince Yusupov believe the mystic was maybe protected by some unseen force. I believe is more likely someone became afraid and switched cyanide poison with some other harmless liquid. This is more likely story, but it does not truly matter. Rasputin is not affected, so the prince demanded gun from Pavlovich and shot two times into Rasputin's belly. Maybe or maybe not this is true, but what happened next in story is undisputed. Prince ran from palace into courtyard, and Rasputin followed with blood spilling from belly. Final killing shot was made from very close into Rasputin's forehead by Purishkevich with his own pistol. This is story of Rasputin's death."

I swallowed hard and wondered if I could remember any event in American history with such detail. Irina was proving to be far more than just another pretty face.

Marcus Astor sat slowly shaking his head. "Tell us the rest of the story, Irina. Specifically, the mutilation."

She bowed her head in apparent embarrassment. "This part of story is only rumor and is probably not true."

"Tell it anyway," Astor said.

She sighed and spoke softly. "Is folklore, but maybe Prince Yusupov . . . I do not know word. *Kastrirovannyy*."

I said, "Castrated."

"Yes, this is word. Prince Yusupov maybe used his father's dagger to castrate Rasputin, and is possible remains are inside private museum in St. Petersburg inside sealed jar. Very large jar, if story is true."

Suddenly, the contents of Astor's case were very interesting.

He opened it up and said, "Mr. Chase, may I present Minister Purishkevich's revolver and Prince Yusupov's father's dagger with unquestionable documented provenance?"

I met Astor's gaze and tilted my head toward Irina.

He said, "Of course. But just like before, only with gloved hands."

She lifted each piece of history from the case in turn and examined them with LEDs beaming from her glasses. After a thorough inspection, she placed the items back inside the case and removed her glasses. "Is possible, but I must see documents."

Astor pulled a leatherbound portfolio from a hidden compartment of the case and passed it to Irina.

She opened the cover and thumbed through the pages. "I may take these inside for a moment, yes?"

Astor shot a glance to Mikhail, who nodded ever so slightly. "Certainly, but do not remove the individual pages from their protective covers."

Irina stood. "Of course."

She made her way into the main salon, and Astor said, "What is she doing in there?"

"I don't know, but I pay her well to protect my interests, so it's safe to say she's making sure my money is well spent."

"Speaking of money," he said. "You now own the walking stick with which Grigori Rasputin traveled thousands of miles, following the footsteps of hundreds of Russian Orthodox monks before him, but with one difference."

He paused, and I gave him what he wanted. "What's the difference?"

"Those footprints led the other monks to religious enlightenment, but they led Rasputin to the court of Czar Nicholas II, and the lineage of the Romanovs into the angry fists of the Bolsheviks."

"This is starting to sound expensive," I said.

"Shop around," Astor said. "See if you can find these pieces of history someplace else at a better price."

"Touché."

Astor took another drink and again admired the remaining whiskey. "I don't see any necessity to play the same games as before. When your historian returns and declares the provenance bulletproof—unlike Rasputin—the price is two million dollars."

I tried not to show a reaction as I finished the whiskey in my tumbler. "*If* Irina confirms the validity of the provenance, I'll make you a better offer than a mere two million dollars."

He leaned forward. "I thought you were a one-offer kind of man."

It was my turn to lean forward. "That was before I knew you were the kind of man who could put whatever I want in my hands."

Instead of having me summon Penny again, he reached for the bottle and refilled both of our tumblers. "I think it's safe to assume that the lovely Irina will come back with good news for both of us, so tell me, what is this better offer of yours?"

I took the first sip of my third glass of the best scotch I'd ever tasted. "Since you seem to have contacts east of where the Iron Curtain once hung, perhaps you're precisely the man to find the one missing item I need to become the pinnacle of my collection."

The interest and greed welled up in his eyes, but in a moment of hesitation, he turned to the stoic Russian behind him. "Come sit with us, Mikhail. I think this might interest you."

The man unbuttoned his jacket and joined us at the table.

I asked, "Are you a scotch man, Mikhail?"

"I am vodka man, but as they say . . . When in Rome . . ."

As if clairvoyant, Penny came through the door with a third tumbler and made a generous pour. She gave me the requisite attention and sashayed away.

Our glasses touched, and Mikhail said, "*Zdorov'ye!*"

We drank in silence until Astor couldn't wait another minute. "So, the offer. Let's hear it."

"I want the Third Imperial Fabergé egg."

Astor let out a long, low whistle and leaned back in his seat, but Mikhail didn't budge.

"You and half the billionaires on Earth want that egg."

I shrugged. "The difference between me and those few men who want the egg badly enough to write the check is this. They want the whole world to know they have it, and such publicity always leads back to the previous owner *and* the broker. It's no secret the egg was acquired by, let's say, less-than-transparent transactions."

Mikhail spoke up. "Egg was stolen and has been hidden for many years."

"Exactly. There's no reason to bring such ugly business as thievery and possession of stolen art under the spotlight on the world stage. I want it so I can pull it from my vault in the middle of long, lonely nights and hold it in my hands. I want to know how it felt to be the czar for small moments beneath the same moon Nicholas II watched pass overhead a hundred years ago."

Astor opened his mouth to speak, but Mikhail held up a silencing finger. "Is ten million dollars in numbered account in Zurich."

Marcus Astor laid a hand on the Russian's forearm. "You should really let me negotiate this arrangement, Mikhail."

"There is no negotiation," the Russian growled. "Is ten million dollars."

I watched tiny ripples in the surface of the golden whiskey inside my tumbler and let the number hang in the air before saying, "Seven million for the revolver, the dagger, *and* the egg, plus one million as a brokerage fee to be paid in cash . . . tonight."

Astor said, "I think we need—"

Mikhail glared at him. "What you think does not matter. You do not have access to egg."

I set my eyes on Mikhail's. "You have it, don't you?"

He raised his shoulders. "This does not matter. What matters is you can have it, but not for seven million dollars."

"I didn't offer seven million. I offered seven million *plus* your one-million-dollar fee."

"But that was for also pistol and dagger. Is not enough."

I hooked a finger around Mikhail's tumbler and pulled it toward me. "You have it, don't you?"

The Russian lifted the glass from behind my finger and raised it in a subdued toast. "Not for much longer."

I raised my glass to meet his, and my new window to the world opened wide. "You'll excuse me for a moment. If we're going to conclude our business tonight, I'm afraid I need to visit the *vannaya komnata.*"

He nodded without a word, and I stood on trembling knees, determined not to collapse until I was inside the main salon and behind the smoked glass.

The prayer worked, but just barely.

When I slid the door closed behind me, Penny stuck a phone in my hand. "It's Skipper."

I took the phone from her hand. "I had no doubt who it was. This thing just turned into a tornado in a trailer park."

Chapter 30
A Russian Heart

I stuck the phone to my ear and my butt to a barstool in the main salon. "Go, Skipper."

"Uh, do you know what just happened out there?"

"Yes, I know, and it changes everything. This was never about Marcus Astor. It's always been about whoever Mikhail really is. Did you have any luck with the facial recognition from the airport video?"

"I did, but it doesn't mean anything. The two passengers were low-level bureaucrats from St. Petersburg, and the pilots are no-bodies."

"What about Mikhail?"

"I think he was still on the plane when the tug towed it into the hangar."

I scratched my chin. "Either that, or he was already on the island."

"It doesn't really matter when or how he got here."

"You're right, as usual, but what does matter is who he really is. I assume you're on it."

"Of course I am," she said. "But I'm coming up empty so far."

I squeezed my temples between the heels of my hands while

still holding the phone in place. "The looming question is even bigger than Mikhail."

Skipper sighed. "Yeah, I know. The Board played us, but what I don't know is why. They didn't have to point us toward Astor. They could've told us the truth about who they were really after."

"We'll deal with that after we get Astor and Mikhail off our boat. For now, I need you to keep working on who he really is."

"I'm on it, but I need a little more than the video feed from Irina's glasses."

I shook off my anger at the Board. "I'll have at least a good thumbprint for you when he finishes his scotch, and I've got an idea for a DNA sample."

I stood from my stool. "Before I head back out there, are the pistol and dagger authentic?"

"The provenance checks out. They're real."

"Then so is Mikhail."

When I gathered my tools and wits, I stepped back through the smoked-glass door, placed my leather tool bag on the deck beside my chair, and rejoined Mikhail, Astor, and Irina at the table. "I apologize for the interruption, but I feel much better now. Would you care for a cigar?"

I laid four flawless Cuban Cohibas on the table, but Mikhail said, "First, we complete our business, then we can celebrate."

"Fair enough," I said. "I suppose that means you think we're still negotiating."

He slowly shook his head. "No, you made it clear. You do not negotiate. You make offer and wash hands. Deal is done or dead. I respect this, but such silliness is child's play when millions of dollars are on table."

I nodded. "I can respect your position. I'm afraid I'm at my upper limit at seven million plus one on *this* deal."

He almost smiled. "My English is not so good, but you said *this* deal as if there will be another."

I leaned down and lifted the leather bag from the deck and placed it on the center of the table. "Your English is better than you think, Mikhail. If you produce the Third Imperial egg at my price, our next deal will be eight figures. That's eight figures American, not rubles."

He leaned forward, parted the upper folds of the bag, and peered inside. "Those are definitely not rubles."

Mikhail lifted the bag from the table, placed it beside his chair, and stuck out his hand.

I stood and stuck my hand in his. "This calls for vodka!"

Mikhail formed a fist with his left hand and pressed it against the center of my chest. "Inside maybe beats Russian heart."

Penny came through the door with a silver tray bearing an oversized replica of a Fabergé egg. She placed the tray on the table, opened the egg, and lifted the prize from within: four crystal shot glasses and a ten-thousand-dollar bottle of Russian Imperial Collection Vodka.

Mikhail took the bottle from her hand and poured four shots, then he carefully lifted the first shot glass and placed it in my hand. The second went to Astor, and the third and fourth were delivered respectfully to Irina and Penny.

The Russian gripped the neck of the bottle and raised it into the air. "*Zdorov'ye!*"

The four of us with glasses drank with exuberance, and Mikhail pressed the bottle to his lips and drank down at least the equivalent of our four shots. "Now, cigars!"

Irina stood and almost curtsied. "If I am no longer needed, I will leave cigars to gentlemen."

Penny lifted her tray but left the bottle and glasses on the table. "And I'll join Irina inside."

I produced three cigars from my jacket pocket, and Mikhail produced a lighter and punch. The three of us punched and toasted the ends of our Cuban masterpieces that would be reduced to gray ash in half an hour.

Mikhail slipped the toe of his shoe into the top of the leather bag and peeked inside again. "One million American dollars is all there, yes? I do not have to count?"

I asked, "What would you do to me if I dared to count *your* money on *your* boat, Mikhail?"

He pulled the cigar from his lips and tapped a fist against my chest again. "Russian heart, indeed."

We smoked in silence until we'd reduced our cigars to ash, and it was time to fulfill my promise to Skipper.

After pouring three more shots of vodka and sliding a glass to Astor and Mikhail, I stood and hoisted my glass. "*K Russkim serdtsam!*"

They stood, and Mikhail echoed in English. "To Russian hearts!"

Partially out of clumsiness from the amount of alcohol in my body, and partially out of determination, I thrust the sturdy base of my glass against the delicate rim of Mikhail's, shattering his into several elongated shards.

He roared with laughter as blood and vodka trailed from his fingertips and slivers of blood-covered glass landed on the table, creating a kaleidoscope of light dancing in all directions.

Continuing his raucous laughter, the Russian grabbed the bottle just as before and pressed it to his lips. Astor and I drank our shots, but I was the only one at the table happy to see the spread of DNA samples before my eyes.

Mikhail walked to the rail and extended his still-bleeding fingertips into the night air. He poured a generous treatment of vodka across his wounded hand and then sucked the blood and distilled potatoes from his fingers.

When he returned, he said, "Three days."

"Until then," I said, and we shook hands like the honorable men we were pretending to be.

Mongo escorted Mikhail and Astor back up the stairs to the waiting helicopter, and Barbie returned them to Astor's rented hilltop home.

Hunter and Singer followed me into the main salon, where we found the rest of the team perched around a small computer monitor with Skipper's face filling the screen.

"Good," she said. "There you are. We've got a lot to discuss. Did you really just buy a long-lost Fabergé egg for eight million dollars?"

I shook my head. "No! I'd never do something like that. I bought a long-lost Fabergé egg, the pistol that killed Grigori Rasputin, *and* the dagger that castrated him for seven million dollars plus a small tip."

She groaned. "Actually, you didn't buy any of that. The Board did."

"We'll see about that."

Skipper shuffled some paperwork. "Enough about that. Nice move obtaining Mikhail's DNA sample. That was real smooth. Now we just have to hope he's in a database somewhere."

Irina said, "I bagged the samples, and we'll get them to you ASAP."

"No need," she said. "I'm coming to you. Barbie is picking me up on her way back from dropping off Chase's new best buddies."

The sound of the chopper landing was enough to get our attention, even inside the plush confines of the yacht. The pilot and our analyst strolled through the door, and Penny giggled.

I studied my wife's expression. "Have you been dipping into the overpriced liquor?"

Her giggling continued, but she shook her head. "No, I'm as sober as Singer, but it just hit me that I had a Barbie doll when I was a little girl, and I also had Barbie's little sister, Skipper. I just think that's funny."

Skipper rolled her eyes as only she can do. "I wondered when somebody was going to put that together. I had both dolls, as well, but the real Barbie and Skipper are way prettier than our plastic predecessors."

"No doubt!" came Tony's unrehearsed response.

Skipper shook a finger at him. "You better be glad you spoke up, Big Boy. You're still in hot water over your galivanting around on the dance floor the other night."

"I only have eyes for you, baby."

"Don't call me baby when we're working."

"But we're always working."

She touched a finger to the tip of her nose. "Exactly. Now, let's get down to business. Where's Mikhail's tumbler and DNA sample?"

Irina held up two plastic bags. "They are here."

Skipper took them from her hand and passed them to Barbie. "Get these to the lab on the *LD*, and make sure they know how important this is."

Barbie gave a mock salute and headed for her chariot.

I asked, "How long will it take to get a result if he's in the database?"

Skipper said, "That's just it. There isn't *the* database. There are hundreds, if not thousands, of databases that could hold his DNA. We'll have to try them all until we get a hit. Believe it or not, the Kremlin's database is one of the easy ones to hack."

I said, "They're all easy for you."

She gave me a smile, "Yeah, but there's only one of me until I figure out how to clone myself."

"So, where do we go from here?" Disco asked.

Skipper huffed. "From here, we wait, but there is one thing we need to discuss. How much are you going to tell the Board?"

I poured a cup of coffee and took a sip. "I haven't decided yet. I guess it depends on how much more money we need when it comes time to buy ourselves a warship."

"You're keeping the egg, aren't you?"

Irina's eyes turned to saucers. "Are you really keeping it?"

I stared into my coffee. "We'll see, but one thing is for certain. If it's authentic, you can spend as much time with it as you want, and no gloves required."

I thought she was going to cry as the thought of holding the egg in her bare hands flooded through her mind, and I made an irreversible decision at that moment.

The coffee wasn't sobering me up, but it was waking me up. "Here's how I see this playing out. We've got three days to figure out who Mikhail is. The sooner we get a solid ID, the better. I want as much background as possible. We need to know who and what we're dealing with. I'll talk with Clark tomorrow when the twenty thousand dollars' worth of liquor wears off, and we'll decide what to tell the Board."

Singer asked, "What if Clark was in on it?"

I downed the rest of my coffee and palmed my forehead. "I can't tell you how badly I hope you're wrong." I poured another cup. "For those of you who don't know what happened out there tonight, we got hit by a truck. When the Board assigned this mission, they led us to believe Marcus Astor was the target, but after what happened right out there"—I pointed through the glass wall to the stern deck—"it's obvious that Mikhail or someone he works for is the real bullseye on this one. Astor is a minor player. He was just our conduit to the Russian. I don't like it. We're not a squad of junior-enlisted soldiers. We're tier-one operators. When they point us toward a hill, we take the hill, but we need and deserve to know what we're going to find at the top of that hill. That didn't happen this time, and if Clark knew and didn't tell us, that's a more serious issue than I know how to address."

Silence filled the air until I knocked my knuckles against the counter. "Get some sleep. You've earned it, and we've got a lot of work to do tomorrow. All hands on deck at zero eight hundred."

Chapter 31

Two Out of Three

It wasn't the coffee that kept me awake that night. It was the dread of hearing Clark Johnson, a man I trusted, loved, and respected, tell me he knew my team was being set up to get to a target the Board refused to disclose. Sending operators like my team into the field on a different mission than they've been briefed on is like telling an attack dog he killed the wrong bad guy. The dog is left confused, timid, and still wanting a treat.

I lay in my bunk beside the lady in black and felt my blood approaching its boiling point with every passing minute. Finally, I slipped from beneath the sheets and silently escaped our cabin. From within the relative privacy of an unused cabin on the main deck, I dialed the phone and felt my heart pounding in time with the ringing on the other end.

"What!"

"Clark, it's Chase. Did you know?"

He groaned. "Know what? And why are you calling me in the middle of the night?"

"Did you know our true objective?"

Sounds of him escaping his bedroom wafted through the phone until a door closed. "What are you talking about, College Boy?"

"We were set up, and I need to know if you were in on it. You've never lied to me before, so don't start now."

"Men of action have no need to lie to each other, and I can honestly say I have no idea what you're talking about. My first concern is that the team is safe. Nobody got hurt, right?"

"We're physically fine, but we're not taking the slap in the face too well. The Board—your board—sent us out here to wrangle Marcus Astor into international piracy. You and the Board told us to approach Astor and buy an egg to warm him up, but Astor was never the real target. A guy who calls himself Mikhail is the real target. When we shook Astor's tree hard enough, Mikhail, a Russian, fell out."

I heard the sounds of Clark's refrigerator door opening and closing, followed by his mumbled question. "Who's Mikhail?"

"Swallow whatever you stuck in your mouth, and tell me straight that you didn't know we were after someone other than Astor."

He swallowed. "Chase, if I had known the Board was setting you up, I would've pounded them into the ground. There's no way I would've done that to the team."

"You have no idea how much relief that brings into my life, and I'm sorry for doubting you, but a lot has changed in the last couple of years. I know you have responsibilities I'll never understand, but it's nice to be reminded what brotherhood is, even from the top."

He said, "Do you remember the day you pulled me off the top of the Khyber Pass?"

"Of course I remember. I'll never forget it."

He said, "I'm only halfway to where you are."

"What are you talking about?"

"Like you, I'll never forget it, but when you pulled me out of the cave, I was crawling through death's door, and I don't remem-

234 · CAP DANIELS

ber anything about what happened that day. The one thing I know for sure is that you would've walked through the fires of Hell to get to me, and that's what you can always expect from me. Tell me what you want me to do, Chase. Whatever it is, consider it done."

"I'm not prepared to answer that question yet, but when I wake up and meet with the team in a few hours, we'll let you know. In the meantime, I'm sorry for doubting you, brother."

"There's nothing for you to be sorry for. I've been where you are, and it stings. You can rest assured that it'll never happen to you again as long as I'm your handler."

I said, "When all of this is over, we'll swap stories. Good night, Mud Pie."

He chuckled at my use of the pet name his mother called him since second grade. "You know what they say. When the going gets tough, it's not time to walk softly."

"Nobody says that. Go back to bed, Socrates."

With the fear of Clark's betrayal off my chest, I slept like the dead, and Penny had to shake me awake.

"Sweetheart, you should probably get up. It's almost eight o'clock."

I pawed at my eyes and stretched. "What?"

"It's ten 'til eight, and you told the team to be ready to go at eight."

I rolled my wrist to check my watch. "So it is. Thank you. I don't know how long I would've slept if you hadn't roused me."

She leaned down and gave me a kiss. "You called Clark last night, didn't you?" I nodded, and she said, "Drunk calling your ex is a terrible idea in the middle of the night."

I chuckled. "He's not my ex. I'm still seeing him on the side. I thought you knew."

She gave me a shove. "Get up, Rip Van Winkle. You've got a team of operators upstairs ready to kill your ex. You probably should let them in on the good news."

I splashed some water on my face and brushed my teeth before heading up to the stern deck, where everyone was waiting and stewards were delivering breakfast plates.

"Good morning, guys. I'm sorry I overslept."

Hunter checked his watch. "Don't be sorry. Be better."

"Okay, I deserve that one. Listen up. I talked with Clark, and he assured me he didn't know the truth about who we were sent to roll up."

Singer sighed. "I hate to admit that I had my doubts. I was afraid Clark might've become one of the cake eaters."

"I'm in the same boat," I said. "I doubted him, too, but now that we know the truth, we have to tell our handler what we want."

The only reply that came was the clanging of silverware against plates and coffee cups being lifted to lips.

"Come on. You've got to have some ideas. Tell me what you want."

Singer looked up and wiped his mouth. "I think I can speak for all of us when I say we want to follow you where you take us and do what you think should be done. It's that simple. We trust you, Chase."

That's not what I needed to hear ten minutes after crawling out of bed. I wanted to hear what the team wanted, but in true warrior fashion, they proved, once again, why ours was the team that didn't fail. I wasn't worthy of being their voice back then. I hadn't seen and done the things they'd survived, but for reasons I'll never understand, they trusted me, and I swore day after day to never do anything to abandon that trust.

"Okay, if that's how you feel, I'll make the call. Any and all of you are welcome to sit in."

Singer took another bite of eggs. "That's not how trust works. You make the call, and then you brief us."

We finished breakfast, and my mind roiled like the churn of a waterfall as it strikes the pool below. With the last of the coffee swallowed and the final plate scraped clean, I headed for the interior of the yacht.

Clark answered on the first ring. "Let me guess. They told you they'd follow you into the hurricane, and they're standing by for your orders."

"How do you know this stuff?"

"I may not be the sharpest tool in the quiver, but when it's time to pay the piper, I know which side of the butter my cookie crumbles."

"How long has it been since you've had a psych eval? Are you taking any prescription medication? If not, maybe you should."

"You know what I mean," he said.

"No, actually, I don't, but I didn't call for a philosophy lesson. I called to tell you what we want."

"Let's have it."

"Twenty million dollars, the true identity of our target, and the real reason they want him."

"It's not going to happen, Chase. They may give you the money, and they might even tell you his name, but they're never going to tell you why."

I chewed on the flesh inside my jaw. "Then they can take their money and the name and shove them both right up the same hole. I'm not putting my team in harm's way for a mission on which we've not been fully—and I mean completely fully—briefed."

"That's not how it works. We're soldiers, Chase. We follow orders."

I smiled for the first time in hours. "No, Clark, you're wrong. You and most of my team were soldiers once, but not anymore. We're warriors, not mercenaries. Make the call and make the sale. If you can't do it, we're done. The poorest man on the team is Disco, and he's over two million in net worth. We don't need the money. We do what we do because it's always been the right thing to do. We're not going to be sent on some mysterious mission as part of a private war between some fat cat on the Board and some wannabe Russian oligarch. Money, name, reason. Call me back when you have all three."

He made the sound he always made when I drew a line in the sand and dared somebody to cross it. "Okay, get your butts over to the *Lori Danielle*. I'll brief you on a secure uplink in an hour."

With that, the line went dead, and I headed back onto the deck. All eyes fell on me the instant I cleared the door.

"We're headed for the *LD* for a secure briefing in the CIC."

Captain Sprayberry weighed anchor, and we rendezvoused with the *Lori Danielle* forty-five minutes later in the open water southwest of St. Barts.

Skipper took over the combat information center like a Tasmanian devil, and soon, Clark's face filled the main screen.

He said, "Well, it looks like the gang's all here. Couldn't you find anybody else to shove into that little room?"

I ignored his attempt at small talk. "Let's have it. We're secure on this end."

"Right to business, huh?"

"That's right. What's the word?"

He cleared his throat. "The money is in the operational account. His name is—"

Skipper interrupted. "Ilya Mikhailovich Semenov, and he's the only son of Mikhail Vladimirovich Semenov, a former KGB

238 · CAP DANIELS

brigadier general turned arms dealer turned junk dealer turned dead guy floating in the Volga River."

I'd never been prouder of our analyst, and she could see it in my eyes.

She gave me a wink, pointed to herself, and mouthed, "Because I'm Skipper."

I nodded, and Clark said, "It sounds like someone's been doing her homework."

"Now, the why," I said. Clark hesitated, and I said, "All or none."

He took a long, deep breath. "You were right. It's a private war, but a just war. I won't give you names, but the daughter of one member of the Board married the son of another member, and they had two beautiful children. The young family was on vacation in Zurich three years ago, and the children were kidnapped by forces working for the senior Semenov. The ransom was paid, and the kidnappers left directions to a sealed mausoleum where the children could be found. When the security team cut the locks, they discovered the bodies of the little girls. Emily would've been four, and Arista had just turned three. Chase, you do not want to know how they were killed."

I bowed my head and ground my teeth together until the hinges of my jaws were ready to explode. Feeling as though my head would soon burst into flames, I whispered, "How do you want him?"

"Terrified and broken, but breathing."

I said, "I can only promise you the first two."

Chapter 32
The Sins of the Father

Everyone sat in absolute silence until Singer whispered, "Amen."

"I don't know if I can do it," I said.

Skipper looked up. "We have to do it, Chase. We simply have to."

"We're handing Semenov to the Board. There's no question about that. But I'm not sure I can see him again without tearing his throat out."

Singer stood. "Let's go for a walk, Chase."

There would never be a man who understood more about how my head worked than Jimmy "Singer" Grossmann, so I followed him through the secure hatch of the CIC and onto the bow of the Research Vessel *Lori Danielle*.

"I want to tell you a story, Chase, and I want you to listen to every word. Can you give me that?"

I nodded and leaned against the massive winch that managed the incredible weight of the anchors and chains designed to hold the ship where the captain needed her to lie.

Singer began. "We've been to Northern Africa together, so I know you understand how the sun scorches the earth and everything attached to it when the wind refuses to blow down there."

I nodded, and he continued. "My spotter, who was a Sudanese kid named Kazim, and I spent eleven hours crawling up a stone staircase to a rooftop outside of Khartoum and silently building our nest. We were there with one mission. I was to put one fifty-caliber round through the head of a warlord named Abdallah Amani MacHar, who was expected to approach Khartoum in an open jeep within the next forty-eight hours. Kazim and I lay on top of that scalding mud roof for thirty-six hours waiting for MacHar's jeep."

He paused and wiped his brow as if he were still lying beneath that Sudanese sun.

"Neither of us moved any part of our body faster than a snail for that day and a half. We were running out of water, and the bugs—you can't imagine the bugs—they were relentless, and we couldn't swat, wave, or spray anything. We had to simply accept the pests as part of our environment. Believing I'd nearly reached the end of my ability to continue the mission, something caught my eye at the edge of my scope, and I moved ever so slowly, repositioning my muzzle from the dirt road to a blown-out shack, where a man had a young woman by her hair and was throwing her around like a rag doll. I'd whispered, 'Motion ten meters north.' Kazim panned his spotter's scope even more slowly than I'd moved my rifle. He whispered, 'Contact.'"

Singer stopped talking again and turned his face to the morning sky. He pulled a bottle of water from his pocket and emptied it down his throat before continuing.

"Kazim said, 'No, Sergeant. You must not engage.' I argued that the man was going to kill the woman if we didn't intervene. I could drop him with one press of the trigger, but Kazim lowered his left hand and laid it against the back of my neck. His clammy skin felt like something nearing death crawling across my skin. He whispered, 'Close your eyes and pray to your God. If you kill this man who is punishing his daughter, you will be forgiven by the God of Abraham, but if you do this, you will destroy our only chance to take the life of MacHar, thereby saving thousands of lives. Tell this to your God, and listen for His voice and heed His guidance.' I did what that young Sudanese spotter told me to do, and when I opened my eyes, the dust trail behind an approaching jeep wafted on the right edge of my scope."

I pulled my bottle of water from my pocket and handed it to Singer.

He swallowed it and said, "I saved thousands of lives that afternoon because of a Muslim kid named Kazim. And do you have any idea what the name Kazim means in Sudanese?"

"No, I don't know any Sudanese."

He looked into my eyes as if he were staring into my soul. "It means one who controls his anger."

Singer was the master of effectively using silence to make a point, and he demonstrated that skill in that moment.

When I believed I'd fully digested his message, I said, "You always know exactly what to say, exactly when I need it. I don't know what I'd do without you, Singer."

As I pushed myself from the anchor winch, Singer placed his hand on my shoulder. "The man punishing the girl in the blown-out shack was Kazim's father. And the girl was Kazim's sister."

A chill ran down my spine as I tried to imagine the mental discipline of that young man who kept his focus when the moment demanded more from him than any man should have to endure, and I was ashamed of my rage. Doing what was required of me to see the mission through to its intended end was my only reasonable choice, and thanks to my friend and spiritual mentor, that reality came into brilliant focus in that moment. But his story had not yet reached its end.

"Kazim was sixteen years old, Chase. His father's throat was cut later that night, and that sixteen-year-old boy became the man of the household. His sister's transgression had been her willingness to allow an American man to see her without her hijab. She'd been burned by a white phosphorus incendiary grenade, and she removed her head covering so an American Special Forces medic could treat the infected wound on her neck. For this sin, her father believed he would've been justified in killing his daughter. That Green Beret medic who probably saved that girl's life with a handful of antibiotics and clean bandages . . . His name was Sergeant First Class Clark Johnson."

Chapter 33
Darned Good Eggs

In the following two days, with Skipper taking the lead, we learned everything that could be known about Ilya Mikhailovich Semenov and his father. What we could not uncover was the reason behind the brutal kidnapping and murder of two innocent little girls. The more I learned about the man and his operation, the deeper my rage ran, but every time I felt it boiling over, I replayed Singer's story in my mind and found the strength to tamp down my anger and turn it into limitless determination to complete the mission.

During a break in our preparations, the same gleaming mahogany powerboat idled to our swim platform, and the same two men occupied the vessel.

"Hey, Disco. Bring your interpretation skills out here. The McFrenchy brothers are back."

Two minutes later, our chief pilot turned from the stern rail. "If you're ready, it's on. Seven o'clock tonight. Right here."

I swallowed the ire in my throat. "Set it up."

The boat motored away, and Disco took a seat across from me. He said, "Are you ready?"

"I'm ready, but we've got a lot to do in the next four hours. Get your girlfriend over here. We'll need her to get the money right."

"She's not my girlfriend, yet, but I'll go get her. How about the transportation for tonight? Do you want Barbie?"

"No, definitely not. I want you. We're finished playing look-at-my-butt. It's time to be all business."

"I got you."

"Did the messenger mention Astor?"

Disco said, "Yeah, they'll both be here. Is that what you were expecting?"

"I kind of thought Mikhail might come alone or maybe with another Russian. I'm sure he's got some muscle following him around."

He slapped the arms of his chair. "I'll go get Ronda. Is there anything else you need?"

I glanced toward the glass wall between the stern deck and the salon. "Check with Skipper and see if she wants to go back to the CIC. I suspect she'll want to stay here, but you never know."

Ten minutes later, the rotor wash from the AW109E blew my hair around and sent a few paper napkins flying around the deck. By the time I cleaned up the napkins, Disco was back with the CPA, and it was time for a powwow.

Skipper, Ronda No-H, and I sequestered ourselves in the chief engineer's office adjacent to the engine room and sealed the hatch behind us. Ronda looked like a POW who was next in line for interrogation.

"Relax," I said. "Everything's fine."

"Then why are we locked in whatever this place is?"

Skipper took the helm. "You'll get used to it soon enough. There's enough electrical and mechanical interference in this room to defeat any recording device in use by almost any intelligence agency on the planet."

"And why do we care about that?" Ronda asked, still pie-eyed.

Skipper chuckled. "Like I said, you'll get used to it. Chase is a little paranoid when he talks about certain topics. Spending seven million dollars falls into that category of 'certain topics.'"

"So, I've not done anything wrong?"

I couldn't resist having a little fun with our bean counter. "Do you *think* you've done something wrong?" I gave her one of Singer's silent pauses until I was afraid her head was going to explode. "I'm just messing with you. We couldn't be happier with you. Especially Disco."

Her expression fell from near panic to full blush in an instant, and she reverted to her initial assessment of our chief pilot. "He's sweet."

"Yes, he is. Now, let's talk about money. A man named Ilya Mikhailovich Semenov—he'll call himself Mikhail—is going to be on board this evening with an extremely valuable item. Irina is going to examine the item, and if she validates its authenticity, you're going to transfer seven million dollars from our operations account at Cayman International into a numbered account that's likely Swiss. While you're doing that, I need you to make it look harder than it is."

Ronda frowned. "I'm not following you. Transferring money is a snap. There's nothing to it."

"I know. But I need you to make it look like it's taking longer than it should. You'll be using a laptop Skipper will give you, and just like everything else in your new world, the laptop isn't what it appears to be."

"What is it, then?"

Skipper jumped in. "It's a laptop, but that's not all it is. While you're stalling, I'll grab every morsel and crumb I can find inside Mikhail's account. I should be able to identify the bank, and with some luck, I'll find some account numbers for previous transfers into and out of that account. That'll give us a place to start constructing a snapshot of his financial network."

Ronda tilted her head. "There's no way he'll leave the seven million in that account if this is a nefarious transaction. It'll fly away the instant it hits the account. At least that's what I'd do, and you'd never get the money back."

"We don't care about the money," I said. "We care about where and to whom it goes. For us, the money is just a shiny object to distract Mikhail while Skipper is prowling around in his accounts."

Ronda smiled. "This is kind of cool. Is it legal?"

"It's legal-ish," I said. "But we're the good guys."

She seemed to accept my answer, and for the first time, I saw that glimmer Disco described in her eyes.

I said, "You're going to fit right in around here, No-H."

"Thanks, but I do have a question. If we know Mikhail's account number, why are we waiting to stick our noses in it until we make the transfer?"

"That's the thing," Skipper said. "We don't have the number, and we won't have it until Mikhail gives it to us at the meeting tonight."

"Ah, gotcha. Will he write it down or just tell us the number?"

I shrugged. "There's no way to know."

"I know you guys are the spies, but I've got a suggestion if you want to hear it."

Skipper and I answered in stereo. "We're not spies!"

Ronda flushed. "Sorry, I didn't know what word to use."

I chuckled. "No worries. Disco's the spy. The rest of us are good guys. What's your idea?"

She said, "I'm not bragging or anything. That's not me. But you should probably know something about me. I have an eidetic memory for numbers. Once Mikhail says the account number, or if he writes it down, once I've seen it, I'll never forget it. Never."

I laid my hand across a manufacturer's identification plate on a piece of machinery above my head. "What's the serial number beneath my hand?"

She never took her eyes from mine. "A-B six, seven nine four, T-R eighty-eight hundred P. Manufactured in June of nineteen ninety-one in Berlin."

I glanced at Skipper, and she nodded. "No-H, you're my new favorite human, and don't you dare tell another living soul you can do that. It's our little secret."

"Whatever you say. You're the boss's boss, but the boss already knows."

"That's okay," I said. "Captain Sprayberry's job is to run a taut ship, not catch international arms dealers and baby killers."

Ronda gasped. "Baby killers?"

"It's just a figure of speech," I said. "I need you to focus on the task at hand. Stall as long as you can during the transaction, and when you see me scratch my nose, let Mikhail know the transfer is done. Got it?"

"Yes, sir. Stall until you scratch your nose." She looked around as if on the verge of telling a dirty joke. "So, is this Mikhail guy really an arms dealer? Is that really what we're doing? Buying weapons?"

I stood and gave her a wide smile. "Nope. He's just a chicken farmer, and we're buying eggs."

She said, "Those better be some darned good eggs for seven million dollars."

"I guess Irina will let us know."

* * *

The sun blew St. Barts a goodnight kiss at the same moment Disco kissed the helipad with the landing gear of our chopper, and my prediction turned out to be spot-on. Three men stepped from the helicopter, and none were strangers. Marcus Astor followed Mikhail, and the third man was one of the two we watched step off the Gulfstream a few days before. The third man was carrying a metal case about the size of a shoebox, and a pair of padlocks adorned the side opposite its hinges.

Our high-definition cameras captured and recorded every feature of the three men, from the distance between their pupils to the almost imperceptible limp in Mikhail's gait.

I kept my seat as the three of them joined me.

Mikhail waved an open hand across the table. "What? No more bourbon and vodka?"

I said, "Not tonight, I'm afraid. We plan to spend some real money this evening, and I prefer sobriety when eight figures are on the table."

"I can respect this," Mikhail said.

I motioned toward the strongbox. "Let's have a look."

Mikhail motioned with two fingers, and the man guarding the case laid it on the table and slid the small metal fortress toward his fellow Russian.

Mikhail spun the dials on the face of each lock and then pulled a pair of keys from his inside jacket pocket. A key went into each lock, and soon the case was spread open with one of the most beautiful objects I'd ever seen.

I reached for the ornate egg, and the man who'd carried the case leapt to his feet and grabbed my wrist with a vise-like hand. Mongo sprang from the base of the stairs and caught the man's elbow with his right hand while lacing an enormous arm around his neck. Mikhail went for his waistband and drew a Makarov pistol, but before he could level the weapon at either Mongo or me,

Singer materialized behind him and stuck the muzzle of his Glock against the base of his skull.

Astor's hands disappeared beneath the table, but before he could produce a weapon, Hunter stuck the front sight of his pistol beneath his chin and raised his head through forty-five degrees.

Playing the part I'd designed especially for Ronda No-H's benefit, Disco appeared beside me with an MP-5 submachine gun slung from his shoulder. "This is the part where everybody gets real cool, real quick."

Mikhail laid his Makarov on the table, and Disco slid it to me. I raised both hands as if I didn't want the filthy weapon to touch my hands, so Disco slid it into his waistband.

Russian security boy reclaimed his seat, and Mikhail squirmed in his chair and straightened his jacket.

I said, "I'm going to take the egg out of that box with my bare hands, because if it's real, it'll be mine in half an hour, and if it's a fake, I'm not going to diminish its value by touching it. Agreed?"

Mikhail nodded once, and I eyed my team. They lowered their weapons and stepped back from the table as I lifted the egg from its cradle. The weight surprised me, and the craftsmanship was astonishing. I instantly understood Irina's fascination with the piece, and I said, "Bring out the historian."

Chapter 34

What Is It You Desire?

Irina stepped through the door with her magic glasses in her gloved hand and stopped a foot away from the table. The expression on her face was unmistakable disbelief. "You're holding it without gloves."

I gasped and returned the treasure to its case. "You're right. Let me have yours."

She pulled the white cotton gloves from her hands and laid them on the table in front of me.

I ignored them and pushed the metal case toward her. "It's all yours. Tell us what you think."

She reached for the gloves, but I slapped a hand down on them. "You can't feel it with those on. Go ahead. Pick it up and tell us if it's real."

She licked her lips and moved in slow motion toward the egg. Her eyes darted back and forth between me and the box as she inched ever closer.

"Go ahead."

She placed her glasses on her face and carefully cradled the spectacular piece of art in her cupped hands. With measured precision, she examined every inch of the egg and then withdrew a pair of small calipers from her pocket. She made several measurements between features and compared them to a laminated sheet of precise dimensions from Fabergé.

She placed the egg on its base and turned back for the door. She returned with a wooden case and produced an electronic scale, then zeroed the instrument and placed the egg on the pad. When the digital numbers stopped, she let out a sigh. "It's a little heavy."

"This is preposterous!" Mikhail roared, but Irina held up a hand. "Is okay. Is good it is heavy."

Mikhail and I had the same look, so Irina became our professor. "Because of many angles, uh . . . *slozhnyy*."

I said, "Intricate."

"Yes, is intricate work and many pieces of, uh . . ."

Mikhail huffed. "Speak Russian, for sake of God. We all speak Russian."

Irina breathed a sigh of relief and continued in Russian. "Thank you. Because of many angles and intricate work, the piece collects dust, skin, and particles of almost everything that touches it. Over time, this adds weight to the piece, so it would be a sign of a forgery if it weighed exactly the same as when it was produced."

Mikhail turned to me. "I understand now why you have this woman. She is brilliant, and I should steal her away from you."

Irina smiled at him. "*Ty ne mozhesh' pozvolit' sebe menya.*"

Mikhail laughed loud enough for the whole island to hear him, and Astor threw up his hands. "Not all of us speak Russian. What is going on?"

Mikhail said, "She told me I could not afford her."

Irina said, "I must now test purity of gold. You understand this will slightly damage piece."

Mikhail shrugged. "As Mr. Chase says, if it is forgery, you cannot hurt it, and if authentic, it is his."

I said, "Run your test."

Mikhail's agreement to the handling and testing gave me the confidence to believe he had faith the egg was authentic, but I wasn't interested in buying his confidence. I was interested in an authentic egg, and eventually, a warship.

Irina scratched a small sample from the underside of the ornate base and produced a small vial of liquid. I didn't understand the test she was conducting, but when it was over, she said, "Egg is authentic and original Fabergé Third Imperial egg. And now for surprise."

"Surprise?" I said. "What surprise?"

She carefully opened the hinged egg to reveal what looked like a gold pocket watch. Her eyes lit up as if she'd just seen the Earth at creation, and Mikhail put on his glib, knowing smile.

"What am I missing?" I asked.

Irina lifted the timepiece from inside the egg and rolled it over in her hands. More measuring, followed by another gold test, and she looked up. "Inside many of eggs was surprise. Inside this one is Vacheron and Constantin Lady's watch."

"So, what's your answer?"

She gently placed the watch back inside the egg, closed it, and returned the piece of exquisite art to its metal case. "There is no question. Egg is authentic, and is complete just as it was when czarina opened it on Easter morning of eighteen eighty-seven."

"Thank you, Irina. Please send the financier."

She offered an elegant bow and returned to the main salon. Ronda No-H came on deck with the laptop Skipper provided and set up shop between Mikhail and me.

She slid her glasses up her nose. "Are you ready to authorize the transfer, Mr. Chase?"

"I am."

She glanced at Mikhail. "And your institution is prepared to receive the deposit?"

"Yes." He quoted the account number.

Ronda typed furiously and then pursed her lips. After a pause of several seconds, she said, "And the account is in Zurich?"

Mikhail answered before realizing he shouldn't. "No, Geneva. Why?"

No-H ignored him and began typing again.

The Russian demanded, "What are you doing? This is simple transaction."

Ronda rolled her eyes. "Oh, silly me. The last five digits are seven four seven one, not seven four seven four. My mistake. I'm sorry."

I relaxed and ran my fingernail across the tip of my nose. She hit a key like the final note of a concert pianist's concerto and spun the screen to face Mikhail. "There you go. It's done."

The Russian huffed and pulled his cell phone from a pocket. Thirty seconds later, he reached across the table, and I shook his hand.

He said, "Business is done. Now we can have drink and cigar together."

I turned to Ronda. "Send Irina back out, if you would."

She closed the laptop and walked away. Irina replaced the accountant, and I said, "Please secure the crowning jewel of my collection."

She lifted the case and carried the treasure inside the yacht. I hoped it would land in one of the safes on board and not in Irina's luggage.

I spoke in Mikhail's native Russian. "If you truly wish for our business to be complete, we can indeed smoke and drink, but I have more money to spend . . . if you have more to sell."

He smirked. "Cigars and vodka can wait."

"That's what I was hoping you'd say, comrade. I have a request, but there are far too many ears on deck. Wouldn't you agree?"

He made a shooing gesture with the back of his hand, and his security man stood, but Astor stayed in his seat.

Mikhail glared at the wannabe aristocrat. "You will go away."

I looked up at Hunter. "Take them inside, and have someone bring them a cocktail. We won't be long."

Seconds later, Mikhail and I were alone, as far as he knew. But Skipper was recording every breath.

He leaned back, trying to appear relaxed. "So, what is it you desire, my friend?"

"I desire a great many things, but those will come in time. For now, I want a little piece of Spanish history the Moroccans have in their possession at the moment."

"I am listening."

"The Spanish Navy sold a corvette called *Descubierta* to the Moroccans, and they converted it into a nearshore patrol boat."

He squinted. "Yes, I know of this ship, but the barbarians in Morocco would call it a *coastal patrol vessel*, not a *nearshore vessel*."

"As you said, they're barbarians, so why would I care what they call their worn-out, secondhand boats?"

He repositioned in his seat. "Why would you want a vessel you describe this way?"

"Forgive me, Mikhail. Or should I call you Ilya? Either way, why I want the boat is none of your business, but what I'm willing to pay for the boat . . . now, that's something you should care about."

He slid down in his seat until he was looking over my head, into the darkening sky, where the first hint of long-ago supernovas offered their blinking, dancing lights.

My pitch was made, and anything else out of my mouth would serve only to spawn more questions. The Russian was envisioning the acquisition of the vessel and already counting American dollars.

In an attempt to make my brain do anything other than count the passing seconds while Mikhail worked out his plan, I pictured Penny Fulton in that spectacular black dress and allowed my mind to follow itself to the natural conclusion of just how astonishing she looked when that dress hit the floor at her feet.

"What makes you believe I can get for you this ship?"

Ah, a stalling tactic. I can have some fun with this.

"If you can't do it, I'll find someone who can, but when I spend eight million dollars and build a rapport with a man, I like to consider that man a one-stop-shop for all my buying needs. You might even call me a brand loyalist."

He stargazed for a few more moments, then said, "Twenty-five million dollars."

His calm, Russian-accented English yanked me from my desire to play with him. He'd taken the bait, and it was time to let him run with it before setting the hook.

"Twenty-five million dollars? My God, man. I can have a ship *built* for twenty-five million dollars."

"This is price. Stealing for you warship of sovereign nation is dangerous business. For the danger, I must be paid handsomely."

It was my turn to stare into the heavens while my trophy sailfish swallowed the hook and ran for the darkened depths. He was expecting a counteroffer, but instead, I changed the rules.

I steepled my fingers. "Maybe a partnership is in order."

"*Partnerstvo?*"

It was time to set the hook and turn my fish around. "Perhaps, but only if you're certain you have the ability to pull it off."

Mikhail leaned in and narrowed his gaze. "For right price, I can get for you trigger for Chinese nuclear warhead and panties from your president's wife. Ship is easy."

"In that case, here's my proposal. I don't want to buy the ship. I just want to rent it."

"What does this mean, rent it?"

"It means you get me the ship, and I'll keep it for six weeks. When its usefulness to me is depleted, I'll give it back to you, and you can collect your handsome recovery fee from the barbarians in Rabat."

"Ten million dollars."

Hook well set. "Four million dollars."

His chest swelled with a long, deep breath, and my fish was turning for the surface. "Six million. Three now, and three upon delivery."

I stood and headed for the glass door.

Mikhail said, "Where are you going?"

"To find us an even better bottle than the one we shared on our first meeting . . . partner."

Chapter 35
Two Questions

By the time the cigars were smoked to the filter and our postcoital pillow talk was over, I was Ilya Mikhailovich Semenov's new best friend. We stood, shook hands, and Disco whisked the Russian and his entourage back to the island. Before the sound of the chopper's blades disappeared into the night, I was in Skipper's makeshift CIC aboard the *Moscow Mule*.

"I've got two questions," I said.

The brilliant analyst held up a hand. "Fine, I'll get your answers, but first, I have to tell you . . .That was amazing! You just bought a Moroccan warship from a Russian arms dealer, on the deck of a yacht you stole from a dead Russian oligarch, who your former SVR assassin girlfriend killed. You are a steely-eyed missile man, Chase Fulton!"

I rolled my eyes. "You got it all wrong. Well, not all of it, but you got one thing wrong. I didn't buy the ship. I just rented it."

"Whatever. You're still the alpha in this pack. That was awesome."

"Can I let you in on a little secret?" She raised an eyebrow, and I said, "Don't tell anyone, but I was scared out of my mind. Especially when everybody on deck, except me, had a gun."

"Who needs a gun when you've got this team backing you up? Now, what are your two questions?"

"What language do they speak in Morocco?"

Without hesitation, she said, "Arabic and Moroccan Berber."

"That sounds like the name of some obscure carpet. Do we have anybody who speaks either of those?"

"Is that your second question?"

"No, it's a sub-question of question number one."

"It must be nice to be able to make up rules as you go."

I stuck my thumb in the center of my chest. "Steely-eyed missile man, remember? I do what I want."

"Yeah, okay, but when the sun comes up tomorrow, it's a whole new day, and that title goes away. To answer your sub-question, Singer and Clark speak Arabic, but I don't know about Berber."

"Still sounds like a carpet. Here's question number two. Who runs the country, and can you get me into his office?"

"That's two questions, and the answer is complex. Morocco is technically run by King Mohammed VI, but he's more of a figurehead than a governing official. Abbas El Fassi is the prime minister, and I don't think you can just make an appointment to see the prime minister of Morocco."

"Great. That must mean he takes walk-ins."

"Stop it," she said. "That's State Department stuff, and believe it or not, it's over my head. Even I have limits. But tell me what's going on in your head. Why do you need to talk to the prime minister?"

"Because while my frontal lobe was negotiating with Mikhail, the rest of my enormous brain was hatching a plan. I want to help King Mohammed and company protect one of their naval assets."

Skipper's eyes widened. "Oh, Chase, I love it! I'm pretty sure I can get you in to see the American ambassador to Morocco. Will that work?"

Coming down from my adrenaline high, I planted myself in a chair. "Maybe. Do we know the ambassador?"

She spun around, and her fingers danced the rhumba on her keyboard. "His name is Thomas Thomas Riley, Bush appointee, born in San Mateo, California, BS from Stanford in industrial engineering, MBA from Harvard, and a pretty sturdy net worth. From all indications, he has a great relationship with the king and the prime minister. What else do you want to know?"

I scratched my head. "Thomas Thomas Riley? Is that like Forrest Forrest Gump or Boutros Boutros-Ghali?"

"That's it. You just lost your steely-eyed missile man crown. You're still an idiot."

"Words hurt, you know?"

She ignored me and said, "Give me twelve hours, and you'll have your audience with the ambassador."

* * *

Irina spent the remainder of the evening cradling the Fabergé egg and whispering to it in Russian. I thought it was odd, but apparently, the thing was talking back to her, so I didn't interrupt.

I made a call to Clark and spent thirty minutes enduring a berating for failing to keep him in the loop until I told him what we'd accomplished.

At that point, he said, "Disregard everything I just said. Nice job, College Boy. What's the delivery date?"

"Two to four weeks is what Mikhail told me, but we agreed to talk again in three days. I suspect he's laying the groundwork and putting together a team of would-be pirates."

"Excellent. Do you need anything else from me or the Board?"

"Not right now. I just wanted you to know that I'm a steely-eyed missile man."

He made a noise I couldn't identify. "That's how I have you stored in my phone. Do you need somebody with a necktie to hold your hand in the ambassador's office?"

"No neckties or hand-holding required. But I'd appreciate you having somebody grease the skids for me."

"We can do that," he said. "Have Skipper let me know as soon as the appointment is set."

"I'll make sure she keeps you posted, and we'll do a secure call tomorrow to discuss my plan. What time works for you?"

I could almost see him checking his watch.

"I'll sleep 'til nine, so let's plan for ten."

I laughed. "I know you need your beauty sleep, so we'll chat at ten. Goodnight, Sleeping Beauty."

"Good night, sleazy-eyed missile man."

* * *

By noon the following day aboard the *Lori Danielle*, Clark knew every detail of my plan, and Skipper's promise was fulfilled. My appointment with the U.S. Ambassador to Morocco was less than thirty-six hours away, and I wasn't going in alone.

"Mongo, do you own a suit?"

"I've got a bathing suit and a birthday suit. Which one would you like to see?"

I palmed my forehead. "Pick the one you want to wear into the ambassador's office tomorrow."

"Oh, that kind of suit. I've got a couple, but they're a long way from here, and I can't exactly buy off the rack."

"I've got a better idea. We're all going, and the uniform of the day is cargo pants, T-shirts, and boots. Skipper, get Clark back on the phone."

Moments later, he answered. "What is it, College Boy? Isn't one call a day enough for you?"

"I need a government Gulfstream and crew. I'm taking the whole team to Rabat as a show of force."

To my surprise, he said, "I like it. I'll put the airplane on deck at St. Maarten, ASAP, and you can consider the skids well-greased. The secretary of state himself did the greasing. They'll roll out the red carpet for you when you land in Rabat."

The seven of us climbed the Gulfstream's airstairs four hours later, and the crew pointed the nose northeast.

It was no surprise when Skipper said, "I think we need to trade the Citation in for one of these. This is nice."

"This is expensive," I said. "And I don't know if Disco can fly it."

Our chief pilot, who I thought was fast asleep, raised his cap above his eyes. "It's got wings, doesn't it?"

Clark was wrong. There was no red carpet waiting for us when we landed at Rabat–Salé Airport, but there was a pair of blacked-out SUVs with diplomatic plates, grill-mounted police lights, and serious-looking drivers.

It should've taken half an hour to get to the embassy from the airport, but diplomatic plates apparently trump speed limit laws in Rabat—just like every other world capital.

The Marine guard opened the embassy gate without checking any identification or peering inside either vehicle. The driver had no comment, which appeared to be his unspoken personal mantra. We were ushered up the stairs, through the back door of the U.S. Embassy, and down a long corridor until we reached an ornate open area the Marine called "staging."

I soon learned that when the secretary of state greases skids, they become remarkably easy to pull. The ambassador opened his office door and waved us inside. He eyed my team as if sizing them up for picking teams for an intramural basketball game. I silently wondered if he'd pick Mongo first.

His eye finally fell on me. "You must be Dr. Fulton."

I stuck my hand in his. "Just Chase, sir."

He nodded and motioned toward a collection of chairs and sofas. "Please make yourselves at home. You come highly recommended by the secretary, but you'll have to forgive me. With such short notice, I've not reviewed your dossiers or learned your names yet."

I settled into an oversized chair that was more suited for Mongo's backside than mine. "Thank you, Ambassador, and I suspect you'll never read our dossiers or learn our names. We prefer it that way."

"Indeed. May I get you anything before we begin?"

"No, sir. We're on a bit of a tight schedule, so with your permission, I'd like to get right down to business."

"Of course, of course. Just let me call in the others, and we'll get started."

"The others?"

"Well, yes," he said as he thumbed a button on his desk phone. A female voice answered, and he said, "Send them in."

Before I protested further, two men in decent off-the-rack suits came through a side door.

The ambassador waved a hand. "Dr. Fulton, this is Kyle Lawton, the defense attaché, and this is Paul Forrester, the commercial affairs officer. Gentlemen, meet Dr. Chase Fulton and his team."

I shook both of their hands and held Forrester's an instant longer than Lawton's. "Commercial affairs officer, huh?"

He shrugged. "Among other things."

I hadn't expected the CIA station chief to sit in on our briefing, but with the international implications of our mission, I suppose it was reasonable.

Ambassador Thomas T. Riley crossed his legs and gave me a nod. "The floor is yours, Dr. Fulton."

I cleared my throat. "Please, sir, just call me Chase. May I assume you know what we are, Mr. Ambassador?"

"You may. I've known teams like yours exist for some time, but to my knowledge, this is the first time I've ever seen one. And this is all of you? Just seven?"

"Hardly, sir. The six of us constitute the direct-action team, and the young lady to my left is the intelligence analyst and operations center commander. The remaining hundred or so members of our team are support personnel, administrative, and technical specialists. The bulk of those are steaming eastward across the Atlantic as we speak to support our planned mission."

"I see," the ambassador said. "So, tell me about this planned mission."

I began. "At the core of the mission is the Moroccan ship, the *Descubierta*. She's formerly a Spanish corvette refitted as a coastal patrol vessel."

Riley held up a finger. "Kyle, are you familiar with this vessel?"

The defense attaché nodded, and the ambassador said, "Please continue, Doct . . . Chase."

"I've made arrangements with a Russian arms dealer to commandeer the *Descubierta* for a couple of months and then ransom it back to the Moroccan Navy."

Riley squeezed his eyelids closed and massaged his temples. "You've done what? You want me to go to the prime minister *and* the king with that story?"

"I don't care what you do with the story, sir. I'm merely here to brief you on the plan, and I believe the secretary of state has been in contact with your office with encouragement for you to support our operation. Was I misinformed, sir?"

He pulled a plastic bottle of antacid from his drawer. "So, are you suggesting that the Moroccan Navy is to willingly surrender this ship . . . What's her name?"

"The *Descubierta*, sir."

"Yes, the *Descubierta*. You want me to talk the king into just handing over one of his warships?"

"No, sir, not at all. What the American secretary of state—and by extension, the president—wants is for the prime minister, and/or the king, to authorize my team to board and defend the *Descubierta* during the assault by the Russian's team."

"We're talking piracy here, aren't we, Chase?"

"We are, sir, but my team and I are well trained, and there's very little chance we'll lose the ship to the Russian."

"Very little chance? But there is a chance."

"There's always the off chance that something goes terribly wrong in any operation, but we have a solid track record of success."

He drummed his fingers on his desk. "And just how many times have you successfully defended a warship against Russian pirates?"

"I'll put it this way, sir. We've never lost a ship that was under our protection."

He popped two more chalky tablets onto his tongue. "That wasn't my question, Chase."

"Yes, sir, I know, but that is my answer."

He chewed and swallowed, then poured himself a glass of water from a pitcher on his credenza. "Let's assume I can sell this idea to the prime minister, and let's assume you successfully defend the ship. What then?"

"Then we capture or kill the Russian arms dealer."

"Capture, you say."

"Yes, sir. That's always the preferred outcome."

"What will you do with him after you've captured him?"

"We'll turn him over to the authorities, sir. That's how these things work."

"Which authorities?"

"I don't know, sir. That's not up to me. Those decisions are made by people who sit behind ornately carved desks and wear neckties instead of flak jackets. My team and I are the sword, Mr. Ambassador, and the sword doesn't get to choose its wielder."

"I see. Well, let's get Mr. Forrester's thoughts on this operation of yours. Paul, what do you think?"

Instead of addressing the ambassador, Paul Forrester locked eyes with me. "So, you're SEALs?"

I held his gaze. "We're tier-one operators, and you're the CIA chief of station."

"That's right, Chase. I'm the COS. Was it the JCPenney's jacket or the shoes that gave it away? GS-fourteen pay doesn't go as far as it used to."

I ignored the question. "Mr. Forrester, we're not bureaucrats. We're the very sharp point at the tip of a very long spear. This is an opportunity to take one of the world's nastiest guys out of circulation. When it's over, we don't get our pictures in the *New York Times* or plaques for our love-me walls. We move on to the next mission while the GS-fourteens and such get to use our successes as bullet points on their performance appraisals."

Forrester turned to the ambassador. "I like this guy, Tom. Let's run the thing up the Moroccan flagpole and see if it'll flap in the wind."

Riley put more antacids down his pipe. "Okay, but if it goes south, it's your butt that'll be flapping in the wind."

The seasoned case-officer-turned-station-chief smirked. "You know that's not how it works, Tom. I'm the commercial affairs officer. As long as Americans aren't getting shot in grocery stores from Casablanca to Tangier, I'm bulletproof. It's the honorable secretary of state who'll follow the *Descubierta* to the bottom of the Atlantic for this one."

Thomas Thomas Riley rose from his seat. "It looks like you've got yourself a warship to defend, Chase. Maybe Mr. Lawton knows where your ship is this time of year."

I stood with the ambassador and checked my watch. "She's in the Bay of Tangier—exactly where my support vessel will be in seventy-two hours."

The same Marine escorted us back to the waiting SUVs, and the same drivers returned us to our waiting Gulfstream. We climbed aboard, and I produced my sat-phone.

Clark answered on the third ring. "Yeah, I know, and King Mohammed says you're buying him a new Navy if you screw this up."

"What was the last thing I screwed up?" I asked, but before he had time to generate his list, I said, "Never mind. We won't screw it up. It looks like it's time to do what we do best."

"What's that?" Clark asked.

"Hang out on the beach and drink piña coladas until it's time to go to work."

"Don't forget the sunscreen. Cheers!"

Chapter 36
To Bow or Not to Bow

As it turned out, Tangier is not the Mediterranean paradise I expected. We'd lived in the lap of luxury aboard the *Moscow Mule* with stewards waiting on us hand and foot for too long. Compared to the treatment we received aboard the yacht, the best resort in Tangier felt more like the Highway 64 Motor Lodge in Dump Truck County, Alabama.

When a pair of bugs big enough to qualify as small rodents ran across the bathroom counter while I was brushing my teeth, I peered around the partition, to the bed where Penny lay pulling herself from what barely qualified as sleep.

"I've got an idea," I said.

"Please tell me it involves moving back aboard the yacht, or even the *Lori Danielle*."

"The *Mule* is still three thousand miles away, and the *LD* isn't exactly luxury digs, but I've heard good things about a little island called Ibiza off the coast of Spain."

She sprang upright. "Oh, Chase, please tell me you're not kidding around. I've wanted to go to Ibiza since I was a little girl."

"Let me get a shower, and I'll talk to Disco. I don't even know if there's an airport on the island that can accommodate the Gulfstream."

She threw off the cover and snatched her phone from the nightstand. "I'm on it!"

"Don't get too excited yet. Ah, never mind. Get as excited as you want. I'll be out in a couple of minutes."

After a wrestling match with an enormous piece of sandpaper that apparently qualified as a towel in North Africa, I found Penny packing her bags. "I guess that means Ibiza has a big airport."

"Oh, yeah. Really big. But you can't go, can you?"

I pulled on my shorts and sat on the edge of the bed beside her. "No, and you can't go where I'm going."

"I was afraid of that. How about Irina?"

"She's done her part. The rest is up to the gunslingers, but there's no reason why the two of you can't enjoy Ibiza for a few days while we're doing what we do."

She laid her head against my shoulder. "Maybe when it's over, you and the rest of the guys could take a little vacation."

I ran my fingers through her hair and kissed her forehead. "Maybe. We'll have to see how the timing and logistics work out."

"I know what that means. It means somebody might get hurt."

I squeezed her against me. "I'm afraid that's the nature of the beast. We plan for the worst and celebrate when we're wrong. There are a lot of variables and unknowns. We've not even met the Moroccan crew yet. They may not take the news very well when six American commandos move onto their boat."

"I hate that part of what you do."

"I know," I said. "But we're removing a blight from the planet. What we do is necessary and—"

"I know. I've heard this speech a dozen times, but that doesn't mean I have to like it."

"No, you don't have to like it, but you do need to remember that we're some of the most highly trained operators on Earth.

We're good at what we do. We may come home with a few broken bones, but we usually leave the bad guys counting dead bodies while we make our exit—if there are any bad guys left."

"Tell me what you're going to do," she said.

It came out as a question, and not a command, so I said, "We're going to move aboard the *Descubierta* and use the skills Dre and the SEALs taught us in St. Marys to crush the pirates Mikhail sends to capture the ship."

"That sounds really dangerous."

"I'm not going to blow sunshine up your skirt. It *is* dangerous, but not as dangerous as assaulting the ship. Mikhail's men are the ones in danger. We'll hold a stronger, safer position on the ship, and they'll have to put themselves in a vulnerable situation to come aboard. She's a warship, so she's not easy to catch and even harder to conquer."

"Do you ever get scared?"

"It's not exactly fear, but anybody who tells you his heart rate doesn't get up when bullets start flying is a liar. The thing I fear the most is coming home and telling Tina, Skipper, or Irina how brave the men they love were. We lost some SEALs on the operation in The Bahamas, but I've not had to face the tears when one of our family doesn't come home."

She stared at the floor. "Who will tell me?"

I didn't like the question, but I wasn't willing to dismiss it. "If something happens to me, Mongo will be in charge, but I think Clark would be the one to tell you."

"I'd want it to be Hunter," she said.

"Hunter? Why?"

She wiped a tear from her eye. "I've seen how you two work together. In the shoot house, you move as if you were one person. When you're not with me, you're with him. The two of you are part of each other. It's only right. Please, Chase. If, God forbid, something happens to you, make sure it's Hunter who knocks on my door."

"This is not the conversation I planned to have this morning."

She took my face in her hands. "Promise me it'll be Hunter."

"Okay. I'll talk to him and Mongo."

She stood and shucked off the UGA Baseball T-shirt she wore as a nightgown, wadded it into a ball, and threw it at me. As she turned the corner into the bathroom, she looked over her shoulder. "I like it that you still look at me like that."

"I'll never stop looking when you parade around naked. Not even when we're ninety."

She laughed. "When we're ninety, you'll be blind, and my butt won't look like this."

"It'll still look like that to me."

Breakfast was another family affair for the team, and the primary discussion became a debate concerning what time we should wake up Clark.

I checked my watch. "It's nine here, so that makes it five on the East Coast. All in favor of now, say 'aye.'"

A few seconds later, a cell phone on a nightstand in South Beach rang, and a hibernating bear groaned himself to life. "What?"

"Good morning, sleepy head."

"I should've known it was you. Is this business, or are you torturing me out of some sadistic need you seem to have?"

I pressed the speaker button. "It's business, and the gang's all here. Do you have a rendezvous time and place for us yet?"

He grunted. "Give me a minute."

We listened as Clark crawled from his bed and his Green Beret joints popped and creaked as he repositioned from the horizontal to the vertical.

"Okay, here it is. You're meeting Captain Aref El Amrani at the headquarters building on the Royal Moroccan Navy Base Tangier today at noon. Don't pile on him, though. From what they tell me, he's a stickler for formalities, so call him captain until he tells you not to."

"What's he going to call me?" I asked.

"Probably a lot of things neither one of us can pronounce. Just be respectful, and don't start any fights with his crew. They're likely to be on edge."

"On edge? Why?"

"Wouldn't you be a little upset if a team of foreigners showed up and told you that your boat was about to be attacked by pirates?"

"I don't think I'd be upset. That's a little nugget most captains would want to know before it happens."

"Maybe so," he said, "but you're not a Moroccan patrol boat captain. The egos and attitudes are a little different in that part of the world. Just show him the same respect you show me. No, don't do that. That's a terrible idea. Just be respectful. We don't need this turning into an international incident."

I chuckled. "We set up a pirate attack on a Moroccan warship. That is, by definition, an international incident."

"You know what I mean."

"I rarely know what you mean, but I'll be nice to the captain. Is he a captain by rank or just the captain of the *Descubierta*?"

"What difference does it make? Just call him captain, College Boy."

"Aye, aye, sir."

He groaned. "Is there anything else? I'm going back to sleep."

"Just one more thing. I'm going to send Penny and Irina to Ibiza on the Gulfstream. I don't want them here if or when this thing turns into something nasty. Are you okay with that?"

"That's good thinking. I've been to Tangier *and* Ibiza, and there's no doubt which one I'd pick."

"Thanks. That's all I have."

"Good. I'm going back to bed. Call me after the meeting with Captain El Amrani."

Neither Penny nor Irina put up any arguments when I told them to get out of Tangier before lunch.

Skipper was a different story. "I'm going with you," the analyst declared.

I grimaced. "I don't think that's a good idea. We're not going to make any headway in a Muslim country with a Christian woman in our midst."

"But I need to be on that ship."

"I know, but that's not going to happen. I want you to go to Ibiza with Penny and Irina. We'll pull you out when the *Lori Danielle* gets here, and you'll be back in the CIC, where you're right at home."

"I don't like it," she said.

"I know, and I feel the same way, but we don't have the home field advantage on this one. We have to play by their rules, and there's no way the Moroccan Navy will take you aboard the *Descubierta*."

"All right, but I want it known that I'm going to Ibiza to live in a luxurious, five-star resort under protest."

I laughed. "Somehow, I think you'll survive."

The Gulfstream whisked them away to the east, and I secretly envied the next week of their lives.

Getting onto the Royal Moroccan Navy Base Tangier was an exercise in frustration and attempted patience. After a half hour, we were finally granted escorted access to the ground floor of the headquarters building. Finding Captain El Amrani began to look hopeless until a young sailor behind one of the many desks scattered about the building declared, "I speak English. Perhaps I can help."

His British accent and perfectly maintained uniform granted him an element of professionalism most of his comrades lacked.

"Thank God. My name is Fulton, and I have a noon appointment with Captain El Amrani."

The sailor shook my hand. "Yes, Captain El Amrani is waiting for you down the hall."

He turned to our armed escort and spoke in a language both of them obviously knew, but I did not.

After a bit of negotiation, our English-speaking sailor became our escort, and he delivered us into a conference room near the end of a long corridor, where we found a thirty-something dark-skinned man with close-cropped hair and a beard. His epaulettes bore two thick stripes topped with a closed circle and one thin stripe.

Our escort said, "May I present Capitaine de corvette Aref El Amrani."

The officer rose, inspected my team, then glared at the sailor who'd delivered us into the room. Without a word, the sailor vanished.

I extended a hand. "Good afternoon, Captain El Amrani. I'm Chase Fulton, and this is my team."

The sixty seconds he spent examining the faces of my team felt like hours, and I wondered if there was some protocol I didn't know to progress our meeting past the silent stares.

The young sailor who'd escorted us came through the door with a silver tray holding eight glasses that were only slightly bigger than a shot glass. He poured coal-black coffee into the glasses and placed one in each of our hands. The sailor disappeared again, and Captain El Amrani raised his glass barely enough to suggest we should drink. And we did.

With the coffee glasses empty, the captain said, "Sit, gentlemen."

His Arabic-accented English was good, but not as clean as the coffee bearer's.

"You are here to take command of my ship."

It wasn't a question, and I said, "No, sir. That's not why we're here at all. We're part of an international sting mission to capture a man named Ilya Mikhailovich Semenov, a Russian arms dealer."

He glared beneath enormous black eyebrows. "And for this, you are here to take command of my ship."

"Again, no, sir. We're not here to take command of your ship. We're here to protect your ship."

His dark eyes bored into mine. "You are here to protect my ship from an attack you orchestrated."

I said, "No . . . Well, yes. But it's not that simple."

"It is very simple to me, Mr. Fulton. You arranged to have a warship of the Moroccan Navy assaulted by Russian forces, and then you demand to come aboard my ship for the supposed purpose of defending it from the same Russian forces. Would it not have been easier to simply not arrange for the piracy in the first place?"

"Yes, sir, it would have been easier, but easy isn't what we do. You're not losing command of your ship. The *Descubierta* will remain solidly under your command. We are nothing more than well-trained fighters who intend to apprehend the Russians who assault your ship."

"Apprehend," he said. "Not kill?"

"Apprehend, if possible. Kill if necessary."

"And you are American Special Forces. Perhaps SEALs."

"No, sir. We are—"

"Mercenaries, then."

I cleared my throat, stood, and bowed. Although I had no idea if bowing was customary in Morocco, I believed the universal gesture of respect and subservience couldn't hurt the proceedings. "Captain El Amrani, forgive me. My men and I humbly request to come aboard your formidable vessel for the purpose of apprehending or eliminating the Russian arms dealer, Ilya Mikhailovich Semenov, a godless infidel bent on capturing your ship of war, sir."

El Amrani nodded and motioned to my seat. "Thank you, Commander Fulton. You and your men are welcome aboard His Majesty's ship, the *Descubierta*, for your noble purpose. My security forces are at your service, of course. However, all of you must first be instructed on proper Moroccan etiquette and protocol before boarding. This instruction will take place here in headquarters and will be conducted by an officer of protocol."

I reclaimed my seat. "Thank you, sir. We look forward to the instruction."

He rose, and my team stood with him. "Please be seated, gentlemen. The protocol officer will arrive shortly, and you will be escorted to the *Descubierta* upon completion of the required instruction."

The captain left the room, and before the door was fully closed, Hunter slapped a palm on the table. "What was that?"

"Improv," I said. "We weren't getting anywhere, and Clark warned me to be respectful."

"Respect is one thing, but groveling ain't in our playbook. When was the last time any of us bowed to anybody?"

I said, "I'm thinking of implementing it into our standard operating procedure. I think you bunch of knuckle-draggers should bow to me before you speak."

"Yeah, give that a try. That should go over really great, especially with Skipper."

Before I could continue abusing my team, a uniformed officer of indeterminant rank pushed through the door and took the seat at the head of the table. The class took almost two hours, and I'm certain I was the only American in the room who didn't fall asleep at some point.

"Are there any questions?" the officer asked.

No one said a word.

"Very well. Wait here, and your escort will arrive soon."

The only thing more dependable than the scalding sun in Morocco was the punctuality of the Naval forces. Before we had time to discuss the bizarre rules under which we'd live for the coming days, another officer opened the door and ordered, "Come with me."

It took a great deal of negotiation, but we eventually talked the driver into stopping by our hotel so we could reclaim what gear we had. His impatience was apparent, but he maintained his professionalism and dropped us at the foot of the *Descubierta*'s gangway at the Port of Tangier, where we were welcomed aboard without ceremony. But after the training we'd endured, my team exercised extreme diligence in avoiding the left hand of every man on the ship.

Chapter 37
A Giraffe?

We spent the afternoon familiarizing ourselves with the layout of the *Descubierta* and drawing our weapons. When the ship's armorer handed an M4 and a Beretta 92 through the bars, I breathed a sigh of relief until Singer made his way to the window.

"Do you have anything long?"

The armorer turned to me as if I was supposed to translate for him.

Disco saved me. "Point to Singer and say '*Qanaas.*'"

I did as instructed, not having a clue that *quanaas* meant *sniper*, but the man behind the bars of the armory seemed to understand immediately. He turned, unlocked a safe, and pulled out a weapon I'd never seen. When he slid it through the bars, butt-first, Singer accepted the weapon as if it were a newborn baby. Then he checked the chamber and performed a function check as if the rifle were an old friend.

The armorer blurted out a long string of Arabic, and I vowed to learn the language soon. Not understanding a word, I turned to Disco. He said, "I didn't get it all, but he said something about zeroing the weapon at sea."

Singer turned back to the armorer and gave him a knowing nod. The man returned the gesture and held up a thumb-and-index-finger pistol. Singer nodded and accepted the offered sidearm.

With the weapons and ammo drawn, I assembled the team on the stern deck. "Let's have it."

Hunter went first. "I like it. There's plenty of cover, and we've got nice weaponry."

Singer said, "I agree. I'll put a couple dozen rounds through this thing once we're at sea."

I motioned toward the rifle, careful to use my right hand, per Moroccan custom. "What is that thing?"

Singer held up the impressive-looking weapon. "This is the PGM Ultima Ratio. It's a French rifle built specifically for sniping. This one is chambered in seven-six-two by fifty-one."

Hunter leaned in to examine the weapon. "French, huh?"

Singer said, "Yes, it's French, and it's an excellent rifle. The name Ultima Ratio came from the Latin phrase, *ultima ratio regum*. That means *the last resort of kings*, and rumor has it that Louis the Fourteenth had it engraved on his cannons."

After two and a half days of running drill after drill and learning every inch of our temporary home, I declared us fit for battle and made a sat-phone call to the *Lori Danielle*.

Captain Sprayberry reported, "We'll be off the coast of Tangier by noon tomorrow, but we need fuel."

I said, "Lay in at the Port of Gibraltar. You can bunker fuel there and pick up Skipper."

"We'll let you know when we enter the strait," he said. "Is there anything else?"

"Negative. Now that you're in the neighborhood, we're ready to dance."

It was time for a conversation with the captain, so in the respectful fashion I was taught, I approached the pimple-faced officer of the watch. "Sir, when duties allow, I request permission to speak with the master of the vessel."

His only acknowledgment of my request was a curt nod. I didn't know if that meant I'd see the captain in an hour or a week, but regardless of the timetable, I was left at the mercy of protocol.

To my surprise, I was summoned to the wardroom before I'd returned to my team.

A young sailor called to me in what qualified as English, but just barely. "Sir, is um . . . in wardroom. Is now."

I picked up my pace and grabbed Mongo. "Let's go. We're meeting the captain in the wardroom, and it appears to be happening right now."

Without a word, he fell in behind me, and we made our way through the small hatch and into the wardroom, which was only slightly larger than a Porta Potty and smelled similar. In addition to the captain, two more officers sat with disinterested looks on their bearded faces. The captain began the briefing even before Mongo and I claimed our seats at the stainless-steel table.

"Word has come through your State Department that we are being pursued, but only loosely."

"When did you receive this word?"

The captain's expression changed from a disinterested briefer to an angry father. "Were you not told by the protocol officer never to interrupt a superior officer? When I want questions, I will solicit them. Until then, it is your responsibility to listen with great attention and nothing more. Is this understood?"

I gave Mongo a sideways glance, and he shook his head. I swallowed the argument that was on the tip of my tongue and lowered my head in submission.

"As I was saying. The American State Department has funneled intelligence through the Delegate Ministry to the head of Moroccan government in charge of the National Defense Administration that an attack on this vessel is imminent, and this vessel is now a sovereign vessel under my exclusive command as ordered by the king."

I turned to Mongo and mouthed, "What does that mean?"

The smartest man I know held up one finger as if to say, *Shut up, and I'll tell you when this is over.*

The more I ran the phrase through my head, the more confused I became.

The captain slapped a hand on the table, rattling the surface as if it had been hit by a bomb. "Mr. Fulton, you are solely responsible for the safety of this vessel concerning any act of piracy. This condition will remain until such time that I no longer have faith you are capable of defending the king's vessel, at which time you will be dismissed. Is this understood?"

Again, I turned to Mongo, and he put on that discretion-being-the-better-part-of-valor face and nodded slowly. I mirrored his action, and the captain appeared pleased.

To my surprise, Captain El Amrani dismissed everyone in the wardroom except me.

He said, "Now that we are alone, please feel free to speak frankly, but do not forget your standing aboard this sovereign ship."

"Thank you, Captain. Our support vessel will arrive tomorrow, bunker fuel, and pick up our intelligence analyst in Gibraltar. She is the *Lori Danielle* and an impressive weapon of war masquerading as a research vessel."

"This analyst of yours, why is he not here aboard my ship with you?"

"Our analyst is an American woman."

My answer told him everything he needed to know about why I'd chosen to board without her.

I asked, "Did the State Department offer any insight on when the attack might be planned?"

"We are a warship, Mr. Fulton, and as such, we are constantly in a state of readiness to defend our vessel and our nation."

"Yes, of course, sir, but often, there are indicators of an aggressor's timeline. Were you briefed on any such indications?"

"My answer is the same. We stand constantly ready."

The captain had obviously not been fully briefed on everything the State Department knew, so I didn't push the issue any further. By early afternoon the next day, Skipper would know more about the world around the *Descubierta* than the ship's own captain.

I stood. "Thank you for seeing me, Captain. It is always an honor."

He rose and spoke softly. "Mr. Fulton, give me your vow that you will protect my ship from the barbarians when they come."

I looked him squarely in the eye. "Sir, you will not lose your ship on my watch."

The remainder of the afternoon was spent out of sight of other vessels, with Singer bonding with his favorite new plaything, the PGM Ultima Ratio rifle. As with every other long gun the world-class sniper cradled in his arms, the PGM became an extension of his own body, mind, and soul.

* * *

With the moon's traverse of the darkened sky complete, the sun reclaimed her eastern throne as the Mediterranean yawned and stretched to life. Like most days of my adult life, I watched the dawn gently consume the night and cast its long-reaching shadows across the sand and sea. The shadows, though visible and blatant, were nothing. In fact, they were merely the absence of light. And just as those shadows appeared with every dawn, they vanished at midday, with the sun at its zenith, and when the absence of light no longer casts itself onto the endless earth and sea. For that fleeting moment, a man could believe the shadows were gone forever, but the eternal revolution of the globe would leave such a man doomed to realize the relentless shadows would return and haunt the eastern reaches that had previously known only the light of the morning sun. Such is the eternal rise and fall of evil forces faced by men of valor—men who wage war against all that humanity cannot face. Such men battle the willowy shadows until beating them back into their moment of absence, but those men know that peace is fleeting and their rest only momentary, for their battle resumes and rages on with the undefeatable passage of time.

I found myself and the team facing that daunting truth, but none of us would wither in its face. We'd pour our hearts and might into the coming battle, knowing full well our victory would come. But that victory would be short-lived, with demons waiting in the wings to descend and pour themselves into the void left by the evil we would destroy in the coming days.

* * *

My sat-phone trilled at two bells on the afternoon watch aboard the Moroccan warship, and the element we'd missed for the previous two days appeared, making us, once again, whole.

"Chase, it's Skipper. I'm aboard the *LD*, and I've just logged the CIC operational. All internal systems are up and running. Satellites are coming online, and I should have solid comms with U.S. Fleet Forces Command within the hour. Carrier Strike Group Ten, including the USS *Harry S. Truman*, is in the Med, and according to Clark, they are standing by to support our mission should this thing turn into a giraffe."

"A giraffe?"

She scoffed. "Yeah, you know, a giraffe. The long-necked animal. In the early days of traveling circuses, the whole show traveled by train, and the animal handlers would have to lasso the giraffe and drag its head down into the animal car every time the train went into a tunnel. It was a lot of work and frustration."

I shook my head. "You're cut off from talking to Clark. He's starting to affect you, and I can't have that. Anyway, what is Fleet Forces Command?"

"That's what the U.S. Atlantic Fleet Command became last year. I don't know why they changed the name, but they still have the same mission. It's nice having them in our back pocket, just in case."

"It certainly is. Are you bunkering fuel?"

"Yes, they should be finished with that in the next half hour or so, and we'll be fully operational."

I said, "Good. The captain briefed us that the State Department informed Morocco that we were being loosely tracked. I'm not sure what that means, but with you in the CIC, I'm sure we'll have a sitrep within an hour, right?"

"Oh, yeah. Probably before that. As soon as the satellites make their way to this side of the planet, I'll have a good picture of what you're facing."

"We're ready on this end, but things are still a little tense between us and the captain. I'm playing it cool, but I'm afraid he's going to get antsy and throw us off his boat if we don't knock this one out of the park."

"We always knock it out of the park. Tell him to chill out. We've got this."

"How about you call him up and give him that message?"

"Give me his number, and I'll give him an earful."

I laughed. "I have no doubt. While I've got you, how was Ibiza?"

"It was amazing! I'm going back as soon as this is over. It's as close to Heaven on Earth as anything I've ever seen. You'll be lucky to get Penny and Irina to leave."

"I'm glad you had a good time. Let's go to work."

Chapter 38
CQB, Baby

The mission of the *Descubierta*, since her conversion to coastal patrol boat, consisted of a routine patrol route along five hundred miles of coastline from Saïdia on the Algerian border to Casablanca on the Atlantic, and I was under no illusions about my ability to influence the captain's route. He would do what he had always done, and predictability would be the death knell for the captain's illustrious career if I didn't find a way to put the ship where Ilya Mikhailovich Semenov, the U.S. State Department, and I needed it to be in the coming hours.

Leaving Tangier, the captain put us on an eastbound offshore patrol through the Strait of Gibraltar, altering our course and speed as we went. The tactic was a good one for a routine patrol since it left onshore observers unable to determine when the ship would arrive at any given point on its route. The route gave us the opportunity to hopefully lure our stalkers into the strait. With Carrier Strike Group 10 in the Mediterranean, any attempt by the pirates to escape in that direction would produce disastrous results for the bad guys. Likewise, with the *Lori Danielle* patrolling the entrance to the strait, no vessel the pirates could use would have the capability to win a fight against the deceptively demure research vessel.

"Here's the rotation," I said. "Starting now, we're on a four-hour sleep/watch schedule. That way, no one is ever more than four hours past a period of rest, even if he didn't get quality sleep during his four hours off. I'm lead for team number one, consisting of Hunter and Tony. Mongo, you're lead for team two, with Disco and Singer. The rules of engagement are simple. We do not initiate contact with the pirates. We defend this vessel as if it were our own backyard, but we never engage without the full team."

I tossed a black box about half the size of a pack of cigarettes to Mongo. "That never leaves your body. Got it?"

He examined the device. "Sure, but what is it?"

"It's a pager, of sorts. If I need you, I'll press and hold the two recessed buttons on the top and bottom. After three seconds, the device will vibrate and sound a shrill alarm. Trust me. You won't sleep through it. If that thing goes off, it means only one thing—we are under attack, and I need you to jump into the fight."

Singer shoved the pager into his pocket. "We'll take first watch, if that's all right with you."

"I was going to flip a coin, but I like volunteering even better. Skipper will be on remote comms. Everybody on watch keeps the earpiece in place at all times. When you come off watch, stick your radios on the chargers. Any questions?"

Hunter said, "Let's catch us some pirates."

I raised a finger. "That reminds me. Our orders are to capture Mikhail, if possible. Shooting to wound is not what we do, but if you can take him alive, do it. There are a couple of guys at Guantanamo Bay who can't wait to sink their claws into him."

The stoic faces around me represented the dramatic shift from a training mentality to battlefield readiness.

"When they hit us, they'll hit hard, but we've proven we can take a punch and stay on our feet. Let's make sure we land our first

punch and send them to the mat. Does anybody else have anything to say before we check in with the CIC?"

Tony said, "Forgive me for asking what's probably a stupid question, but do I understand correctly that the shipboard security
forces are standing down on this one? Are we really on our own?"

"We are," I said. "And honestly, I think Captain El Amrani
hopes we fail. He wants the victory for his men. I don't know if
it's him thumbing his nose at Americans or if he's just an ass.
Maybe both, but I looked him in the eye and swore he wouldn't
lose his ship on our watch. Don't make me out to be a liar, boys."

The grunts and growls of a team like ours sometimes sounded
more like a pack of vicious predators than humans, and that's
what they became when the bullets started flying.

I pressed the button on my commo gear. "CIC, Alpha One."

Skipper's voice sounded in each of our earpieces. "Alpha One,
CIC."

"Show the team operational, and send the intel."

She said, "Roger, operational. The captain's information was
spot-on. You're being trailed by a pair of fast intercept vessels, and
they either have satellite capabilities or there's a GPS tracker on
your vessel."

"How loose are they?"

"Twelve to fifteen miles, and they're matching your speed."

"Do you have any video?"

She typed a long string of characters on her keyboard. "Not
yet, but I'm working on it. We're paralleling your course, but we're
westbound, so we'll put eyes on them before sunset."

"Send the graphics as soon as you get them in sight. We want to
know what's coming as early as possible."

She said, "Stand by. I'm receiving inbound traffic from Fleet
Forces Command."

We waited in silent anticipation of what the good ol' American Navy had to say.

Skipper came back. "Good news. FFC reports the Carrier Strike Group is operating off Palermo, so big brother is in the neighborhood with four squadrons of F-Eighteen Super Hornets in his pocket."

"Nothing about that is bad news," I said. "We're in two three-man teams. I've got Hunter and Tony, and Mongo has Singer and Disco. We'll be on four-hour watches, but don't hesitate to wake us up if something doesn't smell right."

"You've got it. Who's on first?

"Mongo has the first watch."

"Okay, that's all from here. Do you have anything else for me?"

I scanned the team, and no one flinched. "That's it for us. Alpha One, out."

"CIC, out."

We wasted no time getting to work. Singer hoisted his borrowed rifle, still in its case, across his shoulder. "I'm headed upstairs. I'll be in position in less than five."

Mongo nodded. "Disco and I will be on the stern. That means you have the bow."

Singer nodded and trudged up the ladders toward his perch at the highest point on the ship that was large enough to accommodate his nest.

Hunter, Tony, and I left Bravo Team on deck and hit the sack. What little sleep I got wasn't meaningful, but my body rested, even if my mind refused to do so.

In yet another example of Skipper's perfect timing, she radioed only minutes after I stuck the earpiece in place. "Bravo One, CIC."

Mongo's voice filled my ear. "Go for Bravo One.

"I just sent you a dozen pictures of your pursuers. Have Alpha One call when you change watches."

I keyed up. "Alpha One is on. I'm looking at the pictures now. Other than their potential speed, I don't see anything particularly ominous about our foe."

"Agreed," she said. "But the *Lori Danielle* looks harmless, too."

"I'd like to have Dre's assessment of the threat those little boogers pose."

She said, "I can make that happen."

"Do it."

"Consider it done. I assume you're changing watch."

"We are, and I'll keep you posted if anything changes here."

"I'll do the same," she said. "Sleep well, Mongo."

The big man groaned. "We'll try. Bravo One, out."

"Alpha One, out."

"CIC, out."

Mongo briefed me in, and he sent his crew to bed. The routine continued for eighteen hours until we reached the Algerian border and the captain turned the ship south, and finally west, to patrol the northern coast of Morocco at just three miles from the shoreline.

At shift change, just after the course reversal, I gathered the team. "I'm concerned. There's no chance they're going to hit us this close to the shoreline. We have to find a way to convince the captain to run offshore. Any ideas?"

"Have you tried reasoning with him?" Singer asked.

I huffed. "It's like trying to reason with Clark, except worse."

Singer pressed a finger against his chin. "Maybe I could talk with him."

"I have no idea how to set that up, but I'm willing to give it a try. What's on your mind?"

He said, "I don't know, but it'll come to me when I sit down with him."

"Let's give it a shot. Are you ready now?"

Singer handed his rifle to Disco. "There's no time like the present. Let's go."

We met a young officer on the portside wing, and I asked, "English?"

The man held up a thumb and index finger an inch apart. "A little bit."

I flattened a palm against my chest. "We request to see the captain, please."

It may not have been fear that came across his face, but it was at least hesitation. He puffed out his cheeks and exhaled as if dreading the coming spectacle. "I will ask, but probably no will see."

"All you can do is ask. Thank you."

He seemed to muster his courage before stepping through the hatch and back onto the navigation bridge. He returned several minutes later and said, "Uh, yes. Go to, uh . . . *ghurfat almaeisha.*"

I turned to Singer.

He said, "I think it means wardroom, but I'm not certain."

The young officer lit up as if discovering English for the first time and pointed to my sniper. "Yes!"

I asked, "Now?"

He nodded.

Singer and I descended the stairs into the wardroom, where the officers took all their meals, and we found the captain sitting with a bowl of ice cream in his hands and two more small bowls on the table.

He motioned toward the bowls. "I will listen until my bowl is empty."

Singer took a seat immediately across from the captain and dug into his bowl of ice cream. "Thank you, sir. It's very good."

Captain El Amrani tilted his bowl so we could see the meager remains, and his point was clear: there was no time for small talk.

Singer wiped his mouth and returned his bowl to the table. "Captain, if you were going to assault a ship with the intention of taking her as a prize, would you do that two miles from a coastline that was friendly to the ship's crew?"

He let his spoon fall into his empty bowl, stood, and walked from the wardroom, leaving Singer and me alone and bewildered.

"Well, that went better than I expected."

Singer laughed. "At least he didn't throw us overboard."

"Yet."

By the time we made it back topside, the Moroccan coastline was growing more distant by the minute.

"It worked," I said. "I can't believe it."

Singer just shrugged and reclaimed his rifle from Disco.

The pilot handed over the weapon. "It looks like we have a new team diplomat. Nice work. How'd you do it?"

Singer said, "I appealed to the pirate inside him. Every sea captain has a little."

I brought Skipper up to date on our new course.

She said, "I noticed the northbound turn. Well done. Your tails crossed the Algerian border and picked up some extra manpower and a third boat. It looks like they're gearing up for war."

"If that's what they want, that's what we'll give them. Can you get me a headcount?"

"Five, five, and four in three nearly identical boats. Captain Sprayberry wants to tighten the noose. How do you feel about that idea?"

I took a moment to consider what the extra boat and manpower might mean. It could simply be a crew change, and they planned to pursue us with three boats all along. Maybe the third boat was being repaired. If I was wrong, I could be on the verge of stepping into the furnace without a fire extinguisher.

"Tell Captain Sprayberry to move in but to stay between us and the mouth of the Strait of Gibraltar. I want to keep this fight inside the strait."

"Will do. We'll be on our way shortly."

"There's one more thing," I said. "Are there any SEALs in Carrier Strike Group Ten?"

"Probably, but I don't know for sure. Why?"

"It wouldn't hurt to put them in the air in case this turns into more fight than we want. Fourteen men against six of us are pretty good odds for the good guys, but if they pick up any more trigger-pullers, we may have our hands full."

"I'll make the request," she said. "But no promises."

"Do what you can. Alpha One, out."

I took a seat on a deck box. "Mongo, what's your thought on when they'll hit us?"

"I think they'll strike after dark, and the extra men and boat say they're ready to dance. I think they'll watch for us to get established on our patrol route and hit us before the moon comes up."

"That's what I was thinking," I said. "If I were going to steal this boat, I'd do it in the dark and with as much help as I could find."

No dissenting ideas arose, so I gave the order for the whole team to stand down and sleep if they could. "Mongo and I will take the watch until an hour before sundown, then it's all hands on deck and stand to."

Mongo and I climbed to Singer's little nest, high above the deck. The afternoon passed without incident as we traced westbound on the same course we sailed in the opposite direction. When we climbed down from the sniper's perch, my earpiece came alive.

"Alpha One, CIC."

"Go for Alpha One."

Skipper said, "Man your battle stations. They're making their move. Boat three is running at thirty-five knots a mile north of your course, and boats one and two are making twenty-two knots from astern. And they're doing something I don't understand. They put fabric covers over the bow of each boat and rigged it to cover about two thirds of the vessel. I don't know what it is, but I'm working on it."

"I know what it is," Mongo said. "It's radar-absorbing blanketing called RAB. It does two things. First, it reduces the vessel's radar returns and makes them almost invisible outside a mile and a half, but the second thing they do may be more valuable than that. When the sun goes down, the RABs will make them especially hard to see in satellite imagery."

"That doesn't sound good," Skipper said. "We'll be reduced to thermal imaging, but at least that's better than nothing at all."

Mongo said, "If they were smart enough to obtain the RAB material, they're likely smart enough to stitch some thermal blankets underneath to mask at least some of the engine's heat signature."

Skipper sighed. "This keeps getting worse by the minute. I'm starting to think we've underestimated these guys. They're more sophisticated than we thought."

"How about a submarine?" I asked. "If we can get the Navy to cast their net a little wider than usual, the sub's sonar can designate and track surface targets. Why can't we park a sub beneath us and let him be our eyes and ears?"

Skipper said, "It's not going to happen. I haven't told you yet, but the SEALs are a no-go. The Navy is only willing to assist after an act of piracy is underway, not before."

Singer said, "Look around, Chase. We don't need the satellites or radar once Mikhail's men hit us. At that point, it's CQB, and who's better than us at close quarters battle?"

Chapter 39
Men Overboard

With over three hundred ships traversing the Strait of Gibraltar every day, there's never a good time to assault a ship and expect to be alone. If Mikhail's men had the guts to try and take the *Descubierta* with other ships in sight, we were facing an enemy of fearless lunatics.

I tossed my handheld GPS to Mongo. "What do you make of that?"

He studied the screen for a moment and looked up. "He's turning back for the coast."

I keyed my mic. "CIC, Alpha One. We're making a turn to the south. Tell me what you see."

Skipper said, "I was just about to call you. The third boat that broke off to the north made a drastic turn to the south, and it looks like he's headed for El Jebha."

"What's El Jebha?" I asked.

"It's a port town at the southern end of the hook of Morocco, where it turns north into the strait."

I closed my eyes and drew a mental map of the area. "How far is it from El Jebha to the latitude of the strait?"

"Stand by . . . It's fifty-five miles from the coastline at El Jebha to the shipping lanes."

I grabbed Mongo's sleeve and shook him. "Get 'em up!"

He was on his feet and sprinting for our quarters before I could explain my urgency.

"He's getting us as far away from the shipping lanes as possible. There's no privacy in water this congested, but Captain El Amrani is running for the darkest spot he can find, and he's inviting them in."

"Why would he do that?" Skipper asked.

"It's what I'd do," I said. "He wants us off his ship as soon as possible, so the sooner we get hit, the sooner it's over, and the infidel Americans can go home—if they live through it. Either way, we'll be out of his hair before sunup."

The sun touched the western horizon, and darkness fell on the Med. Singer scampered up the rigging to his overwatch position, and Tony passed out night-vision equipment.

I said, "It's time to rock and roll, gentlemen."

My earpiece crackled, and Singer's smooth baritone made me believe everything was going to be all right. "Overwatch is in position."

The five of us took our positions and waited for updates from Skipper. Minutes passed like hours before the call finally came.

"It's on, guys. We're ten miles northeast of your position, and the fast-movers are converging on you. Captain El Amrani won't talk to me, but one of the male technicians has been in comms with him, and he says this will be the only opportunity he gives the pirates. If anyone screws it up, it's over."

I said, "I'm not sure he has that authority, but hopefully it'll go exactly as we planned and the good captain will get his wish."

She said, "Mongo was right. With the sun below the horizon, those boats are hard to see with the satellite imagery. We're advancing on your position, and we'll be there to provide close support by the time you get hit. Let's go to open-channel comms."

We switched our radios to open channel so everyone could hear everyone else without keying up. The comms would be all but useless when the bullets started flying, but the coming fight was going to require both hands and both feet—for those of us who have an even number of feet. From me, the pirates would get one fleshy foot and a robot right down their throats.

As I scanned the darkened ocean around us, hoping to catch a glimpse of anything moving in, I was jolted by mechanical sounds behind me. Turning to investigate, I couldn't believe my eyes. The 100-man crew of the ship was piling into lifeboats and lowering themselves over the side.

Before I could ask, Singer said, "Are you guys seeing this? The whole crew is abandoning ship."

Skipper yelled, "What? No way!"

I ordered, "Hunter, Tony, get the crew out of those lifeboats on the port side. Disco and I have the starboard."

We ran to the lifeboats with our rifles raised and yelled, "Get out of that boat, now!"

Hunter was far less polite and even threatened to mow the deserters down if they didn't get back aboard, but our demands fell on deaf ears, and the crew yelled at us in Arabic as they descended to the water below.

Captain El Amrani stepped to the hatch of the lifeboat. "You wanted a fight, you arrogant American. Now you shall have one."

I yelled into my mic. "Tony, get up to the bridge, and get this thing moving. Whatever it takes."

He answered, "Aye, sir," and sprinted for the bridge.

Singer said, "Inbound! Three bogies. Two astern, and one ahead. Do you want me to stop them?"

"Sink the one on the bow," I ordered, and ran to the stern rail. "Dig in, boys, and try not to get dead."

Almost before I'd finished my sentence, the portside hatch to the navigation bridge roared and belched orange flame and black smoke.

I yelled, "Tony, report!"

Nothing.

"Tony! Report! Are you all right?"

Skipper's voice cracked as she said, "What happened, Chase?"

"I don't know yet, but you'll know the second we know."

Hunter sounded almost as terrified as Skipper. "I'm going to find him."

"Thirty seconds," I yelled. "Not a second longer. We need you on the rail."

I could hear his footfalls on the metal deck as he ran with all his might to find his protégé.

Singer reported. "Bogey ahead is dead in the water but still afloat. Do you still want them sunk?"

"Sink them, now!"

The roar of his rifle sending round after round of punishing lead into the hull of the bobbing boat was all the response I needed. When his weapon fell silent, he spoke as if on a Sunday afternoon stroll through the park. "She's on her way to the bottom, and four casualties are in the water."

"Roger. Let them come from astern, but if we get overrun, cut 'em down."

The ship drifted to a stop, dead in the water, and the only man still aboard who had any idea how to get her moving again might have been lying dead somewhere near the bridge.

I called, "Hunter, report."

"I'm coming down. It's blown all to hell up here. There's nothing I can do."

Before I could respond, someone yelled, "Incoming, port stern quarter! Get down! Get down! Get down!"

I hit the deck just in time to hear the rocket-propelled grenade whistle overhead and strike somewhere on the masthead. The explosion wasn't as hot as it had been on the bridge, but the shot drove a spike through my soul. "Singer, report! Singer!"

Nothing.

"All hands, report!"

Their voices came in rapid succession. "Hunter, Mongo, Disco."

The silence after the report of three left me trembling to my very core. "Tony, Singer, report!"

The fight was now ten against four, and our overwatch was gone. My whole world was imploding around me, and the fight had barely begun.

"Skipper, are you there?"

"Yeah, I'm here."

The formality of radio procedures was on its way to the bottom of the ocean, just like the first boat.

"Get us some help!"

She turned from heartbroken widow to hardcore analyst in an instant. "The Little Bird is spooling up, and we'll be on scene in two minutes."

The next two minutes were the longest of my life. The fast-movers raced down each side of the ship, firing grappling hooks as they went. We fired until the barrels of our rifles were glowing cherry red, and we tossed off every hook we could find, but the four of us couldn't defend a ship that size without some Divine intervention. And there was none of that in sight.

"Get to the stern," I yelled. "We'll chew 'em up when they come over the rails."

Disco and Mongo took up position on the portside rail while Hunter and I set up on starboard.

The telltale hiss of a second incoming RPG felt like a thousand demons screaming my name.

I ordered. "Get down!"

We hit the deck, and the grenade sailed harmlessly above, exploding as it contacted the water on the other side of the ship. A second and third RPG raced toward us, keeping us pinned down and praying they wouldn't strike the deck.

"Put some lead on that launcher," I said.

A volley of fire consumed the area we believed the grenades were coming from. The RPG assault was quashed, but it had done what it was designed to do. The decks ahead of us swarmed with at least eight well-armed commandos, and we'd been pinned down just long enough for them to come across the bow rail.

A flurry of full-auto fire exploded from amidships, and I watched Hunter's boots leave the deck as he was knocked backward onto the steel deck behind us. As I scampered toward my partner, I poured lead back at the aggressors as fast as my rifle would cycle.

He was lying on his back and firing between his feet. His aggression gave me time to drag him behind the base of a deck crane.

"Where are you hit?"

"I don't know," he said. "But it felt like a dump truck."

I fired across my shoulder as I ran my hand over his torso, neck, and legs. My hand came back clean and dry. "Roll over."

He struck the deck with an elbow and put himself facedown in the prone position, gunning like a wild man as I palmed his back, butt, and legs. "You're dry."

"They must've just got my vest, but I'm pretty sure I've got a few broken ribs."

I looked up into the night sky as the echoes of automatic rifle fire pierced the air. When I caught my breath, I called, "Ammo count."

Mongo answered, "Three mags."

Disco said, "Two, but I'm pinned down."

Hunter held up one full magazine and pointed toward the one in his rifle.

I yanked a pair of magazines from my pouch and called, "Disco, catch!"

I slid the mags across the open deck, and he let them hit him in his side. "Thanks, but I need two cans, not two mags."

The fear in my voice was impossible to hide. "Skipper, where's our help? This thing is going to be over in sixty seconds if we don't get some support."

Nothing.

"Skipper! Where are you?"

Chapter 40
Will It Ever End?

Hunter rolled toward me. "She's answering you, Chase. Can't you hear her?"

I smacked my ear with a palm to find my earpiece missing, so I felt around my collar and found nothing except Hunter's hand. A second later, he shoved my earpiece back into my canal as if he were stuffing a turkey.

"Go, Skipper"

"Barbie's airborne, and we're thirty seconds from contact. Tell me what you want."

"I want you to blow this ship to hell from amidships forward."

"What about Tony and Singer?"

Will it ever end? Will the day ever come when I don't have to make the decision to rain fire down on my own men? If Tony and Singer were dead, we'd do no harm by destroying the front half of the ship, but if there was any chance either man was still alive, I couldn't risk sacrificing either of them.

"You're right, Skipper. Find a way to get me some ammo and pin down the gunmen amidships. I think there's still one boat out there with two men aboard, or maybe two boats with one man aboard each. I don't know for sure, but we think there are eight on deck with us. Singer put four in the water, so that leaves two, and I need you to find them."

Skipper said, "We'll launch two RHIBs and rake the portside amidships forward with the fifty-cal."

The near-constant thunder of the AK-47s was almost deafening until the night sky ahead of the ship came alive with orange-streaking fire. There was no question in my mind what set the air on fire. It had to be the four Hellfire missiles from beneath the hardpoints on the MH-6 Little Bird in Barbie's capable hands.

My initial reaction was panic, knowing the hellfires would tear Singer and Tony into shreds of flesh and flame if they were still alive somewhere on the superstructure of the vessel. I sent up a silent prayer and watched the answer unfold before my eyes. Instead of ripping into the steel sheeting of the patrol boat, the Hellfire missiles flew wide and sent towering fountains of water into the sky as they exploded on contact with the surface of the ocean.

Barbie knew what she was doing, and I was instantly thankful for her experience and keen battlefield-management skills. The pirates who'd occupied the starboard side of the ship ran from their perilous positions beneath Barbie's hellfires to take cover with their teammates on the port side.

As if the sun itself had risen from the Med, every light on the *Lori Daniel* flooded the patrol boat with relentless white energy as she roared past us at well over thirty knots, pouring fifty-caliber lead into the ship and obliterating anyone standing on deck.

Believing the fight was over, I collapsed to the deck and threw myself back against the base of the crane. My heart pounded as if trying to exit my body until the adrenaline in my veins subsided enough to piece together what had happened. To my horror, I looked up to see a single grappling hook over the stern rail and a hand extending upward. I shouldered my rifle and tilted it to see the bolt locked to the rear and the chamber empty. I dropped the rifle and drew my sidearm. When the face of the man attached to the arm showed itself, I would send him to a watery grave.

The hand grasped the rail, and I thumb-cocked my Beretta, waiting to see the look of horror on the pirate's face the instant before his brains would explode out the back of his skull. With rage weeping from my every pore, I gripped the pistol as if the fate of the world lay in my hands, until a shadowy face of the climber peered between the rails, and I yanked the sidearm off target. I ran to the rail and leaned over, grabbing the wrists of the greatest sniper I'd ever know.

I dragged Singer aboard and helped him onto the deck beside Hunter, who'd shed his flak jacket and was squeezing his ribs. "Where've you been, Singer? You missed one heck of a gunfight."

He caught his breath. "When I saw that RPG inbound, I knew I'd pulled my final trigger if I didn't find a way to either stop it or get out of its way. I sent one round toward it, but I must've missed because it kept coming. I jumped to my feet and threw myself overboard an instant before that thing tore my nest to shreds. I can't believe I got out in time, and that water's colder than you'd expect."

Thrilled beyond words that Singer was alive, I took a knee and let the probability of Tony being dead wash over me. "We've got to look for Tony. The bridge was wired, and I don't think he ever made it inside."

Hunter growled like a wounded bear when he forced himself to his feet against the agony of the broken ribs. I stepped around him and moved from the cover we'd enjoyed behind the crane.

My hand found my earpiece exactly where it belonged, and then my mic. "Skipper? Are you still with me?"

"I'm here, Chase. We're coming about for another pass, but I don't think anyone survived the first run."

"Roger, we're moving forward to find Tony. Singer is aboard and safe. He made a leap of faith and made it into the water."

"That's great news, but please find Tony . . . please."

"We'll do our best. Any luck finding the other boats and men yet?"

"Still hunting," she said.

That's when the crack of the 7.62mm projectile broke the sound barrier thirty feet ahead of us and only inches from the muzzle of the Russian-made Kalashnikov. I saw the muzzle flash and heard the crack simultaneously. There was nothing I could do, even though I instinctually threw myself to the deck. I heard the bullet tearing flesh, but I didn't feel the burn. The sting hadn't come, so I squeezed the trigger of my pistol in rapid succession until the bolt locked to the rear. I wasn't in pain. I wasn't blacking out. I wasn't shot. I turned to see Hunter on his back and Singer shoving his hands against his shoulder.

My partner bellowed in pain, and I yanked the first aid kit from my belt and threw it toward the sniper. Singer had to keep as much of Hunter's blood inside him as possible, and somebody had to put a bullet in the rifleman who'd downed him.

Disco's voice filled my ear. "We're moving forward, but we're still blind from the lights on the *LD*."

I said, "Roger. I'm moving, too. We have to find that guy and put him down."

A long arcing ribbon of sparks flew from the deck just ahead of Disco and Mongo, and they dived for cover. I followed the sparks and sent five rounds into the darkness where I believed the shots had originated. The gunman had to be stopped. Hunter was hurt too badly for any of us to keep him alive on the doomed, abandoned ship. Getting him into the sick bay aboard the *Lori Danielle* within minutes would mean the difference in him dying on the cold deck or surviving to return home. Tony—or Tony's body—lay somewhere aboard the ship, and the gunman was standing between me and my downed man.

I called into my mic. "Find a way to get Hunter to sick bay. I'm going after the shooter."

Reaching back, I yanked Hunter's sidearm from his holster and sprang forward, running as fast as my legs would carry me across the aged deck. With every third stride, I sent a pair of rounds downrange to keep the aggressor's head down while I closed the distance between us.

I heard Disco's voice as I advanced. "Mongo's moving to Hunter and Singer. I'll cover the move, then I've got your six, Chase."

I breathed into the mic. "Roger."

As cautiously as possible, I made the corner of the superstructure and cut the pie, just like I'd practiced thousands of times in the shooting house, taking small slices of the environment into my line of sight until I encountered the enemy or discovered the area clear to advance. With every lean and slow shuffle of my left foot, I took in more information until I saw I could move ahead.

Realizing I was stepping into a pitch-black pit with a potential viper, I retreated to relative safety and whispered, "I need some light on the portside amidships."

"We're coming," Skipper said. "Just hold on. We'll turn it into a tanning bed in thirty seconds."

Almost before she'd finished, a blade of brilliant white light sliced through the darkness, spraying a beam across a ten-foot area of the ship. I glanced up to see the Little Bird in a hover a hundred feet away with her searchlight glowing beneath the nose. Taking full advantage of the light, I pressed forward with pistols raised until I heard a series of shots ring out, and the searchlight swung away. The momentary darkness left me afraid I was in the open with no cover or concealment other than the blackened sky.

The shots continued, and I sent six or seven rounds toward the belching rifle as it poured lead into the sky, desperately trying to bring down the chopper. At least some of my shots found their mark, and the rifle clattered to the deck. Barbie apparently saw that the weapon was silenced, and she brought the light to bear on the ship one more time.

In the center of the glowing beam, a man stood with one arm shielding his eyes from the searchlight and the other reaching for the rifle. I moved faster than I thought possible and kicked the rifle overboard. Well within the man's reach, I squared my stance to face him and shoved the muzzles of my pistols beneath his chin.

As my eyes adjusted to the light, I put on a demented smile. "Hello, Ilya Mikhailovich Semenov. I'm surprised you're brave enough for this business. I pictured you to be the back-office type."

He scowled, and in his course Russian accent, said, "I should have known. All of this was too easy. The money, the women, the yacht. None of it fits you, Daniel Chase . . . if that is your name."

I growled. "Get on your knees, and I will let you live."

"I have other proposition for you. How about you put down weapons and we end this like real men? Or maybe you are afraid to fight me man to man, yes?"

I lunged forward, shoving him into the bulkhead. I wanted him alive, and the only way I could see that working out was for me to give him what he wanted. To my surprise, though, the shove didn't disorient or discourage him. He bounced off the hard steel and came up with a knife in his right hand. I leaned back, barely dodging the upswinging blade, and I chopped across my body with my pistol in a futile effort to knock the blade from his hand.

He moved like an experienced, trained street fighter. His movements were small and efficient, and he showed no fear.

I raised one pistol to bear on his forehead. "Haven't you ever heard that you're never supposed to bring a knife to a gunfight?"

"This is not gunfight," he said. "You have wasted all your ammunition. You have now brought useless guns to knife fight, you weak, American imbecile."

Instinctually, I glanced down at my pistols to find he was partially right. The pistol in my left hand waited with the slide locked to the rear and the magazine empty. I dropped the two-pound chunk of metal to the deck and took a stutter step backward, clamping my remaining pistol in a powerful two-handed grip. "Don't make me kill you, Ilya. I have injured men who need medical care. This doesn't have to end like this."

Obviously unwilling to surrender, he bounded forward, thrusting the knife toward my pistol. I lowered my weapon a foot and pressed the trigger. He'd given me no choice. I had to end it.

To my horror, the hammer fell, and the recoil never came. I slammed my palm into the bottom of the magazine and racked the slide in an effort to clear the misfire and cycle a new round into the chamber, but the slide locked open, and the sickening feeling of holding an empty weapon filled my gut.

I threw the pistol at Mikhail to give myself an instant of an advantage, but he was too fast. He sidestepped the flying block of plastic and metal and sprang toward me with the knife extended. I cleared the centerline between us and shot a hammer fist to his wrist. The blow should've disarmed him, but it seemed only to fuel his fire. Changing to a backhand grip, he spun and brought the knife diagonally up and across my chest. I spun to avoid the attack, but the back of my right hand took the blow of the razor-sharp fighting knife, and the flesh opened up.

I didn't feel the pain, either because the adrenaline was flowing or the five surgeries I endured to repair my hand over a decade before had left the nerves only partially active. But pain was not my fear. The blood loss would be massive if I couldn't end the fight and get some pressure on the gaping wound.

I stepped inside and threw a series of battering punches to his ribs, finishing with an uppercut that sent my blood mixing with his as my fist sent his lower jaw crashing into his upper teeth. There was no way to know whose blood was whose, but I couldn't think about that. There was still an eight-inch knife in the air above my left shoulder, and I had to make my exit before the blade found its home between my cervical vertebrae.

Rolling to my right, I shoved him away from me and threw a powerful front kick as soon as I was in position. The blow sent him backward against the rail, and I moved in. I was cut and bleeding, and I was going to be cut again. There was nothing I could do to avoid my fate. Clark's admonition of "The only thing guaranteed in a knife fight is that everybody is going to bleed" kept running through my mind. I just had to make him bleed more than me.

With him off-balance and against the rail, I made my desperate move and raised my foot, sending a roundhouse kick straight for his head. Just as he'd been trained and practiced endlessly, he blocked the kick with his knife hand, obviously intending to sever my foot if he could, but he was almost two years too late for that. A hack doctor in Western Africa beat him to it, and Mikhail's blade lodged in the hinge of my robotic ankle. My follow-through ripped the knife from his hand, and I let my rotational energy carry me through the arc and landed a backfist to his neck.

The blow to the vagus nerve sent Mikhail to his knees, instantly dizzy, confused, and disoriented, and a left cross sent him collapsing unconscious to the deck. I planted a boot on his neck to ensure he was down to stay and examined my right hand. It was a nasty cut, but nothing Dr. Shadrack couldn't stitch up in a few minutes. I tore off a piece of my shirt and wrapped it around my hand as an improvised pressure bandage, then leaned back against the bulkhead.

After catching my breath, I said, "Shooter is down. Somebody give me a sitrep."

Skipper's voice came. "We're laying along the stern now. We'll have Hunter on board inside two minutes. Are you injured?"

"No, I'm fine, but our old friend Mikhail is going to have a nasty headache in the morning. Send a couple of guys up here to get him to the stern. He's unconscious, but I don't know for how long."

Disco appeared in the next instant and grabbed my hand. "What happened?"

"It's nothing. Help me get him to the *LD*."

We each grabbed a wrist and dragged his limp form across the deck, where we saw Hunter being carried inside the *Lori Danielle*.

I asked, "Is Hunter alive?"

"He was when we lifted him over the rail," Mongo said. "Now, let's find Tony before Skipper tears this ship apart with her bare hands."

Singer, still soaking wet, joined us, and we moved toward the navigation bridge hatch, where the first explosion had been.

"Be careful," I said. "There could still be active trip wires."

Mongo produced a flashlight and led the way toward the burnt and blackened hatch. "It was definitely a booby trap. Most of the blast was directed outward."

I said, "There's no sign of him here on the ladder. The blast could've blown him overboard."

Mongo hung his head. "If that's the case, he would've been unconscious and couldn't have survived."

"I hope you're wrong." I stepped through the blackened hatchway and onto the narrow bridge. Mongo stuck his flashlight in my hand, and I shone it around the deck of the bridge.

Disco shoved past me. "There he is!"

I followed his movement toward the starboard side of the bridge and saw Tony's legs extending from beneath the console. Disco hit the deck beside him and shoved a pair of fingers against the flesh of his neck. He looked at me with defeat in his eyes. "I can't find a pulse."

Mongo reached down and grabbed Disco's collar, then lifted him out of the way. He knelt beside Tony's body and stuck his head under the console.

We waited in terrified impatience until Mongo said, "Get a gurney. I've got an extremely weak pulse and sporadic, shallow breathing."

Skipper screamed into our earpieces. "Get him out of there and down to sick bay, now!"

Mongo scanned the bridge until his eyes fell on the chart table, six feet long and two feet wide. The monster of a man grabbed the table and ripped the top from its base, then threw it onto the deck beside Tony. With gentleness like I'd never seen, he pulled our rescue swimmer from beneath the console and onto the makeshift gurney.

The big man looked up. "Well, don't just stand there. I can't carry him down that ladder by myself."

Disco grabbed the foot of Mongo's gurney, and the big man lifted the head. They carried him down the ladder as if they'd done it a million times, and they quickened their pace once they reached the main deck. Tony and his tabletop gurney were over the rail and into the waiting hands of a couple of paramedics with a real gurney.

Mongo, Singer, Disco, and I collapsed to the deck, and our Southern Baptist sniper began one of his soft, familiar prayers to his best friend somewhere up above.

When a chorus of amens rose, Singer said, "Too much went wrong tonight. We missed too many signs, we've got two men clinging to life by their fingernails, and we almost lost the whole team. How many more times is it going to take until we leave widows and loved ones crying over our coffins? If either of those good men in that sick bay dies tonight, what did he trade his life for? Are we really keeping our country free, or are we settling old scores for a pack of men we call the Board, who hide behind a veil and send us to make these sacrifices because they're too busy, or too important, or too scared to do it themselves?"

We sat in silence, considering the wisdom of a man we loved, who'd spent countless hours of his life nested high above the action and keeping us alive. Jimmy Singer Grossmann wasn't God, but he was the closest thing we had to an all-seeing, all-knowing protector, and if he was ready to turn in his rifle, the rest of us had some immense soul-searching to do before we stepped foot into harm's way again without the faith that we were noble men doing noble work for a noble purpose greater than the sum of us all.

Epilogue

Ibiza, Spain

I sat under the shade of a young palm and stared out over the vast Mediterranean Sea with a cigar between my teeth and a glass of twenty-year-old bourbon in my hand.

Tony Johnson gingerly nestled onto the sand by my side. "Sorry I missed the fight, boss."

"Me, too. You would've enjoyed it, and we certainly could've used the help. How do you feel today?"

"I remembered my name when I woke up this morning. That's progress."

"How about Skipper's? Did you remember hers?"

He grinned. "I knew hers the second I came out of the coma. That's pretty strange, wouldn't you say?"

I took a sip. "No, that makes a lot of sense, actually. You can't remember my name right now, can you?"

He shook his head, and a tear came to his eye. "No, sir, but I know you're the boss."

"I'm not the boss, Tony. I'm just the one who's foolish enough to take the responsibility. My name's Chase."

He nodded slowly. "Yep, that's it. It was on the tip of my tongue."

"I know it was."

He looked over his shoulder. "How about Air Force? How's he doing?"

"Hunter," I said.

He shrugged. "If you say so."

"Stone W. Hunter is his name, and it's going to be a long time before his left arm works again. Broken ribs are bad enough, but a seven-six-two round in the shoulder is a tough way to go down."

"Tell me what happened, boss. I may not remember tomorrow, but I need to hear it."

I leaned back against the palm and pulled the cigar from my lips. "It's the age-old story of greed and lust for power. The captain sold out his country and his ship for the promise of a million dollars from the Russian arms dealer, Ilya Mikhailovich Semenov. They shot Captain Aref El Amrani for treason. The Navy took Semenov into custody, and I guess he's in Cuba at Guantanamo Bay, getting the five-star treatment from his CIA interrogators. They'll probably turn him over to the World Court in the Hague when they've sucked him dry."

I took a long draw on my cigar and looked into Tony's glassy eyes. "Marcus Astor was never the real target of our investigation. It was all a ploy to get Semenov for his father's role in the murder of Emily and Arista, the young grandchildren of two of the Board members."

Tony slowly shook his head. "I don't remember who any of those people are, but if two little girls were murdered, I guess it's worth whatever the team and I had to go through to get at their killers."

For a moment, I envied his amnesia. Being able to forget may have been an unthinkable hell for Tony, but I couldn't count the things I'd pay any price to forget.

"As you already know, Hunter took a round in the shoulder, but he'll be all right . . . in time. You wound up on the bridge underneath the console, and none of us can figure out how that happened."

He stared into the sky as if searching for answers that would never come. "I remember Mr. Hunter, but only sometimes."

"It'll all come back," I said. "What happened to you aboard that ship should've killed you. You got a second chance at, well, everything."

I paused, just like I'd done the nine previous times I'd told Tony Johnson the story of our latest mission. I hoped that would be the day he remembered how he got onto the bridge without tripping the explosives, only to barely survive when they finally cooked off. That wouldn't be the day he'd remember, but I'd tell the same story every day until it stuck and he could remember. I guess that's the cost of being the boss.

Mongo pulled Singer aside on our tenth day on Ibiza and asked, "You're ordained, right?"

Singer smiled, knowing what was coming next. "Yes, I am, and I'd be honored to marry the two of you right here on this beach."

The ceremony was simple. Mongo wore linen pants and a white shirt that actually fit. Irina cried through the whole thing and only stopped when Singer pronounced them man and wife. The only person happier than Mongo and Irina that day was Tatiana, Irina's daughter and prima ballerina of the Juilliard School Ballet Company.

Later that night, I placed a small, ornate wooden box with a ribbon tied around it on the floor at the door of the honeymoon suite and knocked gently.

I hid around a corner and waited. Someone opened up, lifted the box, and closed the door. Ten seconds later, Mrs. Irina Malloy screamed like the happiest woman on Earth when she opened the box and held her wedding gift in her ungloved hands—the Third Imperial Fabergé egg, presented to the Czarina Maria Feodorovna on Orthodox Easter Sunday in 1887.

About the Author

Cap Daniels

Cap Daniels is a former sailing charter captain, scuba and sailing instructor, pilot, Air Force combat veteran, and civil servant of the U.S. Department of Defense. Raised far from the ocean in rural East Tennessee, his early infatuation with salt water was sparked by the fascinating, and sometimes true, sea stories told by his father, a retired Navy Chief Petty Officer. Those stories of adventure on the high seas sent Cap in search of adventure of his own, which eventually landed him on Florida's Gulf Coast where he spends as much time as possible on, in, and under the waters of the Emerald Coast.

With a headful of larger-than-life characters and their thrilling exploits, Cap pours his love of adventure and passion for the ocean onto the pages of the Chase Fulton Novels and the Avenging Angel — Seven Deadly Sins series.

Visit www.CapDaniels.com to join the mailing list to receive newsletter and release updates.

Connect with Cap Daniels:

Facebook: www.Facebook.com/WriterCapDaniels
Instagram: https://www.instagram.com/authorcapdaniels/
BookBub: https://www.bookbub.com/profile/cap-daniels

Also by Cap Daniels

The Chase Fulton Novels Series
Book One: *The Opening Chase*
Book Two: *The Broken Chase*
Book Three: *The Stronger Chase*
Book Four: *The Unending Chase*
Book Five: *The Distant Chase*
Book Six: *The Entangled Chase*
Book Seven: *The Devil's Chase*
Book Eight: *The Angel's Chase*
Book Nine: *The Forgotten Chase*
Book Ten: *The Emerald Chase*
Book Eleven: *The Polar Chase*
Book Twelve: *The Burning Chase*
Book Thirteen: *The Poison Chase*
Book Fourteen: *The Bitter Chase*
Book Fifteen: *The Blind Chase*
Book Sixteen: *The Smuggler's Chase*
Book Seventeen: *The Hollow Chase*
Book Eighteen: *The Sunken Chase*
Book Nineteen: *The Darker Chase*
Book Twenty: *The Abandoned Chase*

The Avenging Angel – Seven Deadly Sins Series
Book One: *The Russian's Pride*
Book Two: *The Russian's Greed*
Book Three: *The Russian's Gluttony*
Book Four: *The Russian's Lust*

Stand Alone Novels
We Were Brave

Novellas
The Chase Is On
I Am Gypsy

Made in the USA
Las Vegas, NV
01 November 2022

58577218R00187